Nora, Nora

Also by Anne Rivers Siddons

FICTION

Low Country

Up Island

Fault Lines

Downtown

Hill Towns

Colony

Outer Banks

King's Oak

Peachtree Road

Homeplace

Fox's Earth

The House Next Door

Heartbreak Hotel

NONFICTION

John Chancellor Makes Me Cry

Nora, Nora

A Novel

Anne Rivers Siddons

HarperCollins*Publishers*

HarperCollins books may be purchased for educational, business, or sales promotional use. For information please write: Special Markets Department, HarperCollins Publishers Inc., 10 East 53rd Street, New York, NY 10022.

FIRST EDITION

Library of Congress Cataloging-in-Publication Data
is available upon request.

ISBN 0-06-017613-X

00 01 02 03 04 10 ❖/RRD 9 8 7 6 5 4 3 2 1

This book is for Patsy Dickey,
heart friend.

Nora, Nora

Prologue

The Losers Club met every weekday afternoon at four o'clock in the toolshed behind the Methodist parsonage on the corner of Peyton McKenzie's street. Peyton would be out of her seventh-grade classes at the Lytton Grammar School and sometimes through her homework by then; her father would be cloistered away in the study he had fixed up for himself over the garage behind the elephantine McKenzie house on Green Street; and Clothilde would be grumbling to herself and moving ponderously about the kitchen preparing supper for them. Peyton would not be required of man or woman for at least another two hours. She would have shed her school clothes and carefully stored them in her nunlike closet, and skimmed gratefully into her soft, faded, milk-blue jeans, or flapping cotton boxer shorts and a T-shirt in the summer, looking like a starved pullet, all frail, air-light bones and translucent razor angles.

Ernie Longworth, the second member of the club after Peyton, would be dressed in the bursting coveralls he wore all day in the pursuit of his duties as sexton of the Methodist church. Ernie was thirty-four years old, pursed and peevish as an old budgerigar, sullen and

1

rude to almost everyone but his darting tarantula mother, the parsonage housekeeper, with whom he lived in a little house behind the official minister's residence, and the members of the Losers Club.

Ernie was very fat and pale and fish-eyed behind his thick glasses, and sometimes reeked with what he called, with a loving flirt of the tongue, grave dirt, as he also kept the Lytton Cemetery on a part-time basis. But he read voraciously, and fiercely loved classical music and a sort of obscure theater that had nothing to do with the traveling road companies that performed "light modern classics" on the steps of the Erlanger Theater in Atlanta, twenty miles away, to which Frazier McKenzie dutifully took his daughter and one or two parent-appointed children—not friends; Peyton had no friends of her own age and gender—once or twice a year.

Ernie had been Peyton's friend ever since she was old enough to toddle up the street alone and discover him pottering fussily around his lair, a meticulously kept corner of the toolshed that held a bookcase made of bricks and boards, a gut-springing easy chair with a tape-mended ottoman, a black Franklin stove with a flue that ran out the window, and a coal scuttle beside it. Ernie kept a small white plastic Philco radio on a shelf there, and there was usually a Tupperware pitcher of his mother's grudging pastel iced tea, or three Coca-Colas in an old red metal ice chest, waiting for the club members when they congregated. Ernie invariably looked up in elaborate annoyance when Peyton entered the shed; he would set aside his paperback with a slap, face down on the ottoman, and give her a pale-blue swimming glare of sorely tried forbearance. Though he treated her as an equal, talking to her as if she were his age, or he hers, he was generally so waspishly ineffectual that no one, including Peyton, took him seriously. But she was still proud to have him in the Losers Club, because of his obviously superior mind and lofty taste and opinions on cultural matters, and she often parroted these to Clothilde, who only snorted.

"What good they do him if he can't get himself no further than that ol' toolshed and his mama's supper table," she would say, banging the iron down on the sweet-steaming percale pillowcase on her ironing board.

"He *likes* what he does," Peyton would say. "He *wants* to do what he does. It leaves him more time for cultivating the mind than a real job in Atlanta would do. Ernie cares more for things of the spirit than of the flesh."

"Look to me like he care plenty about his flesh," Chloe said, but she said it good-naturedly, for her. Chloe did not see anything amiss with the time Peyton spent in the parsonage toolshed with Ernie Longworth, nor did anyone else in Lytton . . . not yet, at any rate. Everyone knew Ernie was harmless, if strange. Everyone knew that Peyton McKenzie was nothing but a thin, frail, queer, "nervous" child; the Peytons, which her long-dead mother had been, had always been aristocratically nervous and frail. Lila Lee Peyton had, indeed, died of that frailty at Peyton's birth.

Chloe did not even mind that her own grandson, eight-year-old Boot, was the third member of the Losers Club. Boot had been born with a clubfoot, and was still too young to be left alone, so Chloe had been bringing him to work with her to the big house ever since he was two, when his own mother vanished into the haze of the neon light that was Atlanta, and on up through the spangled chain of eastern cities toward New York, to be seen no more in Lytton. Boot, almost dwarfishly small for his age, was sadly persecuted by the healthy children of the kind, slow-moving women in the Bottoms who might have willingly minded him for Clothilde, and in any case, Chloe wouldn't have dreamed of leaving him behind. He was flesh of her flesh, bone of her bone. But she was grateful that he had a place to go afternoons for a couple of hours, so that she could prepare the McKenzie supper in peace. To most of Lytton, Boot affected a close, mulish, sullen, subservient demeanor that demanded no engagement by any onlooker, but with Chloe and Peyton and Ernie he was himself, a bright, sweet-tempered fatalistic child who was older and wiser by eons than his tender years.

Boot was always the last one to appear at Losers Club meetings, because his infirmity slowed him down, and the toolshed lay at the far end of the garden. This was an overgrown jungle of amok rose bushes, crazed and rampaging wisteria, and kudzu-shrouded cement benches and plaster statuary, the decayed remnants of an ambitious "Garden of Inspiration" conceived by some unremembered minister and executed with loathing by Ernie. He was only too glad to let savage nature strangle out the pruned and seemly Methodist inspirational artifacts and flora. Boot had a hard time threading his way through the virulent green maze; they could hear his floundering in the undergrowth, and the clump-scrape of his heavy leather boot on the gravel path long before his cheerful caramel face appeared in the doorway. It gave them time to change the subject if they had been talking about him, or about some topic that might be offensive to him. In Lytton, Georgia, in 1961, there were many of those, though in truth Boot would not have been offended if they had reached his flaring Dumbo ears; no one else in Lytton, black or white, thought to spare the tender sensibilities of a silent, gimpy little Negro boy. Wise, pragmatic Boot did not mind. He knew that Peyton and Ernie edited their conversations sometimes when he approached. His ears were as keen as his foot was useless. They were, like an insect's antennae, instruments of his survival. He appreciated the gesture of the stopped conversations, though, and always pretended that he had not the faintest idea what they had been talking about.

"Awright," he would pipe, heaving himself down on the ottoman and breathing deeply from the effort of negotiating the Garden of Inspiration. "Who done the dumbest thing today?"

1

Peyton McKenzie changed her name when she was six years old, on the first day of her first year in elementary school. For all her short life she had been called Prilla or sometimes Priscilla, her first name, the latter usually when she was In Trouble, but that stopped with rocklike finality when the first scabby classmate began to chant, "Prilla, Prilla, mother-killer." By the time the entire first grade in the Lytton Grammar School had taken up the refrain, Peyton McKenzie had been born, and there was no chance at all that she would return to the womb.

"It's a man's name, for heaven's sake, Priscilla," her Aunt Augusta said in exasperation for the fourth or fifth time, after Peyton's father had given up on her. "What's wrong with 'Priscilla'? It's a lovely name. Generations of your mama's family have named their daughters Priscilla. I believe the first was Priscilla Barnwell, who came over to Virginia well before the American Revolution. You should be proud."

"Peyton is my middle name," Peyton muttered. "It's as much mine as Priscilla." Both she and Augusta McKenzie knew there would be no changing of Peyton's mind, but Augusta saw it as her duty as the dominant woman in Peyton's life to do battle with the granite streak of willfulness in her niece. On the death of Peyton's mother at her birth, Frazier McKenzie had tacitly placed the day-to-day shaping and pruning of his daughter in his sister-in-law's hands. By the time of Peyton's first great rebellion, aunt and niece were old and experienced adversaries. Each knew the other's strengths and vulnerabilities. Augusta McKenzie knew full well she wasn't going to win this one. But she would never know why, because Peyton never told anyone about the cold, whining little chant at school that morning, not until much later, and none of the other children would tell, either. Her beleaguered teacher soon forgot about the name change entirely. She was the first in a long procession of teachers to forget about Peyton McKenzie for long stretches of time.

Only Peyton remembered, each day of her life and deep in her smallest cell, that she had, indeed, killed her mother. If her father never so much as hinted to her that he held her undistinguished being responsible for the extinguishing of the radiant flame her mother had been, Peyton put it down to Frazier McKenzie's natural reticence. He had been, all her life, as politely remote as a benign godparent. He was so with everyone, except Peyton's older brother, Buddy. When Buddy died in an accident in his air-force trainer, when Peyton was five, Frazier McKenzie closed up shop on his laughter, anger, small foolishnesses, and large passions. Now, at twelve, Peyton could remember no other father than the cooled and static one she had. Her father seemed to remember her only intermittently.

She told the Losers Club about the name change on a February day when it seemed as if earth and air and sky were all made of the same sodden gray cloth. It happens sometimes in the Deep South when winter can no longer muster an honest cold but will not admit the warm tides of spring lapping at the gates. It is a climatic sulk, not a great tantrum, and like any proper sulk it can last for days and even weeks, exhausting spirits and fraying nerves and sucking open hearts with its sluggish tongue. Ernie had been so petulant that Boot had told him to shut up if he didn't have anything to add to the day's litanies of inanities and abasement. Even Boot seemed more dutiful than enthusiastic over his contribution to the club's itinerary, a lusterless account of wiping out the Canaday children's hopscotch grid with his orthotic boot.

"Well, if I couldn't do better than that, I just wouldn't say anything," Ernie sniffed, affronted. Ernie was plagued this day by demons. His small shed was so humid that the lone window was sweated over and the pages of his copy of *The Inferno,* laid casually with its title up on his bookcase, were glued together. His overalls stuck to him, and his thinning, spindrift hair frizzed with the damp, and he was starting a sinus infection. He had also forgotten to return his mother's library books.

"You *ain't* said anything," Boot pointed out. "And I jes' as soon you didn't. You as mean as an old settin' hen today. Peyton gon' have to come up with something really fine to make up for you."

Two pairs of cool eyes turned toward her. Peyton, who had planned to recount the deliberate serving to her of the last helping of tepid turnip greens in the school lunch line while a steaming pot of spaghetti and meat sauce awaited those behind her, swiftly changed her mind.

"I killed my mother," she said, her heart beating hard with the sheer daring of it, and the first opening of the pit of that old pain. The others were silent, looking at her. She looked back, feeling for an instant only the heedless joy of a great coup.

"You ain't, neither," Boot said finally.

"You flatter yourself," Ernie said.

But they knew they were bested by a long shot.

"I did, too," Peyton said. "She died not a day after I was born. She bled to death. Everybody knows that. I've always known it."

"Then why didn't you say?" Boot asked. He was having a hard time relinquishing his sultancy of humiliation.

"You'd have only said I was showing off. Ernie, you did say it. And not only did I kill her, but when I was in first grade I changed my name to Peyton because the kids were singing a song about 'Prilla, Prilla, mother-killer,' and I made it stick, too."

She folded her arms over her thin chest and looked at them com-
placently. Nobody was going to touch her on this day, and perhaps
not on any of the following ones.

"Well, I guess she certainly must have had a fleeting moment of
deathbed regret for her actions nine months before," Ernie said in
elaborate distaste.

"What do you mean?" Peyton said. She could feel her crown slipping away from her.

"He means he bet she sorry she fucked your daddy on the night she
got you," Boot said, his good humor restored. "Yeah, man, that was
one sorry fuck. That was a killer."

"My mother did not fuck," Peyton said, her face flaming with the
audacity of the spoken word as well as the sheer idiocy of it. Of course
her mother had fucked; here she sat, didn't she, on this gray day years
distant from the fatal fucking? Peyton knew what fucking was. You
could not live in a small southern town in deep farm country, in the
company of strapping bus kids from the farms who not only knew
what it was but were actually doing it, and not know. It was just that
she did not know how it was accomplished, and simply could not
imagine. Her cousin Ben Player had shown her their old bull humping
a cow once, on the Player farm, when they were both eight or nine,
but Peyton still could not translate that ponderous, sucking, backward
mounting with people. Most especially not her father. Her mother she
could not remember, of course, but she had been told often enough
what an ethereal sprite she had been. It was inconceivable to Peyton
that she would participate in such a huge, clumsy, wet thing.

"Well, if she didn't fuck, you must have been the result of an
immaculate conception, and from what I hear, it was way too late for
that," Ernie said snidely.

"What are you talking about?" Peyton said, knowing she was
going to hate whatever she would hear.

"Nothing. Forget I said anything. Everybody knows your mama
was a saint," Ernie said, and would say no more. In truth, he was
appalled at his own meanness, but he was not about to admit it. He
leaned back in the spavined armchair and picked up *The Inferno*.

"Meeting adjourned," he said coldly. "I have better things to do than sit around with infants and talk about fucking."

They watched him for a couple of minutes, but he did not look up, and finally Boot said, "Come on, Peyton. He just mad because you outdone him. Let's go to your house. Mamaw gon' make apple butter this afternoon, only I ain't supposed to know it."

At the edge of the gravel sidewalk that gave over to the front walk of Peyton's house, he looked up at her.

"You really kill your ma?" he said.

"I really did."

"Holy shit, if that ain't something," Boot said, and he clumped into the house in search of forbidden fruit.

That night Peyton lay in bed waiting to become a woman.

She had felt it coming all afternoon, small at first, a nudging pressure under her heart, but it had increased steadily, and now it was a huge old tidal surge, smelling somehow of sea brine, tasting of clean lake fish in her throat, something loosed from the tight, cold sac she had pierced that afternoon, something that would drown her and cast her up utterly changed, something that would divide time. Because she could imagine no change more profound than the one from what she was now into womanhood, Peyton thought that must be it. She lay on her back in the quiet dark of the little room that had been her nursery, the lair she would not relinquish no matter what amount of shame her Aunt Augusta heaped on her, and ran her hands over her body, down to her hips and up to her face and down again, wondering where the change would start and how it would feel.

Peyton did this almost every night. It was as immutable a part of the ritual of sleep as brushing her teeth, washing her face, and the hasty whispered recitation of "Now I Lay Me," which had been the first prayer she had ever heard, taught her by Clothilde.

"If you don't say your prayers, ain't no telling what gon' come git you in the night," Clothilde said, mixing theology and pantheism with a fine and careless hand. For a long time the prayer had made Peyton feel safe, but by now she knew that the Lord was no more apt

to keep her soul than to take it. Nevertheless, she always parroted the
nursery prayer. It was a part of the shapeless thing that kept her sleeping in her old nursery, that kept her clinging to her long braids when
every other girl in her class had opted for flips or the Lytton Locksmith Shop's version of the Jackie Kennedy bouffant. It was this,
rather than a budding and secret eroticism, that moved her hands
robotically over her body in the quiet nights. As long as the nubs of
her breasts remained just that, as long as her hipbones were sharp
and bird-fine under her fingers, as long as the small, secret smear of
silky hair down there remained thin and sere, it was all right. Afterward Peyton could relax her stiffened muscles and slide gratefully
into sleep. But on this night sleep would not come. The scanty topog-
raphy of her body had not changed, but she could feel the new green
force rising and rising. She clung fiercely to wakefulness. Whatever
transmutation she underwent, she did not want to be surprised by it
in the morning.

What if I turn out to be beautiful and all the boys want to do it with
me, even the seniors? she thought, and she smiled in the dark, a sort of
smile that her lips had never made before. But then she shuddered. No
matter how many boys wanted to do it to her, she would never do it.
Never. Not ever. One of the farm girls had told the softball group at
recess one day that when a boy did it to you you wanted to do it back
so much that your underpants got all wet and you yelled out dirty
words. Standing on the sidelines, Peyton heard and turned away, nausea rising in her throat. If she lived to be a hundred, she knew that she
would never dampen her chaste cotton Rich's basement pants, never
shout out dirty words in the back of a parked Roadmaster. If she had
to do that she would kill herself, or become a nun.

But what if I wanted to do it? What if that's part of this? she thought.
The green tide probed restlessly between her thighs. She stiffened, and
then leapt out of her bed and padded in the dark to the bathroom
down the hall. After she had urinated she looked into the mirror, seeing a greenish, underwater image in the thin radiance from the street-
light on the corner. No woman, beautiful or otherwise, wanting to do
it or having done it, looked back, only tall, unfinished Peyton, aching

for transformation, terrified of the loss of her self. When she got back into bed, she pulled the covers entirely over her head. She was surprised and alarmed to find that she was shaking all over, a fine trembling that ran in her veins the length and breadth of her.

Now, for the first time in her life, Peyton did not run, either metaphorically or physically, from fear. She felt as if her back at last pressed hard against rock; she must face the fear or be consumed by it. What? she thought, feeling perspiration start at her hairline and on her neck. What am I so afraid of?

But nothing and no one answered. She felt anger bloom in her face and chest. It was, for once, clean and cold and untempered by the need of a child to disown its rage. It was an entirely adult anger, perhaps the first that she had ever felt.

So you can be afraid when there's nothing to be afraid of, she thought. There can't be any God, then. Of all the unfair things in the world this is the worst, and if He's there I hate Him, and if He isn't I'm glad.

Once, long before, swinging alone in the rope swing her father had put up for her in the branches of one of the two great water oaks on either side of the front walk, Peyton had felt a flash of fear so profound and debilitating that she could not slow the swing and had to hang on until it stopped itself. She ran into the house, blind with terror. Her father was sitting at the downstairs desk in the cubbyhole behind the stairs, where Clothilde had said her mother had had a little household office. He was searching through the desk drawers and did not notice Peyton at first, and then the very intensity of her silence drew his eyes up and around to her.

"What are you crying for, punkin?" he said, putting his hand on her shoulder. Her father did not hug and kiss her, but he did, on occasion, touch her gently, and Peyton knew that he did so out of his thin but real affection.

It was only then that she realized she had been crying soundlessly. She gave up and wailed, and he patted her awkwardly on the back.

"Did you fall out of the swing?" Frazier McKenzie said.

She shook her head and then blurted it out.

"Daddy, I don't believe in God," she sobbed. "Do you think He minds?"

"Not too much," her father said equably. "He knows you're only eight. Eight is hard. I suspect He'll make allowances."

She had been soothed then, but she never quite forgot the scope of the fear. This new fear felt like that, only she could not blame it on God or being eight. Under the smothering covers she began to cry. It had been a very long time since she last cried.

I've almost forgotten how, she thought.

Her father's sister-in-law, Augusta Tatum McKenzie, had come for supper earlier, bringing white rolls from the A&P. Peyton knew this made Clothilde furious; she prided herself on her light, melting biscuits and rolls. But Augusta had pronounced that they were made from lard, and that that was very unhealthy, as well as being common. "Common" was an important part of Aunt Augusta's lexicon.

"Where's Charles?" Frazier McKenzie asked, taking the box of rolls from her. "Thanks, Augusta. These look very good."

"Charles has gone fox hunting with that lowlife Floyd Fletcher," Augusta snapped. "It's the second time this week. No matter that it's out of season. If Floyd weren't chief of police Charles could have been in jail long since. Sorry, that's all Floyd is. Sorry as a yard dog."

Augusta Tatum had been born in the mill village down the highway in Franklin, and when, in her candy-box prettiness, she had captured and married one of the McKenzies, from the only distinguished family in Lytton, she had set about shedding the stigma of the mill village. Every now and then, though, it put its red dirt fingers into her mouth and drew out a plum.

"Charlie always did like to hunt," Frazier said. "It's good for a man to get out in the woods sometimes. I ought to do it more often."

"I know you're too busy, Frazier," Aunt Augusta said. She used a different voice with Peyton's father than with anyone else. "It's been a long time since you've had time to fool around in the woods with Floyd Fletcher and that poolroom crowd. You've given up a lot for the law and your family. At least one of us knows it."

Her father said nothing. Peyton stared at her aunt. In all her memory she could not recall a single time when her father had picked up his rifle and donned his boots and gone off into the woods with Floyd Fletcher to slay foxes.

"I don't see how you can give up something you never did anyway," she said. Her aunt brought out the mulish worst in Peyton. In her presence, Peyton turned into just what Augusta thought she was: a tall, shrinking, sulking, ungrateful preadolescent badly in need of a firm womanly hand.

"There are a lot of things about your father you don't see," Augusta said. "I do believe it's deliberate. You're old enough now to think about some of the sacrifices he's made for you. You're old enough now to say thank you once in a blue moon."

Peyton got up and slammed rudely out of the breakfast room and into the kitchen, where Clothilde was whipping cream for strawberry shortcake. Chloe only looked up at her, but Peyton could feel the warm surge of her sympathy. Clothilde fared little better at Augusta's hands than Peyton did. In the breakfast room Peyton heard her father say, "She says thank you often enough, Augusta. She's not an adult, after all. All that will come later."

"You think?" Augusta replied relentlessly. "Have you really looked at her lately? She's taller than her mother already, taller than me. She's getting dark hair on her arms and legs. It's time she shaved her legs, but who is there to teach her how? And that hair. I'd get that hair cut and curled in a jiffy. You remember Lila Lee's hair, so lovely. . . . I wish you'd let me take her in hand, Frazier. She'll never have any friends, boys or girls, unless we do something about that attitude. The only people she sees are that awful Ernie Longworth and that poor little Negro boy."

Her father did not reply. Peyton stood silently, looking at Chloe. She could not get her breath.

I will not grow up, she thought. I will not. Not with her on my neck. I'll run away first.

But she knew that she wouldn't. Peyton had never even taken a Greyhound bus into Atlanta alone. She didn't know where any public toilets were.

She knew, too, that in a terrible way her aunt was right. She would never be part of the twittering, lipsticked girls around the Kotex machine in the girls' bathroom at Lytton High, would never join the crowd of jostling, large-handed boys at the soda fountain after school. Yet each new inch of height brought her closer to a forced exit from the Losers Club. Augusta would see to that. Peyton would be isolated from the only confidants she had in her world, the only living souls to whom she could say anything peevish and perverse that she pleased.

So if not Peyton the woman or Peyton the child, then who?

Peyton stood on a frail bridge between two worlds and stared into an abyss.

"Tell me about my mother," she said to Chloe the next morning at breakfast. It was Saturday, but Frazier McKenzie had already gone out to the office above the garage, and Peyton was heavy with the shapeless hours ahead of her. There was no Losers Club on Saturday.

"I done told you about your mama a million times," Chloe said, but she said it softly. She had long sensed that the private mythology Peyton had spun around her mother was as necessary to her as air and food.

"Well, tell me again. Tell me what she looked like. Tell me what made her laugh. Tell me if she and Daddy went to parties. Tell me if she could cook. Tell me what she and Daddy and Buddy did on weekends."

This last was said with an averted head. Her older brother had been gruffly gentle with her, and even teased her absently sometimes, but he had not spent time with her. All his time, after school, had been spent on the playing fields of Lytton High and in the company of their father. Their hard, bright male laughter rang even now in Peyton's ears. She had always known she was not a part of the laughter or the communion, and would not be. But she had loved hearing it. It had meant, to her, that everything was all right. "Everything is going to be all right" were words that still had the power to soothe her, no matter who said them or how patently inapplicable to the situation they might be.

Chloe took away the uneaten toast and marmalade and slipped eggs and bacon in front of her.

"Eat that," she said. "Eggs give you breasts. Everybody knows that."

"I'd rather eat dog food," Peyton said, near tears.

"Well, that's easy enough to get," Chloe said. She did not push the eggs. She sensed, though she could not have articulated it, that Peyton was going to need her childhood for a long time yet.

"So, she looked like . . . what?"

"You know what she looked like. You've seen her pictures. You've seen that picture Miss Augusta painted of her."

"If she looked like that, her mother and father must have had inferior genes and chromosomes," said Peyton, who was stumbling woozily through what passed at Lytton Grammar School for Preparatory Sex Education.

"What you mean by that?"

"I mean her folks must have looked like idiots, if she looked like that picture Aunt Augusta painted. It's awful. Mother looks stuffed. No wonder Daddy keeps it out in the garage. He keeps all her pictures out there. It's like she was never my mother, only his wife."

"Well, she was real pretty," Chloe said, considering. "She was little and slim, light as milkweed silk on her feet. She had hair that kind of spun around her head, real fine and blondlike, and curly. She never had to go to no beauty shop. She used to sing and dance around the house even when she by herself, and she and your daddy and Buddy used to act silly all the time, and put on plays and things, and play games. It always seemed to me that she was more one of your daddy's chirrun than his wife. She was real popular; she went out all the time, to lunch at the country club, or to Atlanta to shop, or to play tennis at the club. And she volunteered to do a lot of work for poor folks. She was gone 'most every afternoon."

"I'm not like her at all, am I?" Peyton said in a small voice. She knew that she was not, but it was as if she had to hear it regularly lest she start to imagine a relationship that could not have been, and then feel the loss of it in her deepest heart.

Peyton had not known her grandparents George and Priscilla Peyton, from College Park just up the Roosevelt Highway. But she knew about them. Aristocrats, they were, people upon whom the sun shone sweetly, people who got for themselves a dazzling dryad of a daughter, people who gave her to Peyton's father, along with the gift of this great old house in Lytton, with thinly disguised apprehension.

Peyton could imagine why. Her father's family were Scots who had backed the wrong horse at the Battle of Culloden and then departed hastily for the Americas in the middle of the night. They had nothing then but their flinty reserve and the fireshot passions just beneath it that smoldered like burning peat, and the only legacy they brought with them from their wild homeland was their own private mythologies, dark with stunted gods of water and mountains, pierced occasionally by a glinting flash of the Sight. Time had mellowed the passions out of the McKenzies and smoothed the gods into mere amorphous nubs, so that by now they were respectably Presbyterian, not given to singings and revival shouting. Peyton would not have known the dark Hebridean side of her family if it had not been for her paternal grandmother, Agnes MacLaren McKenzie.

Nana McKenzie was a throwback, a genetic sport, a raven among the pale, fluttering female birds of Lytton. She lived alone now, since Peyton's grandfather had died ten years before, in the farmhouse at the edge of town that once had gleamed smartly with paint, its yard and fields wildfires of color and bounty. Nana walked into town when she wanted something, spurning her son's offer to drive her and his invitation for her to come and live with them in the big house.

"Surely you know that wouldn't do," Aunt Augusta had said to Frazier when he first proposed it. "It would be a terrible influence on Peyton. Your mother's half crazy, and the whole town knows it. She makes a commotion every time she comes to town. She makes prophecies. We all know it's just hokum, but she scares the Negroes. Ed Carruthers at the hardware store said his Negro boys have started carrying charms around in their pockets, to ward off the evil eye or some such nonsense. She stood in the middle of Monument Square the other day yelling 'Go tell the Devil!' at a flock of crows. Floyd Fletcher won't do anything because she's your mother, but believe me, he'd like to."

"It would not be advisable for him to try it," Frazier had said tightly. "She's not crazy, you know, Augusta. The things she says and does have come down a thousand years in the Highlands. They make sense to her and to me, too, though I wish she wouldn't do them in the middle of town. When I was little I thought she had the Sight. She still says she does."

He looked levelly at Augusta, who fell silent, dropping her eyes. Then he turned to Peyton, who was elaborately doing her homework at the breakfast table nearby, and winked. Peyton's heart soared. She loved her Nana McKenzie without boundary or condition, knew her wildness in every drop of her own blood, believed with her whole heart that the old woman had the Sight, and was so warmed and energized by the wink that she said, "Everybody knows that crows watch all week to see what sins we've committed, and on Friday they go down to hell and tell the Devil. Jaybirds do it, too. Haven't you ever heard of Jaybird Friday?"

"I have not, except among the Negroes," Aunt Augusta said. "It's a Negro superstition, Peyton, not a Scottish one."

"They've got crows in Scotland, too," Peyton said rudely, and she knew at once that she had cranked it one ratchet too far.

"If I hear of Mama McKenzie creating one more scene in public I am going to speak to Floyd," her aunt said. "There are ways he could discourage her without embarrassing her or us. This can't continue, Frazier."

"I don't want to hear of your doing that, Augusta," her father said, in a voice as still and austere as his profile. "It is not your place. I can't believe you've stooped to tale-telling around town about my mother. She is your mother-in-law, you know. She is Charlie's mother."

"And he has not invited her into his home for more than a year now. Did you ever wonder why?"

Frazier McKenzie turned his head slowly and looked at his sister-in-law. It was not a glower, and he did not speak, but it struck Peyton that she hoped he never looked at her that way. The sea-gray of his eyes turned to ice, and his thin mouth thinned even further. Suddenly

she could see her wild peregrine of a grandmother in him, the floating smoke hair, the strange light eyes, the narrow head and long,
bladelike features.

Why, he's handsome, she thought in surprise. And Nana is beautiful. Why didn't I see it before? And Chloe says I look like them. Does
that mean that one day . . . ?

But Peyton knew that her own pale McKenzie features would
never draw together into a face like theirs, knew that her own milky
gray eyes would never flame or freeze.

"That is enough, Augusta," her father said, and Aunt Augusta
dropped her eyes. Soon after, she gathered up her ubiquitous shopping
bags and went home. Peyton felt exultation at her aunt's virtual ban-
ishment and decided that she would visit her grandmother that afternoon and tell her about it. She said as much to Clothilde, who sighed.

"What y'all talk about all that time?" she said. "Seem to me your
grandmother don't know no living folks anymore."

"No, but she tells me wonderful stories about our own people who
have . . . gone on, and about the other great clans. . . . Did you know
we're proper clan members, with our own tartan and everything? All
of them were heroes. They all died with honor and glory. And they're
not really dead, not to her. She says they're with her a lot of times
when we don't see them. That's who she's talking to when we think
she's talking to herself. She says one day I'll hear them, too, and maybe
see them. She thinks I'm going to have the Sight when I'm older."

Chloe put down her iron and looked at her.

"Maybe your aunt is right, Peyton," she said. "Maybe you ought
to spend some time with other people, folks your age. I ain't afraid of
your grandmother, I like her, and I believe it when she say she see and
hear stuff. Some of my people did that, too. But it ain't what you
ought to be doing right now in your life. Look at you: you don't talk
about much but your mama and your brother and you don't see
many people but your grandmother and that Ernie and my own po'
little Boot . . . and y'all spend all afternoon in the cemetery. You just
too young to spend your life with dead folks. Pretty soon you won't
know what's real anymore."

"That's just silly," Peyton said, and she went upstairs and put on her blue jeans and climbed the dogwood tree at the side of the house to the tree house where she spent a great deal of her time, and she opened her book. She had just discovered *The Catcher in the Rye* and knew Holden Caulfield's great otherness in her own bones and felt that somehow this book was going to change her life.

But she did not read after all. Instead, Peyton sat in her tree eating an apple and thinking, for the first time, about her life with the vivid dead.

2

*P*eyton *watched her movies again that night after supper, after her* father went out to his office over the garage to polish up the Sunday-school lesson he would teach the next morning at the First Methodist Church of Lytton (if there had ever been a second one, Peyton knew nothing of it).

She went into her room behind the cavernous downstairs bathroom and pulled the old projector out of her closet and hung a white sheet on the door. The nails had been there a long time; her father had never noticed them, and Clothilde never mentioned them. All Peyton had to do was pull out the sheet that she kept folded in her underwear drawer and hang it up. The sheet had had nail holes in it for as long as the nails had been up.

She had volunteered to learn to use the old school projector when she was in the fourth grade, surprising everyone but herself. One or two near-invisible students who never did much else were the official projectionists each year; it gave them a sort of inverted cachet to know how to do something the iron-hard farm kids and the ace softball players and the budding cheerleaders did not. To be a volunteer

projectionist at Lytton Grammar School was to be a pariah, but it
was to be a visible one. None of the others in their short memories
could remember Peyton McKenzie's volunteering for anything.

She proved to be deft and quick-handed with the wheezing old
machine, and for the past three years had been the one excused
from her classes to come and thread up and show the jackrabbitting
films on the agriculture of the Urals and the Battle of Agincourt
and, at Christmas, for everyone except the smallest children, *A
Christmas Carol*. The only films she did not show were the coy
ones entitled *Personal Hygiene* and *Now You're Growing Up*,
which the Fulton County Board of Education had recycled every
year for the past twenty. Indeed, in that year of Our Lord 1961, a
few native Lytton youngsters still attained puberty wondering what
the blood and the hair and the nocturnal emissions had to do with
flowers and butterflies and bees.

Peyton didn't care about that, or about any of the other films she
showed in the darkened classrooms. She cared about learning how to
use the projector and how to thread the big spools of film, and what
to do when the film inevitably snapped or frizzled or got caught in
the guts of the machine. By now she could have set up and operated
the equipment in her sleep, and in fact often did do so in the dark,
when her father thought she was sleeping. His bedroom, the one he
had shared with Peyton's mother, was upstairs and in the front of the
house, overlooking Green Street. He might have noticed the glow
from Peyton's bedside lamp reflected on the great oaks outside, but he
could not have seen the silent snow of the film's light.

Peyton showed herself her movies on the average twice a week.
She had found the projector and a screen and the cans of film one
day when she was poking around in the spider room, a forbidden
concrete-floored cubicle at the back of the garage where her father
had once seen a black widow spider. She had asked him about them
that night, and he had said that they were old home movies, so faded
and brittle that no one could make head or tails of them now. He
had, he said, forgotten they were there.

"Movies of what?" Peyton asked.

"Oh, you know. Things around town. This house. The Hendershots' house back behind us. Mr. and Mrs. Hendershot's mules, Cadillac and Hannah. I don't know if you remember them; you were real small when the Hendershots sold them. The church, and Nana's farm. Nana and Grandpa."

"And us? Are we there?"

"Well . . . there are a few of your mother and your brother and me. A dog we used to have, a beagle named Nosy. Some birthdays and Christmases and things. . . ."

"And me? Are there any of me?" Peyton asked. The question was like running a tongue over a sore tooth. She knew the answer.

"Well, you weren't born yet. About that time I moved my office out to the garage and the movie stuff got put away and I just forgot about it. I didn't even remember where it was until you found it today. What were you doing in the spider room, anyway?"

"Just looking," Peyton mumbled. There was warm salt stinging her eyes and nose. She knew that the reason her father had never made movies of her was that the pale little life that had taken that larger, singing one was nothing to be recorded. But after that the movies drew her like a magnet, and it was the next week that she volunteered for projectionist at school. After two or three weeks of practice, she went out to the garage while Frazier was in Atlanta at the Fulton County Courthouse doing a title search, and she moved the projector and the film into her room. She kept the projector behind her long winter coat and raincoat in the closet, and the round, flat cans of film under her bed. Twice a week Peyton lay in the dark and watched a world without her whir and flicker against her wall.

She always thought of these showings as a journey with only one direction in which she could travel. There were no alternate routes and no shortcuts. First she would put on the footage of Lytton and study the flickering images of her hometown as though she would, this time, find something new there, something that would fit her neatly into its small context. She did not know who had made the town films. Her mother or father, probably. They were fairly steady and had a logical progression to them, as if, watching them, you were actually traveling through Lytton coming in from the north on the old Roosevelt Highway from Atlanta. First the Ford tractor dealership, and then Mr. Cornelius Chatteron's filling station, then the town's one prized traffic light and the first railroad underpass off to the left, where the Atlanta and West Point trains crossed through and out of Lytton, their scornful whistles trailing behind. Then the post office and the dry cleaners'—hissing clouds of steam and smelling powerfully of benzine—and then the rest of the small businesses and services that made up Lytton's Main Street, all ranged along one side of the street because the railroad tracks and depots occupied the other, along with a small, ill-kept park featuring a dingy, phalluslike monument to the town's World War I dead. There were a tiny grocery, a hardware store, a barbershop, a butcher shop with its floor thickly felted with sawdust smelling of chilled blood, a lunchroom with a poolroom in back, and a drugstore with a black marble soda fountain and wire racks of comic books where children could and did sit on the floor, hidden from the view of the weary clerk, and read everything new that came in. There were a ten-cent store, the Lytton Banking Company, a seldom-visited insurance office, the town municipal offices, and the solitary wooden movie theater that when Peyton was small, had showed movies from Thursday evening through Saturday, with an afternoon cowboy matinee. The less seemly but still essential business of Lytton was conducted down small side streets, some barely paved. The yellow brick jail was there, with its stinking component of three cells that had harbored Lytton's drunk and disorderly and its out-of-season hunters for nearly a century. And the funeral home, a big, peeling white house that had been someone's home in the last century and still, to Peyton, looked like a place where people lived instead of died. The South Fulton County Public Health Department, where inoculations and not much else were dispensed. The old icehouse, where also in Peyton's childhood, families could rent storage space and hang whole sides of beef and skinned hog carcasses until they were needed.

The individual professional offices were upstairs above the businesses on Main Street: old Dr. Carither's office; another attorney's office to take care of whatever scant litigiousness arose in Lytton; and a dark-paneled dentist's office that somehow always smelled of hot, just-drilled dentin and was universally feared and loathed among the young of Lytton. There was a beauty shop up there, too, to which the ladies of Lytton climbed on dark stairs, their heads wrapped in kerchiefs only to come down again hours later with heads sporting tight, fried Medusa locks, smelling of rotten eggs. Peyton had always heard that there was a pawnshop up there somewhere, but she had never seen it.

She could not have said when the movies of the town were made. They had no human figures in them. It was as if someone had made a tour of the town for posterity and somehow edited out all life; it might have been an architectural travelogue, except that there was little architecture in Lytton to study or celebrate. She rather thought her father had done the filming; it became, in her mind, a kind of loving ritual he had performed early in the life of his family, to record a world for the rest of them so that when they came into the films they would know where they were and be easy with the knowing. Because very little in Lytton had changed appreciably since the middle thirties, aside from the addition of some businesses and another traffic light, the Lytton of Peyton's time was the Lytton of her family's time, too, and that soothed her obscurely. In her mind, when she thought about Lytton, Georgia, it was a town of erratic sepia images bathed in silence, sometimes so vivid that the present-day town surprised her in its eye-jarring garishness and mundanity. Peyton's reel world was also her real one.

When she had reassured herself that the town in the films was still as it had been the last time she looked, she let herself follow the camera down the side streets, where people actually lived; these sequences she knew that her father had taken, from some unremembered automobile, because people on the sidewalks and front porches waved and called out, and she could see, rather than hear, the shape of his name on their mouths: "Frazier McKenzie, put that thing away." "Aren't you a little old to be playing with movies, Frazier?"

He was greeted with familiarity on the shaded street where her parents lived, by children on bicycles in the streets around, by the ice-

man in his truck, by the paperboy, Cooper Freeman, by several trudg-
ing black men on their way downtown to buy groceries, and, finally,
from the doorway of Peyton's house itself, looking almost precisely as
it did now except for the striped awnings over the front porch that
had been there then and now were not, by her mother. Her mother,
Lila Lee Peyton McKenzie, waving from the front door and laughing
silently and doing a pantomime of a movie star being photographed.
As always, when she reached this spot in the film, Peyton felt something loosen in her chest, something open, so that a relief that was so
profound it almost brought her to tears flooded her. Once again she
had traveled the road home, through the town, up and down the
streets, passing by the people who had been the furniture of her parents' and brother's world but not of hers, and had come safely to this
place where her mother smiled and held out her arms in welcome. It
did not in the least matter to Peyton that the welcome was not for her.
In the films and in her mind, it was always a sweet sepia summer, and
time stopped itself on the walkway to her house, and she was home.

Once she was safe, it was easy for Peyton to watch the other films,
the ones she thought of as the Us Films. Most of them were, she
knew, made by her father because they were of her mother, so young
and light-struck and beautiful that she seemed to shimmer with color
even though there was none on the film. Her mother, small and slender with a rounded bosom and delicate hands and feet, her blond
hair a nimbus around her little cat's face, her chin tipped back and
her soft mouth wide open around her laughter. Her mother dancing
to unheard music on the porch, her mother vamping for the camera
in the backyard, where a barbecue was going on; her mother in a
long velvet matron-of-honor's dress at her Cousin Bootsie's wedding
in Gadsden, Alabama, eclipsing the entire wedding party, bride and
all; her mother standing at the net at the little Lytton Country Club
holding a tennis racket and smiling up at a tall, trim young man in
tennis whites who had raised both hands and clasped them over his
head in victory. He was dark and, Peyton thought, brooding and
romantic-looking, as she imagined Heathcliff must have looked, and
the one time she had asked her father about the scene, when he had

showed it for her brother when he was home on his first furlough, he had said the young man was the tennis pro at the club, and had been teaching her mother tennis, and she was such a natural that soon they had played together in tournaments. Her father thought that in the film they had just won the all-club tournament. No, he didn't remember much about the young pro, certainly not what had become of him after he moved on. The boy's name, he thought, might have been Alvin. Peyton, who had fallen instantly in love with the young man and built an entire world around him, hoped not. Alvin was a drip's name, a movie projectionist's name. In her mind she called the young man Gregory.

Soon her brother appeared, fat and blond and toddling stolidly around the big, flower-bordered backyard. Peyton knew that her mother had made these films, because in every one of them Buddy was attached in some way to his smiling father. Frazier McKenzie had been an attractive young man, Peyton thought, a little dour, maybe, with his long Scot's nose and sharp chin, and the peat-dark hair falling over his gray eyes, but when he laughed—and in the films he was almost always laughing—his face lit up with something powerfully magnetic, and he had a loose-limbed, long-armed grace that made him seem a teenager. He almost was: Frazier McKenzie had married Lila Lee Peyton when he was twenty-two and she just eighteen, and he was still only twenty-four when Buddy was born. Peyton studied her father as closely as she did her mother, to try to find something in him that was hers alone, that had not first belonged to her mother or brother. She found nothing, ever, except a physical resemblance that would have better served her brother, who was the low, fair, square image of his mother. Her father's looks had nothing at all to do with her essential Peytonness. On her, his long, thin arms and legs, the sharp, grave face, the light eyes and flyaway, smoky dark hair added up to nothing but plainness. Plainness, irredeemable and immutable.

After an hour of Christmases and birthdays, in which Buddy grew to brick-solid prepuberty and stopped toddling and began throwing footballs and hitting baseballs a country mile, stopped being the heavy-bottomed cherub with his diaper down around his ankles, crowing in the flaccid surf on St. Simon's Island, and became the heavy-jawed, frowning young nimrod, squinting into the distance with his first shotgun broken across his arm—here, Peyton always took a deep breath, stopped the film for a moment, and then set it in forward again.

And there she was, in a Christmas group portrait posed before the big tree that always stood in the high-ceilinged foyer of the Green Street house, along with her father and her brother, all of them older and somehow softened, and a dog she would never know, a setter, looking, even then, faded and arthritic. There she was, in the middle of the tinsel and wrapping paper and the laughter and the soft Christmas morning light: a round melon, a hard knot of darkness in her mother's stomach, the cancer that would soon end the movies for good and all.

In the morning she got up and cut her hair. She did it swiftly and ruthlessly before the bathroom mirror, not meeting her own eyes, grasping each long braid and sawing it clumsily with the kitchen shears. She stood for a long moment, staring at the peat-brown ropes that had bound her to childhood, now lying on the worn linoleum, and then she lifted her head to the mirror.

An apparition looked back. Peyton was breathing hard with the enormity of what she had done, and her mouth made an oval in her pale face, and her eyes looked blind and white like those of an archaic statue. Her hair hung in tattered hanks around her face, stopping a few inches below her ears, and somehow her thin neck stretched out like a Modigliani woman's.

Medusa, she thought suddenly. That's who I look like. Medusa. Well, then, OK. If they try to get all over me I'll turn them to stone.

She grinned savagely into the mirror and nearly vomited with the sheer hideousness of her face and neck. How could the loss of two skinny pigtails have made this insane, malevolent difference in her?

She ran warm tap water over her hands, slicked it onto her hair, and fluffed it out of its limp helmet. Perhaps, she thought, it will be all right after all. It has some curl in it. Maybe it will sort of frame my face. In her mind she saw soft, tumbling waves drifting around her head, full and shining. They would make her eyes larger, soften the severe planes of her face, make her thin mouth bloom. She knew, as she looked back into the mirror, that she hoped to see her mother there.

Medusa still looked back, this time with the snakes.

Peyton took a deep breath to push down the nausea, said aloud to Medusa, "I don't give a shit," and walked into the kitchen.

Clothilde was washing the breakfast dishes, her dark hands slipping birdlike in and out of the sinkful of steaming suds. She turned to look at Peyton and dropped the Fiestaware creamer into the water. Peyton heard it shatter on the porcelain.

"Peyton, what in the name of God you done?" she breathed.

"Obviously, Clothilde, I have cut my hair. Maybe you've heard of haircuts?" Peyton said with a cold aluminum brightness.

"I heard of haircuts," Chloe said. "That ain't no haircut. That look like you took a lawnmower to it. Your daddy gon' have a fit. Your Aunt Augusta gon' have a conniption. What was you thinkin' of?"

"I was tired of it," Peyton said airily. "Pigtails are for babies." She could almost feel the phantom pain in the ragged ends of her hair. Misery rose like bile, threatening to swamp her.

"Well, your daddy gon' grow you up real quick," Clothilde said fiercely, and then her dark face softened. "Why don't you go try to do something with it, maybe wet it and push it back behind your ears, and let me tell him. Get him used to the notion. You can get Miss Freddie at the beauty shop to even it up some tomorrow afternoon. And it'll grow back. We just needs to get used to the idea of you without that hair."

"Where is Daddy?" Peyton said in the new bright voice.

"He out in his office. He giving the Sunday-school lesson this morning. You know, Peyton, you got that pretty straw hat Miss Augusta bought you for Easter last year. You look real pretty in that hat. Why don't you wear it this morning? Maybe with your blue dress. You look real grown-up in that dress."

"I'm not going to Sunday school or church, either," Peyton said. "I'm tired of that, too. I'm going to read all day. Sunday is a day of rest."

She turned and stalked out of the kitchen before Chloe could reply, and got the paperback copy of *Nine Stories* that Ernie had given her for her birthday, and went into her room and closed the door. Seymour Glass would understand.

She waited all day for her father to come to her room, to knock, to open her door and come in, to see, finally, what she had done to herself; waited for whatever he would do. She had no idea. She had never done anything so overtly grotesque before. She was afraid of his anger, but she was more afraid of simple, cold contempt. By suppertime she could stand it no longer, so she smoothed the ragged spikes as best she could and went into the living room, where her father sat with the Sunday paper, the television set flickering soundlessly in the corner. Her father had lit only one lamp, the bridge lamp that stood beside his cracked leather easy chair, and in its pale glow she could see only the side of his face, in profile. It was still and empty. An effigy.

"Peyton," he said, not turning his head. His voice was mild and weary, nothing more. But it cut her to her heart.

"I guess you want to see it," she said, striving for the hard-edged airiness she had found that morning in the kitchen. "We can have the big unveiling."

He turned his head and looked at her then. He was silent for a long while. Peyton felt tears like acid rising in her throat. She knew she would rather die than cry, and also that she probably would.

"Whole lot of crying going on lately," she said chattily to herself.

"We haven't taken you very seriously, have we?" Frazier McKenzie said at last. His voice was still weary, but there was nothing in it of shock or anger. Perhaps it might still be all right. . . .

"Daddy, it was a mistake, I don't know why I did it . . . ," she began, and then clenched her teeth shut over the tears.

"I don't care about your hair, Peyton," he said. "We can get that fixed; Augusta is going to take you into Atlanta and get you all prettied up. It's that you were so unhappy, and needed attention so much, and we didn't notice it—*I* didn't notice it. I wish you had come and talked to me about whatever is bothering you instead of chopping off your pretty hair, but I'm not exactly the kind of father a young girl comes running to, am I?"

The tears began to spill over Peyton's lower lashes.

"I'm not unhappy," she quavered. "I don't need attention. You're a good father, Daddy. I don't know why I did it. It just seemed all of a sudden something I needed to do. . . . But it looks pretty awful, doesn't it? I look like Medusa."

"You don't look a bit like Medusa," he said, and he smiled slightly. Even the smile was tired. "You're a pretty girl. I think you'll be a pretty woman one day. But we're going to have to make some changes. Augusta was right. You're at the point now where you need a woman in your life on a long-term basis. I can't be that to you. Sometimes I think I can barely be a father. You'll be thirteen in—June, isn't it? You can't be a child anymore. You can't just run wild."

"I don't run wild," Peyton whispered, the unfairness of it loosening the tears again. "I've never run wild in my life."

"No, you haven't," he said. "It was a bad choice of words. But you've got to grow up some, and you've got to do it the right way. You may not care now, but you'll want friends and a social life before long, and you'll need to know how to take on some of a woman's responsibilities sooner or later. It's got to start now, and I can't do it, so your Aunt Augusta is going to. It's George Washington's birthday Tuesday, and your aunt is taking you to Rich's for a hairdo and some clothes and maybe to lunch at the tearoom. They have these fashion shows at lunch, I think. You may be surprised to find that you have a good time."

"I won't," Peyton cried, panic rising in her chest. It was too much too fast, too awful, too big a punishment just for cutting her hair.

"You will," he said, and he turned back to his newspaper.

Peyton went back to her room and threw herself across her narrow bed and cried in the winter twilight, knowing that the change was upon her and it was going to be terrible past imagining, and that she and she alone had summoned it with a pair of kitchen shears.

3

Peyton went to school the next day with a scarf tied under her chin.
It had been her mother's; she had found it in the cedar chest that sat
at the foot of the mahogany bed in the big bedroom. It was cream
silk, splashed with huge red poppies and green vines, and must have
looked festive and exotic on her mother. On Peyton, it looked almost
shocking, like a whore's finery on a baby. But it was better than the
hair. Peyton had it all planned: she would tell people she had an earache and had to keep the cold air off of it. "We're going into Atlanta
tomorrow to see a specialist," she would say.

But no one asked, no one except hulking Arlene Slattery, who was
known to be a retard.

"What you got on a head rag for?" Arlene asked.

"I have an earache," Peyton said. "I have to keep the cold air off it.
We're going into Atlanta tomorrow to see a specialist."

"Huh," Arlene breathed adenoidally. "I didn't know it was cold."

"Well, that's what Dr. Sams said to do," Peyton said huffily.

"Huh," Arlene said. In her world a visit to a doctor for anything less than a bull goring or a tractor crushing was as unimaginable as being invited to Buckingham Palace.

No one else mentioned the scarf, and by the time Peyton reached her front walk that afternoon the damp winter sultriness was making her head sweat under the scarf, and her mangled hair itched fierily. She jerked the scarf off, scratched her head, and started into the house. Then she changed course and trotted up the street to the Methodist parsonage. She went through backyards so no one would see her. When she came into the toolshed Ernie and Boot were waiting for her, drinking Coca-Cola. Peyton stood still, heart surging up into her throat, and assumed the old Betty Grable bathing-beauty pose.

"Taadaa!" she cried gaily. Even to her ears it sounded shrill and crazy.

"Holy shit!" Boot said reverently. "You done won the stupidest prize for the next two years. You looks like a picked pullet. What you go and do that for?"

"So I could win the stupidest prize for the next two years," Peyton said, wrinkling her nose like Debbie Reynolds.

"Well, it ain't no contest," Boot said. "Lawdy me. What you daddy say? What did Mamaw say?"

"They said it was very becoming," Peyton said, looking perkily around the toolshed.

"Then they crazy as batshit," Boot said mournfully.

Peyton looked up under her lashes at Ernie, who was sitting still and looking back at her. She knew he could flay her alive if he wished.

Ernie cocked his fuzzy head and closed his eyes to slits and tilted his head and studied her as if she were a museum exhibit. Peyton waited for annihilation.

"You know, it's really not bad at all," he said finally. "I think it suits you. You need to get it evened up a little, but I think when you get used to it you might like it. Yes. I think you might look quite chic. Better than just pretty, really. Perhaps you're going to amount to something as a woman after all. I had just about given up hope."

Peyton felt trembling gratitude swell in her chest, and a kind of hopeful disbelief. Could he mean what he said? Of course not; anyone could see how she looked. But Ernie had never spared anyone's feelings before, in all her experience of him.

She smiled, a silly, quivering smile.

Boot simply stared.

"Well, you little people run on now," Ernie said. "I've got to take Mama to the dentist. Maybe this time he'll drill her tongue out."

Boot and Peyton laughed, and it was suddenly all right again: the Losers Club found its proper place in her firmament, and her life bowled on.

It was early. No one would expect her home for a couple of hours yet. Peyton decided to walk down the highway to see her grandmother. She was forbidden to do this; the Roosevelt Highway, which ran through Lytton, was always thick with Atlanta-bound traffic. But she knew that there was a footpath through the tall weeds on the other side of the railroad tracks, and she followed that. The walk took only about ten minutes. The little wind was cool on her neck. Her grandmother would understand, even if she didn't like the hair.

She found Agnes McKenzie in her dark, cluttered cave of a kitchen, icing tea cakes. They were almost the only thing that Nana cooked well, but they were sublime. She always made them for Peyton at Christmas, and on her birthday. A sweet vanilla smell told Peyton that there was another sheet of them in the old black woodstove. She stood still and breathed deeply. This was the very smell of childhood, rich and simple and succoring.

Her grandmother did not turn around.

"Knew it was you," she said. "Saw it in the washtub this morning. Saw that you could do with a mess of tea cakes, too. We'll talk about it terreckly. Right now I need you to bring me some more wood in from the pantry."

Peyton went into the pantry shed that opened off the kitchen. The wood basket stood there, along with a pristine electric stove and a new washer and dryer. Frazier had given them to his mother two years before. She had never used them.

"You've got arthritis in your hands; I see you rubbing them," he had said in exasperation to his mother. "Why won't you just give the stove and the washer and dryer a try? Cold wash water and heavy iron stove lids are going to cripple you."

But Agnes McKenzie had simply thanked her son sweetly and gone on with heavy, red-hot iron and dark soapy water. Only Peyton knew why.

"I see things in the fire and the water," Agnes had told her once. "The bad things in the fire and the good ones in the water. It's how I know things."

Peyton picked up an armful of lightwood and went back into the warm, dim kitchen.

"If you saw me in the water, that's good, isn't it?" Peyton said to her grandmother. Agnes turned and looked at her, and then smiled her V-shaped kitten's smile. In the dimness she looked perhaps thirty, a smoky-haired, ocean-eyed thirty. Beautiful. Wild.

"Oh, child," she said. "Look at you. I wondered what it was. I knew you'd lost something. I saw that in the fire. Come sit and we'll have some coffee and tea cakes. There's not much that good strong coffee and tea cakes won't put right."

Peyton took the thick cup gratefully and sipped the steaming coffee. It was as black as ink and as thick as the peat bogs in Agnes McKenzie's distant wild mountains. She didn't like it very much—it was sludgy and bitter on her tongue—but no one else let Peyton have coffee. It made another bond with her grandmother. She always drank it in this house.

"Do you hate it?" Peyton said to her grandmother.

"I pretty well do," Agnes said. "You look like you been whupped through hell with a buzzard gut, as our old washwoman used to say. But that doesn't matter. It won't last. You're going to be a handsome woman. You'll have the look of the MacLarens about you. You're going to look a lot like me, I think, when you get really old. And that's pretty good, if I do say so myself. What bothers me is why you did it."

"I don't know," Peyton said miserably. All of a sudden she was desperately, achingly tired. She realized she had been counting on her grandmother to say that she looked fine.

"Big change coming. Is that it?" Agnes said, pouring more coffee.

"You mean becoming a young woman and being proper and all, I guess," Peyton said. "Everybody's going on about it. 'You have to change, Peyton.' 'You're a young lady now, Peyton.' 'You won't have any boyfriends, Peyton.'"

"You think making yourself ugly is going to change that? You'll grow up, my heart, ugly or not. Whacking off your hair isn't going to stop that."

"Well, it just might put it off a while," Peyton said, stung.

Her grandmother laughed. It went with the rest of her, deep and rich and somehow streaked with fire.

"Don't think so," she said. "I see that it's right on top of you."

"Do you see what's going to make me change? Daddy and Aunt Augusta are making me go to Rich's tomorrow and get styled and buy some new clothes. I think that's just the beginning. Aunt Augusta was going on about dancing school. . . ."

"Can't you dance yet, Peyton?" Her grandmother smiled. "I could dance as soon as I could walk; I still do it; it's like playing with the wind; it's like running in water in the sun. But I guess we aren't talking about Augusta's kind of dancing. To answer your question, I do see a woman in your life, for a long time to come. Yes. That much is clear."

"Is it Aunt Augusta? Is it you?"

"I don't think it's Augusta. I wouldn't allow that, in any case. I'd run her off if she leaned too heavy on you. I know how to do that. And no, it isn't me. There's not enough time for that. I don't know who it is, only that she's coming."

"Did you see her in the water or the fire?"

"I saw her in a bowl of Campbell's tomato soup." Her grandmother smiled and reached out to touch the murdered hair gently. "I don't know what that means. It doesn't feel like it's bad, though. Only . . . very different. Maybe I'll see more of her later."

"Will you tell me when you know?"

"No," her grandmother said, pushing the hair off Peyton's fore-head. "I don't believe I will."

When she got home, she found the kitchen dark and the breakfast-room table still not set for supper. The house was very quiet; she could almost hear, as well as see, the dust motes dancing in the last of the afternoon sun on the stairs. She listened hard, in faint unease. She could not remember many afternoons when she had come into this house without the great, warming sense of Clothilde close by.

Then she heard the burring grumble of the old Electrolux upstairs somewhere, and she followed the sound up.

She found Chloe vacuuming the thin-worn carpet in the big upstairs back bedroom that they had always called the guest room, only Peyton could not remember any guests ever being in it. It would have been her room if she had not clung to her small one downstairs. Her father slept in the big front room that had been his and Lila Lee's. He had disturbed nothing of it except to remove, or have Clothilde remove, Lila Lee's toiletries and hairbrushes from the dressing table. Peyton did not know what had happened to them. She often thought she would like to have them, and would ask for them, but somehow she never did. It would be too awful to find that they had been given away, as her mother's clothes and shoes had been, to the Salvation Army.

Buddy had slept in the other front bedroom, and its doors were kept closed, except for when Clothilde went in two or three times a year to clean it. Peyton did not go into it. She scarcely remembered what it looked like.

A thought rooted her in the doorway. They were making her move upstairs. It was a part of Aunt Augusta's ladyhood campaign. She darted into the room, calling to Clothilde, who did not hear her. Peyton shouted and then reached out and touched Clothilde on the back.

"Sweet Jesus Lord!" Clothilde squalled, starting violently and dropping the vacuum cleaner. The snake of its coil thrashed wildly on the floor. "Peyton, you like to scare me to death. Why didn't you call me?"

"I did," Peyton said. "You didn't hear me. What are you doing, Chloe? Because if anybody thinks they can make me move up here, they've got another think coming."

Clothilde turned off the Electrolux and straightened her back, moving her shoulders gratefully.

"It ain't for you, though it ought to be," she said. "Your feet gon' be stickin' out the door of that little old room before long. I reckon we're going to have a guest in the guest room pretty soon, and it looks like the hind axle of hard times. Couldn't nobody sleep in here without choking to death on the dust."

"A guest?" Peyton said stupidly. She could not make Clothilde's words fit into any context she knew. "What guest?"

"Your Cousin Nora coming to see us. She gon' stay a little while. Your daddy called from his office this afternoon; I reckon she called him there. He said to get the room ready and to tell you he had to go into Atlanta to the courthouse this evening and not to wait up for him. He'll see you in the morning. Oh, and your Aunt Augusta said she'd pick you up at nine in the morning, and to wear your Easter dress and straw hat."

Peyton's head spun. She clung to the top of the old cherry bureau, which gleamed now with new polish.

"What cousin? I don't know any Cousin Nora," she said. "I never heard of any Cousin Nora. Who is she? How old is she?" Peyton thought with hatred and alarm of blond curls and rosy cheeks and dancing little feet, and a cherub curled into her father's lap.

"She your mama's younger cousin's girl," Clothilde said. "I never met her. Her mama and your mama had some kind of falling-out right after Miss Lila Lee and your daddy got married, and your mama didn't talk about her, least not that I ever heard. I reckon Nora is your second cousin, and she'd be about—oh, maybe thirty now. Seem to me they lived in Florida someplace. I know she's coming in from Key West."

Peyton felt a great gust of terror, and then anger. What was happening here? Had the entire cosmos gone mad?

"Well, I'm not going to talk to her," she said, her voice trembling.

"She can stay up here in this room, and I'll stay down there in mine. I'll eat in my room. I don't know any cousins, and I don't want any visitors. Does Daddy even know her?"

"Not too good, I don't think she come up here for a visit when she real little, but he wasn't home much. Nora born a long time after your mama and her cousin stop talking."

"Well, why is he letting her stay here if he doesn't even know her?" Peyton cried. "She's not even his cousin, and she's not mine, really. For all he knows she might steal our things, or be coming just to get money from him. . . ."

"Because she your mama's kin, and yours, and it's what you do for kin," Clothilde said severely. "Just listen to yourself, Peyton. Your mama was famous for her hospitality and good manners, and here you think her little cousin gon' steal the silver. You got a nice house and a good daddy; you ought to be glad to share a little of what you got with people not as lucky as you."

"How do you know she's not as lucky as me?"

"Well—" Chloe paused. "I guess I don't. It just seem to me she sounds kind of lonesome-like. She ain't coming with anybody. She ain't married, your daddy said. He'll tell you some more about her at breakfast. And you gon' be nice to her or I'm gon' turn you inside out. She almost all you have of your mama's kin."

"How long is she going to stay?" Peyton asked, figuring in her head how she could arrange her days: breakfast so early nobody would be up; straight to the Losers Club after school; into her room the minute she got home; supper in her room with a book. . . .

"Not very long, I don't think. Your daddy say she on her way somewhere up north for a job. She just need a place to stop and rest on the way."

"There are about a million motels up on the interstate," Peyton muttered.

Clothilde rolled her eyes. "Why should she stay in a motel when she got folks here? Git on now, Peyton, and let me finish. I ain't even started supper yet."

Peyton started to slam out of the room and then stopped.

"Chloe—Nana knew she was coming! She told me this afternoon there was somebody coming, and it was a woman! She saw it in . . . the water."

Peyton was not about to reveal that her grandmother had seen this troublesome cousin bearing down on her in a bowl of tomato soup.

"Huh. Most likely she saw it in a Bell telephone," Clothilde grumbled. "You know your daddy call her every afternoon. Git on now."

"So when is she getting here?"

"I don't know. Two or three days, your daddy says. By the time she gets here you'll be all prettied up and have some new clothes and all. She'll look at her cousin and say, 'Woo-woo!' "

It was Clothilde's most favored superlative. Peyton hated it. She turned wordlessly and stumbled down the stairs and went into her room and closed the door, and she did not come out until Clothilde knocked hard on it and insisted that she eat her supper.

"I ain't carrying no trays to children in a temper fit," Chloe said through the door.

Peyton got up and shambled out into the breakfast room and ate tuna-fish casserole and green beans. In the entire time she ate, she did not look up at Clothilde in the kitchen, and she did not speak.

That night she showed herself her movies again, all of them, the entire tapestry of McKenzie life unrolling on a white sheet in a dark room. If her father came home before she slept, she did not know it. She could not have heard him over the whir of the projector. When she finally did sleep, it was to dream of flying, a wonderful dream she had had only a few times since childhood. She woke with the parabolas of flight still on her skin, wind still in her mouth and hair, and she stretched and smiled with the remembrance of it.

And then she remembered the other thing, that the stranger who was her own blood was coming, and that the only important thing was to manage never to meet her before she left again.

4

Y*ou have a little bitty head in proportion to your neck,"* Mr. Antoine said, standing back and squinting at Peyton in the mirror. "And you're really long and thin through the waist and legs. I think we'll balance that with an extravagant cloud of curls. Really feminine and soft around your face—it's sort of sharp, isn't it? And maybe just a few highlights at the hairline to bring out your nice eyes. How does that sound?"

Peyton, feeling pinheaded and as attenuated as an El Greco, did not answer. Indeed, since Aunt Augusta picked her up that morning in her clifflike Lincoln, Peyton had said as little as it was humanly possible to say without incurring her aunt's wrath.

"That sounds lovely, don't you think?" Aunt Augusta said. She was hovering behind the chair in Rich's Beauty Salon, where Peyton sat dripping-haired and swathed in a pink drape, steadfastly regarding her clenched hands. It was hard to tell to whom Aunt Augusta spoke. Mr. Antoine, probably, Peyton thought. Or perhaps herself. Her aunt kept glancing at her reflection in the huge lighted mirror while Mr. Antoine danced around Peyton like a dervish, darting in to snip, fluff, stand back, snip again. Mr. Antoine was willow-thin and fox-faced, with black hair slicked straight back, and he wore slender black trousers that cupped his little round buttocks, and a white shirt with a black bow tie. A certificate on the wall of his cubicle said that he had graduated from the Peach State School of Beauty and Makeup Artistry, though it did not say when. Very recently, Peyton thought. It was obvious that Mr. Antoine did not shave much yet. She supposed that he was what people considered elegant, even though you could detect, under the fluting of his voice, a whine that spoke of outhouses and pickup trucks.

"So did you get bubble gum in your hair, or what?" he said to Peyton as he snipped. "I see that a lot. Not to worry. You left us plenty to work with. Not like some of the girls I've seen, who didn't leave enough even to make a pin curl. And you have nice, strong, shiny hair. You're going to leave here looking like Sandra Dee."

Peyton closed her eyes then. She did not open them as he worked in the permanent solution, which felt cold on her scalp and smelled of sulfur-scented roses. She did not open them when he pulled her hair smartly onto rollers, or put her under the dryer. Before long the comforting, droning heat inside her own small cave soothed her into a drowse. It seemed hours later when Mr. Antoine shook her awake for what he called the comb-out. Peyton opened her eyes then, but she did not look into the mirror.

He combed and brushed and tugged and fluffed and sprayed. He hummed tunelessly under his breath as he worked. Peyton thought it was "Que Sera, Sera," but she couldn't be sure. She smiled grimly to herself. Truer words were never hummed.

Finally she heard him step back.

"Voilà!" he cried gaily. "The new you. And just *look* at you!"

"Oh, Peyton, it looks just lovely," Aunt Augusta trilled.

Peyton lifted her eyes. Her stomach lurched. She thought she was going to throw up her cereal then and there on Mr. Antoine's elegant pointed shoes.

All you saw was the hair. It was a tall, round helmet with a perfectly smooth exterior, inside which a surf of tiny curls and waves swirled. Crazily, Peyton thought of clothes storming in the porthole of a washing machine, of glinting, voracious fish milling in a round glass fishbowl. Underneath the helmet's surface her hair raged and writhed like the nest of baby snakes she and Ben Player had uncovered one day in their grandmother's rock garden. You could have bounced a nickel off the surface.

And it was blond. Butter yellow. Cadmium yellow.

She could not speak, and lifted her eyes wildly to Aunt Augusta in the mirror. Augusta McKenzie smiled back. Mr. Antoine hovered and fluffed and pursed his mouth and fluffed again.

"You're an entirely different person, Peyton," her aunt said. "You look years older. There's absolutely nothing babyish about you now. You are a blank slate, and we'll make a work of art of you."

Peyton still could not speak. Were they both insane? Could neither of them see what they had done to her? She felt her breathing begin to accelerate until her heart pounded and she felt lightheaded.

"Oh," she said, trying to suck air into her laboring lungs.

"Told you you'd love it," Mr. Antoine said, and he whirled away into another cubicle to answer a telephone.

"Truly, isn't it remarkable?" her aunt said happily, leaving a handsome tip for Mr. Antoine and guiding Peyton out of the chair and toward the salon door.

"Yes," Peyton whispered.

"I think we'll do a little something extra before lunch," Augusta McKenzie said. "Your hair is lovely, but it sort of overpowers your thin little face. I think we'll go down to Max Factor and get you made up. Nothing garish, of course, just a little blush and shadow and pink lipstick, to pop out those eyes and that mouth. Would you like that? Come on, Peyton, we have to hurry if we're going to get you done before the fashion show starts. It's on the first floor."

Peyton found to her horror that she could do nothing but follow her aunt out of the salon. Her legs and arms trembled so that she could hardly stand, and she was giddy from her traitorous breath. Blindly she reached out and took her aunt's arm. All down the interminable escalator ride she held on for dear life.

Augusta squeezed her hand.

"Well, this turned out to be fun, now, didn't it?" her aunt said, smiling. "You seem older already. We're like a couple of girls, skipping school and out for a shopping spree. I haven't had such fun in a long time."

Peyton let her aunt lead her to the Max Factor counter, as docilely as a lamb to the slaughterer's knife. There was nothing more they could do to her. Whatever they did would pale beside the hair. Peyton sat down on a tall stool while her aunt conferred with a skeletal woman whose white-blond hair was pulled back so severely that her eyes and nostrils flared, and whose lashes were laden with black sludge. She closed her eyes again. She would endure. It would be over. They would go home. She would do something to the hair, something, anything. And then she would let herself sink down into J. D. Salinger, hover there, dream there, and from there slide into sleep. She felt a soft brush dancing over her face, and the blond woman's birdlike fingers probing at her eyelids, and a thick smear of something that smelled like bubble gum being slicked onto her mouth. Peyton went far away behind her closed eyes and waited.

When she was small, Peyton had learned a trick. It was to look at things without seeing them. It involved a certain slackening of the muscles around her eyes, a tiny blurring of focus that let her see masses and color but no detail. She did not know how she did it, but it served her well. She stared directly into the face of her angry aunt, looked with dispassion on the bodies of pets killed in the street, watched entire coy reels of female sexual behavior in Hygiene without ever registering either the impact or the import of them.

She did this now when her aunt caroled, "Well, just look at our debutante!" and the skeleton woman said, "You're better than pretty, dear. You're going to be such a distinguished-looking woman," and squirted her with a spritz of something that stung her lips and eyelids and smelled vaguely of Mum's stick deodorant.

Peyton looked, blurring her eyes. She saw nothing but color: the yellow aureole that she supposed was the hair, two pink blotches that must be blush, a slash of deeper pink that was undoubtedly the Tender Rose lipstick that the skeleton lady had extolled. Above the cheeks and mouth were two round black pits that could only be her eyes.

"Wow," she said, not seeing.

"Wow, indeed," her aunt said. "Everybody will think you're in the fashion show. Let's get you these things, and I can help you practice putting them on until you've got it down. It takes a little practice or it looks unnatural."

"No shit," Peyton whispered. All right, then. Just add it to the hair, another dreadful thing that could be fixed when she got home. Only a matter of soap and water. . . .

They ate frozen fruit salad and little chicken-salad sandwiches and watched tall young women, as skinny as Peyton but so different as to have just landed from Uranus, prance and preen down a runway and out into the tearoom, where other, seated women smiled and murmured and spoke to them. The girls held up price tags and smiled back. In Peyton's squinted haze, they all looked like slender black or blue or pink herons, all neck and mouth and stilt legs, all as long and thin as a pencil stroke. For all she knew, they were all offering the same outfit, in different colors.

"Do you see anything you like, Peyton?" Aunt Augusta said. "Not that you could wear these yet; it'll be a while before you can fill them out. But the Tween Shop down on Two has some lovely things, quite grown up and smart. We'll stop on the way out. Your daddy wanted me to get you a couple of dressy dresses and one or two school things. We'll get shoes and bags later. I think this is enough for one day, don't you?"

"Yes," Peyton said, almost soundlessly.

They stopped at the Tween Shop, a terrible place of posturing prepubescent mannequins with impossibly slim waists and gently swollen breasts, most wearing pencil strokes of pink or blue or yellow, a few in shirtwaists with drifts of skirt and neat little collars and belts. A curly, flowered placard said that these offerings were suitable for young misses aged eleven to fourteen. Peyton didn't see any difference between the plastic mannequins and the prancing girls upstairs in the tearoom. She knew that no matter what they put on her face or head or body, she wasn't ever going to look like the women of Rich's Department Store, corporeal or in-.

"You pick something out," she said to her aunt, looking around for a vista that did not contain a mirror. Apparently young misses spent a lot of time regarding their budding selves in mirrors. "I can't decide."

Aunt Augusta and a clucking saleslady riffled along racks of clothes, pulling out a dress here and a skirt and blouse there, until the saleslady was laden with preteenery like a donkey.

"Let's just slip these on in the dressing room," the lady began.

"No," Peyton said. "I'm awfully tired. Aunt Augusta, you pick some things for me and let's take them home and I'll try them there. My head really hurts. . . ."

Augusta McKenzie, who had a keen sense of how far Peyton could be pushed, tutted and shook her head and dug among the clothes like a terrier. She pulled out a horrifying cerise dress and jacket—"Let's get some color into that face"—and a dark, plain sheath with a little coat to match, which she said would be nice for church. She selected two slim skirts and white blouses with little round collars, and one of the shirtwaists, blue-sprigged with tiny flowers and also adorned with a little round collar. It came with a gold circle pin on one wing of the collar.

"A Villager," the saleslady said solemnly, as if she were offering a Fabergé egg. "All the girls are buying them. Our Teen Board wears them. You'll just live in this."

"You can try the others on at home, Peyton, but I want you to go in there and put this little dress on now," her aunt said. "I want you to wear it home. I want your father to see you. He's going to be so surprised and proud."

Surprised is right, Peyton thought. She, too, knew the boundaries of her aunt's goodwill. Obediently, she let Aunt Augusta and the saleslady lead her into a small, curtained cubicle walled with mirrors, and let them divest her of the blue dress with the sash and puffed sleeves that she had worn for Easter for the past two years, and closed her eyes and let the legendary Villager slide down over her rigid hair and down her

body. She stood, desperately unfocused, as the saleslady buttoned up
the front of the bodice and pulled the belt snug around her waist.

"We're going to have to put another hole or two in that belt," the
saleslady said. "And if I might make a suggestion, there are some
sweet preteen bras in Lingerie, with just a little light padding to give
clothes some shape. This would fit a lot better with one of those.
Shall I just run over and pick a few out? I promise they're going to
make such a difference."

"No," Peyton all but wept. "I won't wear one. You can buy five
hundred for all I care, but I'm not wearing any bra. I don't have anything to put in it. I wouldn't wear one if I did."

Aunt Augusta raised her eyebrows at the saleslady and shook her
head, smiling ruefully. The saleslady smirked back.

"It's hard to grow up sometimes," the lady said. Peyton did not
know if she was speaking to her or to her aunt. "We often really
don't want to do it. But it's always easier if we have the right pretty
things to wear."

Then *you* wear them, Peyton shrieked in her head. But she could
not have spoken even if someone had held a gun to her head. Her
stomach lurched.

"Why don't you just pick out a couple that you think would be
suitable and add them to my charge?" Aunt Augusta said. "I guess
the smallest size they have. Do they make them small enough?"

"Oh, yes. Sometimes our girls ask for them at ten or eleven. It
makes them feel grown-up. The sizes start at twenty-eight triple-A. I
think this young lady would do fine in a thirty double-A. It has the
padding, after all. Now, could I just show you a little garter belt and
some stockings? She's really going to need them to look finished in
these pretty things."

"Bring them," Aunt Augusta said. The saleslady scurried away,
happily gorged on a fat charge account.

"Peyton," her aunt said, turning to her in annoyance. "You might
say thank you, at least. That lady has put in a lot of time with you.
I've put in a lot of time with you. Your father has put a lot of money
into this little trip—"

"I think I'm going to throw up," Peyton said.

The trot between the Tween and Junior departments to the restroom seemed endless. Swallowing hard against bile, Peyton plodded dumbly behind her aunt, who was leading her by the hand and saying, "You can hold it, now. You just hold it. You know you don't want to throw up in the middle of Rich's. . . ."

Peyton did hold it, but only just. She lurched into one of the stalls and gagged and vomited before she could even latch the door. She heaved and retched until she thought she would begin to bring up the lining of her stomach. When she finally stopped, she was weak and sweaty and splattered. She leaned against the cold steel of the cubicle and breathed in deep, desperate gasps.

Presently her aunt opened the cubicle and produced a handful of wet paper towels. She began to dab and scrub at Peyton's dress and swiped at her face with the cool brown paper.

"Come on out here and let's wash your face," she said, whether in concern or annoyance Peyton could not have said. "Oh, goodness. Just look at you. Your makeup is all smeared. . . ."

Peyton stood mute, splashing her face in the sink when her aunt told her to, rinsing her mouth, letting Augusta pat her dry with fresh white towels. She did not look in the mirror or anywhere else. Her eyes were firmly shut.

"Better now?" Augusta said. "You're looking better: your color's coming back. Here, let's just touch you up a little. I wonder if it was that chicken salad—you're really not used to rich food. Come on, let's get you home. We'll get a Coca-Cola in the parking lot. That'll settle your tummy."

Peyton found that she could not walk out of the ladies' room without opening her eyes, so she did, looking fixedly away from the mirror. They fell on a middle-aged Negro woman in starched black, with a tiny white apron. The woman sat impassively on a stool beside the end of the counter, a basket full of fresh towels and hand lotions on one side of her and a discreet little china dish full of coins on the other. She looked a great deal like Clothilde, or like Clothilde would have looked if she had been gotten up like a French maid, with a ruffle of white organdy on her massive head and narrow black slippers on her feet. This lady had slits cut into the slippers through which flesh protruded like bubbles in hot tar, and she did not rise from her stool.

Peyton felt suddenly soothed. Here, then, was succor: this woman's stout arms were made for enfolding, her huge shelf of bosom was designed for pressing a hot face into. She wouldn't, of course, but still, the arms and bosom were *there*. She smiled at the woman.

The woman did not smile back. She stared at Peyton with such level malevolence that Peyton almost gasped aloud. She looked into the mirror to see what the woman saw that could engender such contempt.

She saw a ghastly, smirking succubus with wild, stiff yellow hair and smears of pink and black on her white face, the skirts of a silly puffy dress swirling about her, the bodice splotched with damp. She saw what the woman saw: a flossily dressed teenager whose mama had spent too much money on her makeup and hairstyling, who had just thrown up her little ladies' lunch in the toilet and had had to be dabbed and wiped and cosseted like a baby. The woman saw girls like her every day. She hated them.

Peyton read the hate and turned away. She wanted to shout, "This is not me; don't think I'm like this! They did this to me, but I can undo it all. . . ."

But she did not. She followed Augusta McKenzie down the escalator to the basement parking lot and sat there dumbly while their car was brought around, sipping the Coca-Cola her aunt bought her and knowing in her sick heart that there had been nothing asked of her, no test put to her, that she had not, on this day, failed.

In the Lincoln Peyton put her head back against the seat and pretended to sleep.

"You go right ahead," her aunt said. "You've had a busy day. You'll be all fresh when you model the new Peyton McKenzie for your papa."

Nausea stirred like a sleepy snake in Peyton's stomach, and she swallowed hard against it. She turned her face to her window, away from Aunt Augusta. She would never in this world sleep, not on this day, she thought. The helmet of curls itched and was so stiff with spray that her head bounced against the headrest, and in the backseat the green Rich's bags holding the clothes and the loathsome bras and garter belt crouched and pulsed like poison toads.

She heard her aunt click on the radio, and wonderfully, miraculously, Andy Williams's plummy tenor drifted into the car. He was singing "Moon River," and Peyton felt her tight chest ease a little and her eyelids begin to soften. *Breakfast at Tiffany's* was her favorite movie in the world. The hard mica-glitter of New York, the lost sweetness of Audrey Hepburn, the sheer tenderness of George Peppard filled her with a tremulous joy so intense that she often had to close her eyes against it. Peyton knew she would go to New York when she was older, to that New York where, as Holly Golightly said, nothing bad could ever happen to you at Tiffany's. She would look like Audrey Hepburn. "She has a long neck and big feet and funny eyebrows, too," she had breathed to the Losers Club after her first viewing of the film.

"Yeah, and about a million trillion dollars," Boot jeered cheerfully.

"And a waist and at least enough boobs to fill out a dress," Ernie observed.

"Well, she's grown-up," Peyton had said sullenly. "You just wait till I am."

"I wouldn't hold my breath," said Ernie.

But Peyton continued to be charmed and soothed and brought to the brink of joy by the movie, and by its theme song. They became her amulet against the backwater that was Lytton, against whatever in the world was currently pursuing her. Something usually was. Peyton snuggled down into the supple beige leather—"Like being inside a buttered biscuit," she had once told her father—and drifted off down Moon River with Andy and Holly.

She woke only when the car stopped at last, and for a moment she did not know where she was. And then she remembered not only where but who and what, and felt the sour sickness uncoil itself again.

She opened her eyes slowly, keeping them slightly squinted so that if she had to she could call up the invisibility again. Perhaps, if it was still early enough, she could get to her room and lock the door and begin the undoing of the horror before anyone saw her.

What she saw was her father and Clothilde, wrestling a mattress down the front steps and onto the lawn. Her father had on his white office shirt, but the sleeves were rolled and the collar was unbuttoned, and his hair fell over his face. Peyton had never seen him like this. Even on Saturdays and holidays Frazier McKenzie wore his starched plaid shirts with the cuffs and collars buttoned. His forearms were corded and brown, like wisteria vines. She could see the sheen of sweat on his face. Somehow the sight of him made her want to avert her eyes, as if she had seen him naked. Behind him, at the other end of the bouncing mattress, Chloe shone with sweat in the muzzy sun, like basalt. Peyton did not move, and they did not hear the car. Was it possible that they might finish their task and go back into the house without seeing her?

Aunt Augusta tooted the horn gaily.

"Frazier McKenzie, come here and look at your grown-up daughter," she trilled, and then she got out of the car the better to see the first viewing of her handiwork. Peyton did not move.

Her father shielded his face against the sun with his hand and stared. Then he walked slowly toward her side of the car, hand still on his forehead. When he reached the car he stopped and stared in. Peyton could not meet his eyes, and then she did.

Sheer shock and revulsion stared back at her. They were gone in an instant, replaced by the squint of his smile, but they had been there.

"Well, my goodness," her father said. "Get out and let's have a look at you."

Peyton sat rooted in the Lincoln.

"She's had a little upset tummy," Aunt Augusta offered across the roof of the Lincoln. "She probably needs some iced tea and a nap. But first we're going to have a fashion show. . . ."

Peyton jerked her door open and leapt out and ran past her father and the wide-eyed Clothilde and into the house, and into her room, and closed and locked her door. She heard the murmur of voices out on the lawn, a hum like bees, with an occasional fragment of a sentence spiking up: ". . . at least she might have said thank you. All these new things, and before she got sick such pretty makeup. Look, she's just left everything in the car. Frazier, I really think . . ."

More murmuring, and then her father's voice: ". . . maybe a little extreme for her age, Augusta. Let her get used to it. Let *us* get used to it. Good Lord, I didn't even recognize her."

"Well, I guess ingratitude runs in the family," she heard her aunt huff, and shortly after that the solid thunk of the Lincoln's door closing, and the soft growling of its motor.

She jerked off the vaunted Villager and left it in a pile on the floor, and pulled out her soft, faded blue jeans and a T-shirt that said "Daytona Beach" and crawled onto her bed and pulled the faded afghan that her grandmother had made for her at her birth up over her chin and ears. She did not move. She did not hear any more talk, or any sound at all, from outside her door for a long, long time. By the time Chloe came to her door, her windows had darkened with the still-winter twilight, and she was stiff and cramped from lying so long in one position.

"Peyton, you come on out to supper now," Chloe called. "Your daddy gone to a board of stewards' meeting up to the church, he say he want to see you before you go to bed. He say he think you looks pretty as a princess, and he wants to tell you himself. And I think we can fix that hair a little bit so it ain't so hard, and take some of that stuff off your face. It's gon' be all right. Come on out now, and after supper you can show me your new clothes. Your aunt left them for you."

Peyton did not reply, and she did not move. Presently Clothilde went heavily away.

She was back in an hour or so.

"I got to go home," she said. "Ain't nobody with Boot. I'm settin' this tray right here outside your door. You stop actin' like a baby now and come on out and eat it. Your daddy don't have time for this. Your Cousin Nora comin' sometime tomorrow. You don't want her to think you a baby in a tantrum."

Peyton still did not reply. She heard Clothilde mutter, and soon the closing of the front door, and then silence and darkness fell down over the house. Peyton padded to her door and opened it and pulled the tray inside so that her father would not see it sitting there, and set it on her desk and crawled back into her bed under her afghan. The smell of the food pooled thickly in the back of her throat: pork chops and sweet potatoes and green beans that Nana had canned the summer before. She got up and dropped an old T-shirt over the tray and got back into bed. Perhaps she slept. Perhaps not.

She heard her father at her door some time later, dimly.

"Peyton, you awake?" he called softly.

She did not answer. She lay very still, motionless, silent, until at last, eons later, she heard him click off the television set and start up the stairs to bed. She waited another hour, just to be sure, and then she got up and tiptoed through the dark to the big downstairs bathroom and ran a tub of water. She ran it very slowly so that her father would not hear it thundering into the big porcelain tub. It took a long time to fill.

Peyton got into the bath and submerged herself. She felt the hair helmet soften stickily. She got the sliver of Ivory soap from the soap dish and scrubbed her head until it stung. The water around her yellowed like urine. Some kind of rinse, then. Good. One down.

She scrubbed herself all over, then got out of the tub, wrapped her hair in a towel, dressed, and stole back to her room. She sat down in front of the maple dressing table and closed her eyes for a long time, and then she jerked the towel away.

A towering mound of dun-colored Brillo sat atop her head, lightless and dense. She could not get her comb through it. It was already as dry as rabbit tobacco in the fall.

Peyton got up and went out of her room again. She took with her the afghan and a pillow from her bed. She got an apple and some cheese and a Coca-Cola from the refrigerator and went outside into the moony dark and climbed her dogwood tree.

Over the years, since she was very small, her father had constructed a sort of shelter there for her, more elaborate than a platform but less so than a roofed tree house. It had railings and one solid wall at the back, against the tree trunk. Two years before she had dragged an old air mattress up there, and now she pushed it against the wall, and propped her pillow on it, and lay down and covered herself with her afghan. She was not cold except for her wet head; the night was soft and so still that she could smell the faint, rotten curl of sulfur that people in Lytton always said was from the big mills over in Birmingham.

She prepared to cry, but instead she slept.

She awoke with a jolt of body and heart, and pearly morning light was streaming through the tree's bare branches, and her father was calling her from the ground.

Clothilde's voice joined his, shrill and angry.

"Come down from there right now, Peyton," her father said, and his voice was both cold and weary.

"Well, I hope you happy. Your cousin here waitin' to meet you, and you stuck up in that tree like an ol' possum. She drove all night, she say. You git down from there this minute," Clothilde squalled.

Peyton did not look down at them, and she did not answer. She unfocused her eyes into the invisibility squint and looked instead out toward the street. A blur of pure, shocking flamingo pink flamed there against the pitted asphalt. She brought it into focus. It was a Thunderbird coupe, a fairly old one, from what she knew of those exotic cars, covered with road dust and bug-speckled of windshield, but still as fabulous in the morning light as a roc, its pinkness like wet bubble gum, like azaleas, like all the pink things in the world. Nobody in Lytton had a Thunderbird.

There was a rustle of leaves and a creak of the steps to the tree house, and a woman's face appeared over its edge. It could have been any age at all. It was freckled with copper and long and sharp-chinned, and a thick sheaf of dark-red hair fell over one of its pale-green eyes. It was an exaggerated face, almost a grotesque one, and Peyton simply stared. Then the mouth quirked up into a smile, and it was transformed into something near beauty.

"Dr. Livingstone, I presume?" the woman said, and her voice was as slow and rich as cooling fudge, with a little hill of laughter in it. It was a wonderful voice, magical.

The woman swung herself up onto the platform and sat down, legs crossed, chin on hands. Her arms and legs were so long as to look almost simian, and in her blue jeans she was very thin. She looked solemnly at Peyton. Peyton stared back, as mesmerized as a cobra in a fakir's basket.

"I'm your Cousin Nora Findlay," the woman said. "I've driven all night to meet you, and I'm tired and I need my breakfast, and I want you to have yours with me. I don't have any other cousins. Then we'll do something about that hair. Sweet Jesus, what on earth were they thinking? How long have you been up here in this tree?"

Peyton put her head down and began to cry, and her Cousin Nora pulled her over until she was pressing against her shoulder, and Peyton cried and Nora held her until Peyton had cried herself out, and then they climbed down the tree to breakfast.

5

The first thing you noticed about Nora Findlay, Peyton thought, was that she gave off heat, a kind of sheen, like a wild animal, except that hers was not a dangerous ferality, but an aura of sleekness and high spirits. There was a padding, hip-shot prowl to her walk, and she moved her body as if she were totally unconscious of it, as if its suppleness and sinew were something she had lived with all her life. She was tall and a little stooped, with long tanned legs and the same blur of coppery freckles on her arms that her face wore. With her slanted yellow-green eyes and thick, tumbled red hair, Peyton thought she looked like some sort of wildcat: a leopard, a ruddy puma, a cheetah. She had a long Roman nose and a full mouth and small, soft breasts obviously free of any restraint: you could see the nubs of her nipples under the T-shirt she wore. Peyton averted her eyes, but it never seemed to occur to Nora Findlay that her breasts, fettered or otherwise, were matters for concern.

Clothilde had bacon and eggs waiting for them in the yellow breakfast room. It was still very early; dew silvered the grass under the dogwood tree as they walked to the house. Peyton had a couple of hours yet before school. She would have liked to retreat to her room and burrow under her covers and think about the enormities of the past twelve hours, especially this strange, leonine cousin who had arrived in a pink chariot and laid siege to her tree. But she knew that she did not dare. Disapproval of her shone out of Chloe's face like steam off asphalt, and she could still feel the cold weight of her father's eyes on her and hear the steel in his voice from that morning. She was in disgrace, and she knew it. There was nothing for it but to sit down at the blue lacquered table and wait for what would come. For a long time no one spoke, and she did not raise her eyes from her plate. There was only the chink of silver on china as Nora ate.

She smelled cigarette smoke then, a smell so alien in this house that it was as shocking as fresh blood would be, and she looked up at her cousin. Nora sat in the chair across from her father's, where her brother had always sat. No one had occupied it since Buddy's death. Nora was wound sinuously around the chair, her head tipped far back. She was smoking a cigarette from the fresh pack of Salems that sat on the table beside her, and her eyes were closed. Still with them closed, she smiled her wide Halloween smile.

"Have I broken a real taboo?" she said in the rich, slow, melted-chocolate voice. "Am I going to have to sneak behind the woodshed to smoke?"

She opened her eyes then, and swept the heavy hair off her face with one long hand, and turned to Peyton.

"Might as well join you in Coventry," she said. "Two's company, they say."

"Coventry?" Peyton said in a small, tight voice, despite her determination to get through this meal without speaking. All her apprehension had come flooding back at the sight of this bronzy, coiled stranger at her breakfast table. The earlier moment of desperate, cowardly tears and the feel of succoring arms was gone as if it had never been.

"It means disgrace. For some reason, being sent to Coventry means the ultimate punishment; it means shunning. I don't know why. It means we're both of us in deep shit."

Peyton gasped. She had never heard a word such as that used in this house. Frazier McKenzie did not swear, nor did he use slang. It was somehow a part of him, a piece of whatever had buried his laughter deep. The word hung in the warm air like a hovering yellow jacket, and in the ensuing silence Peyton heard the subterranean rumble of the furnace coming on and heard the snorted "Huh!" from Clothilde that meant her direst disapproval. Clothilde did not chide her white family at the time of their indiscretions, but Peyton knew she would hear about this later. She wondered if Chloe would tackle Nora directly.

"I'm sorry, Clothilde," Nora called out. "I have a bad mouth on me. I know I do. I'm trying to do better. I hope I haven't blotted my copybook too badly."

She smiled into the kitchen at Chloe.

"It ain't like I never heard 'shit' before," Chloe said. "It just that Mr. Frazier ain't gon' want Peyton to hear it."

"It's not like I haven't heard it before, either," Peyton surprised herself by saying. And then she looked down at her plate and blushed. She would speak no more to this usurping stranger. Her cousin was not going to charm her with sweet cigarette smoke and soft "shit"s.

Nora seemed comfortable with the silence. She finished her coffee and told Clothilde it was the very nectar of the gods, and Chloe poured her more, and only when she had finished that and smoked another Salem, finally tapping it out on the edge of her saucer, did she move to rise. Peyton saw that her hands were long and beautiful, and her nails were perfectly formed ovals, innocent of polish. The hands were the only thing that did not seem incidental about her Cousin Nora, did not seem, if you would, offhanded. Somewhere in her mind Peyton filed the knowledge. Here was a source of pride, then. Here was a vulnerability.

She was completely unaware of the thought, but still, it warmed her.

Nora stretched and yawned and said, "I have never eaten a better breakfast. I mean that, Clothilde. It is all right if I call you that?"

"What else you gon' call me?" Chloe grumbled, but it was not one of her wholehearted grumbles. Peyton looked over at her. There was something akin to the butterfly beginnings of a smile at the corners of Chloe's black eyes.

"I'm bushed," Nora said, getting up from the chair. Peyton saw that she wore tennis shoes over bare feet, and that her feet were small and neat, out of all proportion to her height.

"You upstairs in the back bedroom on the right," Clothilde said. "Mr. Frazier already took your bags up before he went to work. There's a bathroom next door. Mr. Frazier said to let you sleep as long as you wanted to, that he'll see you for dinner. See all of us, I means."

Peyton would not look up.

She felt rather than saw her cousin come around to stand behind her chair. In a moment those long hands were cupping her head, smoothing back the electric hair, pulling it sleekly behind her head and winding it.

"Got bobby pins? Chloe?" she said, and Chloe produced some from somewhere in her vast necessities drawer. There was a final tug and the feeling of the bobby pins slipping firmly home, and then Nora took her shoulders and stood her up and led her to the old mirrored cabinet hanging over the oak chest that served to hold linens and china and silver.

"What do you think?" Nora said, and Peyton looked.

A small face under a smooth crown of hair looked back at her. The face sat atop a long neck that seemed, now, slender instead of scrawny, and around the sharp chin and slanted cheekbones a few wisps of the horrendous curls lay softly. The eyes were dark with something totally alien, and the sallow skin flushed with a blush that Peyton felt start at her collarbone and surge up. The image was not appalling, not even remotely. But it was not her. She merely stared.

"It's a French twist," Nora said, cocking her head just as Mr. Antoine had done. "It's not really right for you, but it gets that mess off your face and under control, and it shows off those fabulous bones and neck. If you like, we'll work on it some more tonight."

Still, Peyton stared.

Nora gave her shoulders a small shake, then went into the kitchen and hugged Clothilde hard.

"You have saved my life. There's no doubt about that," she said, and yawning, she went up the dim staircase toward her room.

Only then did Peyton look at Clothilde. Chloe was looking back at her, and she was smiling.

"That's right nice, Peyton," she said. "Shows off them eyes."

"I hate it," Peyton said, but there was no heat in her voice. She went into her little room to get dressed for school, and for the first time in her life she felt almost confident, almost anticipatory, about going into the swarm of flips and bouffants that awaited her at school.

Nobody's got a French twist, she thought. This ought to shut up a few of them. Of course, I'm not going to keep it. . . .

She realized as she left the house to walk in the soft, chilly morning to school that she could not wait to show her new hair to the Losers Club that afternoon.

But it was not her hair that the Losers Club wanted to talk about. They did not even mention it. Instead the subject was, first, her night in the tree, and, second, her Cousin Nora Findlay.

"Guess you gets the stupid prize, Peyton," Boot said, eating Planter's peanuts out of the big can from which Ernie doled a grudging inch or two for each of them once or twice a week.

For the first time, Peyton felt no hummingbird dart of triumph in her chest. She felt cross, waspish. The night before had been a source of stunning pain and revelation to her. She was not going to have it cut down to the status of stupidity of the week.

"It wasn't stupid. It was something I planned, a protest. I'm proud of it," she said.

"I should think you might make your point better face to face," Ernie drawled, but Peyton knew somehow that he envied her her flight into the dogwood tree. She realized then that Ernie Longworth would never dare leave his mother to go and sit in a tree all night.

"OK, so it ain't stupid. Tell about your cousin," Boot said, licking salt off his small nimble fingers. "I heard she redheaded as a woodpecker and ain't got no brassiere. Hubba-hubba. What your daddy say about that? What Miss Augusta say?"

"They haven't said anything yet," Peyton said. "Nobody's really seen her yet but me. She has long red hair like a waterfall and green eyes, and real long legs, and she smokes Salems. As for the brassiere, I don't know anything about that," she added prissily.

In her mind, her Cousin Nora Findlay was rapidly being transmuted into something fabulous and strange, a unicorn, a young griffin.

"Sounds like her, all right," Ernie said casually, upending his Coca-Cola. "Little red pullet of a thing, running around half naked, with big cat's eyes and this funny, gritty voice. She stole a bunch of flowers off a grave right here in this cemetery."

"How do you know?" Peyton said indignantly, knowing that somehow he did know. The fine, glinting edge that her cousin's arrival had lent her crumbled like chalky soil.

"Because she was here once when she was little, right after the war started. She was by herself; her mama didn't come with her. We never knew why, but I have my own ideas. I used to play with her some. We're about the same age. I know about the flowers because I was with her. I got the whipping of my life, I can tell you."

"Why, if you ain't the one stole 'em?" Boot said interestedly. His ideas of white people's justice were flexible.

"Because little Miss Nora Findlay told everybody it was me, and then cried when I said it wasn't. She got peach ice cream out of it. I got privet-switch welts all over my legs. Your cousin is as slippery as an eel, Peyton. Watch your back."

"I didn't know she was here before," Peyton said, feeling somehow betrayed. "Daddy never said. Chloe didn't, either."

"Well, your mama wasn't too thrilled about her, I can tell you that," Ernie said. "Likely it was just easier not to talk about her visit. Your mama could be a tiger."

Here was another persona for her mother, then: a tawny, stalking, soft-growling tiger. Peyton knew she would have to think a long time about this before she could fit the image into the grid that held her mother captive in her mind.

At the door to the shed, she turned and looked back.

"How did y'all know about that stuff last night?" she said.

"Huh. Half of Lytton probably know it by now," Boot said. His face was sweetly interested, nothing more. The doings of the folks in the big house on Green Street would provide as much entertainment for the black community as a month of circuses. Peyton saw, suddenly, the terrible pity of this: lives lived on vicarious energy. She turned and went back down the sidewalk to her house.

Nora was nowhere in sight, but her Aunt Augusta was, sitting at the breakfast table with a cup of coffee and a slice of Clothilde's pineapple upside-down cake. She was stabbing the cake and waving it on her fork and haranguing Chloe at the same time; her presence filled the breakfast room and overflowed into the kitchen. Chloe ironed on, unconcerned and uncommunicative. Every now and then she would say, "Uh-*uh*," when Augusta made a point, or "I don't know nothin' about that, Miss Augusta."

Peyton tried to slip past her back and into her own room, but Aunt Augusta rounded on her.

"Well, so here's our grown-up little lady," she said with heavy sarcasm. "The one who, by now, the whole town knows spent the night in a tree after her daddy and her aunt bent over backward to fix her up some. If your daddy doesn't listen to me now about boarding school, I'll be mighty surprised. Just look at that hair! Now what did you do to it? It looks like a little old woman's skinned back like that."

"It's a French twist," Peyton said coldly. "My cousin fixed it for me. She thought that horrible Rich's hair looked like a booger had a fit in it. She's going to fix it some more when she wakes up."

Peyton had completely forgotten that she herself had planned to murder the French twist as soon as she could get to a mirror. In a heartbeat it became a powerful amulet against Aunt Augusta.

"Everybody at school loved it," she said. "Nobody else has one yet. Grace Kelly wore one at her wedding. Some of the girls said I looked just like her."

None of this was true, but Peyton did not care. She had found her aunt's one overweening vulnerability; she would, like Delilah, slay her aunt with hair.

For a moment her aunt was speechless. Then she recovered.

"Oh, yes, your Cousin Nora," she said venomously. "Who drove in here at daybreak while decent people were still in their beds, in a dirty pink convertible with her shorts rolled up to her whatever and no foundation garments, and got in bed and slept all day. Oh, yes, that's just wonderful. What a shining example she sets for you. No wonder your daddy didn't tell anybody she was coming. When I think what her mother did to your mother, when I think what perfect little tramps all those Vandiver women were, I shouldn't be surprised at anything this one does, but those shorts—"

"What do you mean, what her mother did to my mother?" Peyton said in a small voice.

"Well, it's time you knew," her aunt huffed. "Her mother stole your mother's fiancé away from her and ran off with him, and we all heard that she had your famous Cousin Nora way before she ever married that no-good Creighton Findlay. Not that that little affair lasted long; he walked out on her before Nora was two years old. After that she lived all over the place, with one relative or another, dragging that child with her. I guess it's no wonder . . . anyway, she and the child lived with almost every Peyton and Vandiver family except your mama and daddy. Your mama never spoke to her after that business with Creighton Findlay."

"Her fiancé . . . ," Peyton said, her eyes burning oddly. "You mean . . . not Daddy?"

"Of course not! Your daddy is worth a million Findlays. He met your mother just after that and married her the same year. It was the saving of her. Creighton Findlay was just white trash, as no-good as they come, but he was a handsome devil and she was crazy about him. He would have ruined her life. And yours. You wouldn't have had this nice life of yours, or a loving daddy, or a big house like this, or a penny to your name."

"My mother's cousin—Nora's mother—where is she?" Peyton faltered. She knew that her question could have no good answer.

"She died in a sanatorium for alcoholics in St. Petersburg, Florida," Aunt Augusta said with satisfaction. "I hear that nobody claimed her and the city had to give her a pauper's burial."

"Not so," a black-coffee voice said from the stairs. "Everybody knows she married the emperor of Bhutan and is living in splendor in the shadow of Everest. I see her often."

Nora padded into the breakfast room, smiling amiably at Aunt Augusta, her green eyes slitted. Her mane of hair was tangled and hung over her face, and there was the imprint of a chenille spread on one smooth, speckled cheek. She wore a long T-shirt that said "Jesus Is Coming. Look Busy," and obviously nothing else. She smiled at Aunt Augusta. Her face looked more jack-o'-lanternish than ever, luminous and exaggerated. Oddly, it was sweetly appealing.

"Well, Nora," her aunt said, extravagantly avoiding looking at the Jesus T-shirt and the bobbling wealth of Nora underneath it.

"Well, Cousin Augusta," Nora said, the smile widening until her eyes disappeared into freckled flesh. "It is, isn't it? Cousin Frazier's sister-in-law? You look just like I remember."

"I don't recall that we ever met," Aunt Augusta said frostily. She looked at Nora then. Her eyes scanned her up and down like radar.

"We didn't," Nora said, pushing the russet hair out of her eyes and sitting down opposite Aunt Augusta at the breakfast table. There was a small sucking sound as her bare thighs stuck to the wooden chair seat. "I remember you from a picture that was in my bedroom that time I visited here. It was of everybody, all of you, at some kind of carnival or fair. I used to stare at it for hours, trying to will myself into it. I don't think I'd ever seen a fair then. You really haven't changed."

"Well, needless to say, *you* have. You must have," Augusta McKenzie said. "It must be twenty years since we've heard hide or hair of you."

"Easily," Nora said, stretching so that the T-shirt pulled tight across her breasts, and lighting a cigarette. Peyton saw that her aunt's neck was turning dull red, as if she had just gotten out of the beautician's chair after a bad permanent.

"So," Aunt Augusta said. "How long do you plan to be with us?"

Peyton could not imagine that anyone could miss the animosity in her aunt's voice, but Nora seemed to. She exhaled and smiled sleepily.

"I hadn't thought, really," she said. "I just got here. I'd like to look around some. Lytton seems like a nice little town. And then I'd like to see Atlanta. I don't remember that we ever lived there."

"Frazier said you were on your way to a job?" Aunt Augusta said. "What sort of job might that be? Where is it? Not here, I shouldn't think. There aren't any jobs here for a young woman that I've heard of."

Peyton saw Clothilde lift her head from her ironing board and stare at Augusta. She felt a prickle of anger. This was far beyond the boundary of polite curiosity. If I said that, they'd put me in a convent, she thought.

"Clothilde, do you think I might possibly have a sliver of that cake?" Nora said, smiling into the kitchen. "It smells like pure heaven, and it's been a long time since that fabulous breakfast. Well, I don't have any specific plans, Cousin Augusta. I'm just looking around to see what's what. And I wanted to see Cousin Frazier again, and meet Peyton here. I don't have enough family left to spit on."

Chloe brought the cake and poured a cup of strong, hot coffee for Nora. "More where that came from," she said.

Nora smiled her thanks around a mouthful of cake and rolled her eyes. "Bliss," she said. "Nirvana. Maybe you could teach me to cook while I'm here. I really don't have any domestic skills. Everybody's always telling me."

"What *are* your skills, Nora?" Aunt Augusta said. "We never exactly knew."

"Well, I'm good at English, and I write a little," Nora said. "I've been teaching for the past few years, in Miami and Key West. I've really enjoyed that. I taught special English classes to Cuban and Haitian children, and sometimes to adults at night."

"Oh, really?" Augusta narrowed her eyes. Her nostrils flared as if she had smelled something dreadful. "Colored children, you mean."

"Oh, yes. Black as the ace of spades, some of them. It was a real revelation for me to get acquainted with such different cultures. I stayed for a couple of years in one of their homes, with the family. I adored it."

"Well, you won't find much opportunity for that kind of thing here," Augusta said. A faint dew of perspiration started on her upper lip. Peyton would have said sweat, but Aunt Augusta had told her that ladies never sweated, only perspired, and that as seldom as possible.

"My mama used to say a lady misted," Augusta had giggled once. Peyton, who knew something of her aunt's provenance in the mill village, had snickered and told the Losers Club that afternoon about misting. They had laughed about it for days.

"Oh, really?" Nora said, widening her eyes until they shone cat-green in her stippled face. "I've already seen quite a few black people around here. Surely their children go to school?"

"Not our school," Aunt Augusta said. "They have their own school, and it's a good one. Frazier is on their school board, just as he is on ours."

"Strange," muttered Nora, looking ingenuously up at Aunt Augusta. "I thought *Brown versus Board of Education* must be fairly familiar around the South. Hasn't the news gotten to Lytton yet?"

"There's no need to be sarcastic," Augusta snapped. "That rule is all about choice. None of our colored people have chosen to come to Lytton Grammar and High Schools. And why should they? Their own school is just fine."

"Maybe I'll apply there, then." Nora smiled. "You asked about my skills, Cousin Augusta? I am a truly superior fuck. Maybe the best lay east of the Rockies. Lots of people say so. Although it doesn't look like there's much market for that in Lytton. Oh, well. We shall see."

Peyton stared, her mouth open, and Chloe snorted. Aunt Augusta got up from her chair, wheeled on her sensible Naturalizer heel, and sailed in palpitating silence out of the room. Peyton heard the front door slam and the little whatnot shelf near it rattle. She could not speak and only continued to stare.

Nora reached over and ruffled her hair.

"I'm really not all that good," she said. "At least I don't think I am. I don't consider it a skill, more a pleasure. But when I saw your aunt I thought, Now there's a lady with very little to occupy her time, and I think maybe this will do it for a good while to come. Now"— and she looked at Clothilde—"how long do we have before Cousin Frazier gets home? I need to bathe and change, and I thought Peyton and I might work on that hair a little."

"He be home in about an hour," Chloe said, and Peyton saw with astonishment that she was trying to hide a smile.

"Good. Peyton?"

But it had been too much; Peyton could not process it. She wanted to go back to her room and lie on her bed and think this afternoon into her grid. Her cousin's words were disturbing to her, almost shocking, and yet the rout of her aunt had been such a perfect thing. . . .

"I don't think so, thank you," she said primly.

"Later, then," Nora said, and she went back up the stairs. Peyton watched her until she was out of sight. She wondered if growing up meant knowing how to walk like that. Somehow she did not think her cousin knew; she just *did* it.

"Well, I hope she puts on a brassiere, at least," she muttered to Chloe.

"She get herself all fixed up, don't you worry," Chloe said, and the smile that had been twitching at her mouth widened into a real one. "She ain't dumb."

"You like her, don't you?"

"Don't know her yet. But she kind of like a fresh little breeze in here."

"Are you going to tell Daddy what she said?"

"Lord, no. Your aunt gon' do that before he out of his car."

"He's going to be mad," Peyton said. She did not know if the thought gave her pleasure or discomfort.

"I wonder," Chloe said, and she turned back to the slick-shining ironing board. Peyton slumped out of the kitchen to her room and threw herself on the bed to think about it, and instead slid so deeply into sleep that when her father came to waken her for supper she did not, for a moment, know where she was.

They ate that evening in the dining room off the other side of the kitchen, and Nora had indeed dressed for the occasion. Her hair was up in a burnished French twist, and she wore a pink oxford-cloth shirt with the sleeves rolled up, which gave her face the glow of rose on copper, and a pink plaid madras skirt that wrapped around and tied. Peyton had seen the same outfit over and over, both at school and in the dreaded Tween Shop at Rich's, but somehow it was different on Nora. It looked casual and throwaway, instead of self-consciously pretty, and the cardigan around her shoulders looked as if she were merely chilly. Nora looked, Peyton thought, like money, though she could not have said how. According to Aunt Augusta, Nora did not have a pot to piss in.

She liked her cousin better in the much-maligned shorts and T-shirt, she realized. This woman—for in the candlelight she looked like the woman she must be—had no connection with her.

Candlelight. The big dining room, the table set with heavy old silver and the crystal glasses that Peyton could remember being brought out of the cabinet only at Thanksgiving and Christmas. The good china that had been her mother's mother's. Flowers, even: a bouquet of early snowdrops that she knew came from the rock garden in the side yard stood between the candles and smelled of spring evenings. Peyton hated all of it. Her father had bidden it for this unknown cousin, when he had never bidden it for her, not even on her birthdays. She sat in the middle of the table with her Cousin Nora on one end and her father on the other and would not look up.

When Clothilde came in with plates of pot roast and mashed potatoes, her father said, "This was a good idea, Chloe. I'd forgotten how nice this room is with the candles and all. We ought to do this more often."

So it had been Chloe's idea, then. It made no difference to Peyton. She was not going to forgive her cousin this prodigal's feast. If it had not been for her, they would be eating pot roast comfortably in the breakfast room, listening to the news on the old white plastic radio that had stood on the sideboard for as long as Peyton could remember.

"I've never forgotten this room," Nora said, her eyes liquid in the candlelight. "We had dinner here once, with all the candles and the china and silver and everything. I remember thinking that this had to be the safest and most beautiful room in the world."

"It's a handsome room," her father agreed. "Lila Lee had it done not long after we moved here. I don't guess anything's changed since then."

"We never use it," Peyton said into her mashed potatoes.

She was still in disfavor with her father, she knew. He had been formally polite with her all evening and did not often look at her. There would be an accounting for her actions of the night before, though she had some hope that with Nora there, it might wait until the following morning. Some of the edge would have worn off it by then.

Nora ate with the feral delicacy of a big cat. Her father smiled to see it. Chloe, passing biscuits, smiled, too.

"I can't tell you what a perfect dinner this is," Nora said. "I've gotten so accustomed to getting my own meals that I'd forgotten what a pleasure good food and a beautiful table could be."

"What do you usually eat?" Peyton said, forgetting to sulk for a moment. She had absolutely no experience of an unmarried white woman cooking for herself. It seemed to her as exotic as Zanzibar.

"Pizza," Nora said, smiling at her. "Hamburgers. Kentucky Fried Chicken. Anything portable. I've been on the road for a while. I just eat things that I can take with me in the car."

"Oh," Peyton said. She slid a look at her father under her lashes. He did not seem to disapprove. There was a slight knitting of concern between his straight brows, though.

"Why don't you just stay home and eat?" Peyton said, and then realized she had been rude. Her father gave her the remote, level look that meant further displeasure.

"Well, I'm not really sure where that is right now," Nora said, cupping her chin in her hand and reaching out to touch the white bells of the snowdrops. They trembled like new snow.

"You must have a home. Everybody lives somewhere," Peyton pushed it. Her father's eyebrows rose.

"I've lived a lot of places," her cousin said. Her face was serene in the flickering light. She was, Peyton knew, going to refuse to be baited. "I've lived all over Florida, and once in Cuba for a while, and California. I lived last in Key West. Before that I was in Miami. I realized I was getting sort of old for that kind of thing, and so I thought I ought to look around and see if I could find a nest in the East somewhere. I'd really like to settle for a while."

"Nora taught colored children," Peyton said, looking sidewise to see how her father would take it. In the Deep South of her time change had not even swept a wing over the small towns, and the federal government be damned.

"A good thing to do," Frazier McKenzie said. "There are never enough qualified teachers for the children who need them most. I've often wondered what's going to happen to us if we don't educate all our children."

Peyton goggled, her mouth full of apple cobbler. She had had no idea that her father thought about things like that. They never talked of it.

"I thought I might find some kind of minority teaching job around Atlanta," Nora said. "What with Dr. King and all, it's the real epicenter of the Movement. It's what I do best, what I love. And I'm told I'd like the city."

Her father looked at her cousin thoughtfully.

"When was it that your mother died?" he said.

"A long time ago," she said. "About twelve years. But I hadn't lived with her for a while. You know she was sick? She drank an awful lot, and it got so that she couldn't take care of me or herself. One of my father's sisters put her in an institution, and I lived with her family for a year or two. Then I got a scholarship and went to Rollins, and I've essentially been on my own ever since. Don't worry about me, Cousin Frazier. I'm absolutely accustomed to taking care of myself. I'll find a place in Atlanta. I'm looking forward to it."

"It would be nice to have you that close to us," her father said. "I know Lila Lee would want Peyton to know her cousin."

"I'm sure," Nora said, looking down.

When Chloe had taken away the last of the dishes, her father said to Nora, "I'm accustomed to watching a little TV after dinner. It's nothing exciting, but you're welcome to join me. Peyton's going to be doing her homework. Or, if you have something else planned . . ."

"I'd love to," Nora said. "I don't think I've watched a television set in a month that wasn't in a motel room."

"I don't have any homework," Peyton said, giving it one more try. "I did it in study hall."

"I think you probably do," her father said, and he rose from his chair. He held Nora's chair as she stood up. Peyton got up from hers and went through the kitchen and the breakfast room to her room. She was suddenly and powerfully tired, but she did not sleep. Her father would be in, she knew. There was no escaping it.

She heard the television set go on, and then, a little later, incredibly, unimaginably, she heard her father laughing. Nora's rich laughter followed.

I hate her, Peyton thought clearly and roundly.

When her father came in at last, she was awake and staring into the shadowy corner of her room, where a shelf held some of her old toys. He sat down on the edge of her bed, and except for the creak of the springs, there was no sound for a while.

"Peyton, look at me," he said finally, and she did. His face looked cold, carved from granite, in the low lamplight.

"Last night was not acceptable," he said. "I've gone to bat for you with your aunt more times than you can possibly know, but after this I've got to admit she's probably right. You've got to have some supervision."

"No," Peyton whispered.

"Yes. Nothing like last night can happen again, and I can't seem to prevent it. So here are your options. One, you can go to boarding school. Augusta has looked into it and is sure she can find a good one for you nearby. Two, I can put you entirely in Augusta's hands. You'd live here, of course, but she would decide what was best for you and see that you did it. Don't make any mistake about that: I will give her my full blessing."

Peyton felt tears of enormity and betrayal well into her eyes. She could not speak.

"Three," her father said, "your Cousin Nora can stay with us for a while and oversee things. I've asked her if she would consider it, and she's said she'll think about it."

"No. . . ."

"You have three choices, Peyton. You'd better make one soon."

"Nora would mean a lot more work for Chloe," she whispered miserably.

"Not necessarily. Nora would help out, I'm sure."

"It'll cost you a lot extra."

"She'll be finding a job around here. She's adamant about that."

"You'll have to talk to her all the time. You don't like to do that. . . ."

"She's pleasant to talk to. And I'm sure she'll have her own life and her own friends before long. Besides, I work most nights."

Peyton was silent. It was no contest. Boarding school was unimaginable, Aunt Augusta too terrible to contemplate. I wonder why it is, thought Peyton, that when you have choices, none of them is ever anything you want.

Her father got up and walked to her door and then stopped and looked back.

"Incidentally, I like your hair that way," he said. "I can see more than a little of your mother in you."

Peyton turned off her bedside lamp. She burrowed under her covers, feeling warmth that came from somewhere inside her as well as out.

For the first time in a long time, she did not show herself her movies.

6

*P*eyton got up early the next morning, whether to avoid Nora and her father or to encounter them she could not have said. She listened from the bathroom for the sounds of conversation in the breakfast room but heard nothing except the morning news on the radio. She put her head around the door and saw the table set for one and Clothilde stirring oatmeal in the kitchen, a bad sign. She never offered it to Frazier McKenzie, only to Peyton when she ate alone. Chloe was of the opinion that a gluey mass of hot oatmeal was God's own benison to the morning. Peyton hated it.

She shuffled into the kitchen, patting her hair. The French twist had definitely seen better days: wisps and clumps of it had escaped the pins and were rebelling around Peyton's head and neck. She had not combed it since Nora fixed it for her and was halfway hoping her cousin would offer to refresh it. Peyton had no idea how to make a French twist.

"Where is everybody?" she said grumpily to Chloe, who emerged from the kitchen bearing the poisonous chalice of oatmeal. "I *hate* that stuff, Chloe; you know I do. You wouldn't dare serve it if Daddy was here."

"It ain't your daddy needs fattening up," Chloe said, banging down the dish in front of Peyton. "Well, lessee—your daddy's gone to a breakfast meeting of the school board up at the café, and Nora took off early this morning. Say she want to get a look at the town before it has a chance to get a look at her."

"Did she take the Thunderbird?"

"She sho' did. You could hear that little old car peeling off a mile away. She got the top down and the radio going full blast, and she singing along with it and smoking a cigarette. Town gon' get a look at her, all right."

"They'll kick her out of here," Peyton said with obscure satisfaction, not realizing that she hoped this would not happen until after Nora fixed her hair.

"I 'spect Nora could kick back right good," Chloe said. "I hate to be the one who tries to run her off."

"Somebody will."

"Yo' Aunt Augusta ain't able to do it. Who else in this town as bad as that? Look to me like Nora won that round, all right."

Peyton grinned unwillingly. "Aunt Augusta sure did sail out of here, didn't she?"

"Like a ringtailed baboon," Chloe said.

"You think she's already told Daddy what Nora said?"

"Oh, I reckon it's got back to him one way or another. Miss Augusta loaded for bear when she leave out of here."

"What do you think will happen?"

"Not much of anything, I don't reckon. Nora too smart to talk like that around your daddy, and he gon' be right tickled when he hear she run off Miss Augusta. He ain't gon' let you know it, though, so you better just lay low about it."

"Do you know when she's coming back?" Peyton asked. She did not particularly want to see her marauding cousin, but on the other hand, Nora was almost bound to provide her with fresh fodder for the Losers Club.

"She say she be back late this afternoon. She gon' take a nap before dinner. We gon' eat a little early. She going into Atlanta to see a movie later on."

"What movie? Is Daddy going with her? Am I going?"

"I think she mean to go by herself."

"All the way up there at *night*?"

"Nora almost thirty years old," Chloe said. "She been takin' care of herself for a lot of years. She done drive that car from one end of this country to the other. I 'spect she be OK at a movie in Atlanta."

"Huh," Peyton grumped, but in her mind she could see it: the savage little pink car slicing through the dark fields over to the interstate; Nora with the red hair flaming out behind her, singing, a red peregrine riding the wind toward the smear of light that was the city. Something in her heart squeezed.

It was a strange day in school. Everybody looked at her, but they all looked obliquely, as if she held some sort of power that might smite them to stone if they looked full upon her face. At first Peyton thought it was the miserable hybrid hair, but as the morning wore on she heard none of the secret, sniggling laughter that the hair would have engendered. She was puzzled, but it was a heady feeling, too. Peyton had never felt eyes on her back for any reason other than ridicule.

At recess one of the senior boys, a rural Adonis so exalted by age and position on the football team as to be near sacred, said, "Hey, Peyton, I hear your cousin came to see you and that she's a good-looking broad. You tell her that any time she wants a real man's company she can call me. I bet we'd get along real good."

Peyton, who would have passed by this gap-toothed behemoth a day earlier with her eyes averted, looked him full in the face.

"Don't hold your breath," she said. "She's got about a million boyfriends."

Whether or not this was true did not matter: the icon had no way of knowing one way or another, and somehow Peyton thought that there must have been if not a million men in Nora Findlay's life, then at least a spectacular number of them.

"She really got a pink T-bird?" said one of the Adonis's appendages.

"Yeah, she does," Peyton said grandly. "We're taking it into Atlanta tonight to a movie. She's going to teach me to drive it."

There was no reply, and she walked away, floating on power. It may be true, she thought, remembering something she had heard in history class: "Absolute power corrupts absolutely." To Peyton, the prospect of that corruption seemed to shine like diamonds, like stars.

When she got to the Losers Club that afternoon, Ernie and Boot were both waiting for her. Ernie had put out Coca-Colas and a little bowl of the cherished peanuts, and there was a crazed, blackened pan of his mother's gingerbread sitting on the little stove. Peyton knew the feast was a votive offering spread for her, to supplicate the blessing of information about Nora. She smiled and sank down on the ottoman and nibbled peanuts and sipped Coca-Cola. She said nothing. Her corruption was near complete.

"OK," Boot said. "Awright. Tell about Nora. I hear she smokes cigarettes and rolls up her shorts and she told Miss Augusta that she was the best fuck in the country, and Miss Augusta went steaming out of there like the dogs was after her. Did you see that?"

"I did," Peyton said offhandedly. "She said 'shit,' too."

"Whoooeee!" Boot breathed. "What you daddy say?"

"He wasn't there. I don't think he knows about it yet."

"Don't bet on it," Ernie drawled. "Everybody else in town does. I heard it before nine o'clock this morning: Mother heard it from the drugstore lady. By this time everybody from Newnan to College Park will know about it."

"Well, so what?" Peyton said crossly. All of a sudden she was weary of Nora's celebrity. She realized that her own was only a reflection, like the moon's light from the sun.

"So she gon' stay?" Boot said.

"She might. If she does she's going to teach me to drive the Thunderbird, and we're going to take it into Atlanta for movies and things. But I don't know. In a way she's pretty boring. I really don't think I like her very much."

"Look to me like you don't know whether to shit or go blind,"

Boot said affably. This time it was Peyton, rather than her aunt, who sailed out in indignation. They were behaving like infants. Who needed it?

Nora did not eat dinner with them, but she sat at the table smoking and chatting pleasantly. She wore an astonishing outfit of tight black ankle-length pants and a loose, heavily embroidered blouse of some rough, gauzy material, and her hair was down again, obviously freshly washed and burnished. It shone like molten copper in the light from the brass overhead lamp. Her face was innocent of makeup.

"I'll get something after the movie," she said when Frazier McKenzie raised an eyebrow at her empty plate. "I ate lunch real late, and I hear there's a nice little Italian restaurant next door to the movie theater. I haven't had clam linguine for a long time."

Peyton, who had tasted neither fresh clams nor linguine, shot a look at her father to see what he thought of this affectation, but he merely smiled.

"Neither have I," he said. "There used to be a little place down by the courthouse in Atlanta that had it, but it closed during the Korean War. Maybe we'll all go to your place sometime. I don't think Peyton has ever tasted clam linguine."

"I've had clams," Peyton said. "I've had them at Howard Johnson's. I personally think they're overrated. I find that most seafood is."

Even she could hardly believe the affected sentences coming out of her mouth. She looked up at Nora, expecting laughter.

Nora only smiled. "That's because you've never had it fresh, right out of a tropical sea, and cooked over an outside grill, or made into a soup with things you wouldn't believe if I told you about them. I agree with you, frozen fried seafood is ghastly. I'll make you my special *sopa caliente* one day. That ought to change your mind about seafood.

"What's in it?"

"Oh, rice. Sweet potatoes. Fresh coconut milk. Crab and langouste—little warm-water lobsters. Chunks of fish. Broth. Spices that I can't even pronounce. I brought some with me when I left Miami. I learned to make it when I lived in Cuba."

"It sounds hideous," Peyton said.

Her father gave her a look.

"It sounds good to me," he said. "Might make a nice change from plain southern cooking, not that Chloe doesn't do that better than anybody. Sometimes I think we just don't get out into the world enough down here in Lytton."

Nora stubbed out her Salem in the ashtray Chloe had silently put at her place—two days and already it was her place, Peyton thought resentfully, as if Buddy had never been—and lit another. Then she put that out, too.

"This can be pretty offensive if nobody else in the house smokes," she said. "I've been around smokers so long that I just forget not everybody does it. Hispanics smoke like chimneys. I'll confine it to my room, or go out on the porch, if you'd rather."

"No, don't bother," Frazier said, and Peyton frankly goggled. Her father could scarcely tolerate the smells of cooking cabbage, or spare ribs boiling, or even chicken parts simmering on the stove for soup.

"I used to smoke," he said. "I still keep a pipe out in my office. I think smoke after a meal smells good. Maybe I'll bring in my pipe and we can smoke Peyton out of here."

Peyton stared. Her head spun. Her father, smoking? Cigarettes, a pipe? This cool, abstemious man? She felt the world teeter and shift on its axis before it flowed on. In this, her own house, at her own table, she knew no one anymore.

"So, did you have a tour of Lytton like you planned?" her father asked. "It must have taken you all of twenty minutes. What did you do with the rest of your day?"

Nora stretched luxuriously, and the soft breasts surged under the cotton gauze.

Slut, thought Peyton.

"I spent the whole day around town," she said. "It's a charming little town, Frazier. Almost a Disney town. I looked into both churches and parked on the square and walked all over, into all the neighborhoods I could find. . . . The houses aren't grand, but they're so neat, so right somehow. Actually roses on trellises, and vegetable gardens.

I even think I saw a cow down behind the Methodist church. It feels like Oz. It feels like nothing bad could ever happen here."

You ought to try Lytton Grammar School, Peyton thought grimly.

"It's a pretty little town, and most of us like it," her father said mildly. "But it's not Oz, not by a long shot. We have our share of bad business, bad doings. There are a lot of things that need changing in Lytton, but somehow nobody seems to have a go at them."

"You mean like the separate-but-equal drinking fountains by the monument? Or the 'Colored' and 'White' entrances to the movie theater? Maybe you could start with those."

"It'll come," Frazier McKenzie said. "But it's going to have to come in its own time. If you tried to force that kind of change on Lytton all at once you'd hit a brick wall. Nothing would ever change then."

"But Frazier, it's the law of the land. . . ."

Her father put down his coffee cup.

"Yes. It is," he said. "And we're lucky to have those laws in place at last. There's great change going on in the cities; you know that. But out here, in the little backwaters, we're a hundred years behind the cities. It's going to be a matter of years. It's going to happen one mind at a time, one heart at a time. Meanwhile, we try, and we measure our victories in inches."

Nora regarded him thoughtfully. "Like what?"

"Well, like something I want to talk to you about. We talked about it at the school-board meeting this morning. The county education folks are about to get all over us for making no move toward compliance, and if they do that they'll never get any. So I thought—*we* thought—that a compromise might work for a while. Lytton isn't going to integrate its schools by itself; the blacks don't want that, either. They know they'd get the short end of the stick. But maybe one shared class, maybe an honors class so that everyone could see the idea working. You could hold it one week at Lytton High and the next at Carver High, and so on. I think maybe, once it got going, everybody might be able to live with that."

"What kind of class?" Nora said, studying her perfect nails.

"What do you think of English? An honors English class that maybe addressed the literature of blacks and whites alike. A small class, so there could be a lot of discussion. . . ."

Nora raised her head. The bell of coppery hair swung forward over part of her face.

"I want that class, Frazier," she said.

"I thought you might," he said. "I sold you and the class as a package. It would be only an hour a day every day, but I said you might be willing to do some intensive tutoring, too. The black children are going to need it."

"I would *love* it," Nora breathed. "It's just what I've hoped I'd find, but I never dreamed it could be here. When will you know? When will I?"

"The chairman's going to take it to the county meeting this next week, but I don't anticipate any problems. The county is going to be so relieved to see that we're making some sort of effort, and your credentials really are unique."

"I even have a certificate somewhere," Nora said excitedly. "And of course I'd get my own place."

"No, we'd want you here if you'll stay," her father said. "You remember, we talked about it. That is, if you're still willing to spend some time with Peyton."

"I can't think of anything I'd like more," Nora said. "We will teach each other wondrous things. As long as we all understand that I'm not trying to be a mother or a disciplinarian. Just a friend who'll be underfoot a lot."

"It's all we ask, isn't it, Peyton?" her father said. He was smiling.

Peyton thought about boarding school with halls the color of liver and girls with their perfect Sandra Dee noses in the air, and about an endless replay of the horrific shopping trip with Aunt Augusta.

"Uh-huh," she said.

"So I'll let you know as soon as I do," her father said. "But I should think you might plan on starting in a couple of weeks. You'll want to do some lesson plans or whatever it is teachers do, won't you?"

"I've never used lesson plans, exactly," Nora said. "I like to sort of let things go where they want to. But I do want to look through some books, mine and the library's. Maybe I'll go into Atlanta and look through the Carnegie up there, too."

"Whatever you want to do. You mustn't feel that we have full claim on your time. You're a young woman in a new town. You'll make friends. We want you to do that."

Who on earth in this town would be Nora's friend? Peyton thought in honest wonder. But maybe someone would. Good, it would get her out of Peyton's hair once in a while. . . .

"Right now you all are enough for me," Nora said, smiling. "I'm really not used to having family. I just want to luxuriate in that awhile."

They sat in silence for a small space of time, and then Nora said, "I met your grandmother today, Peyton. Your mother," and she nodded at Frazier, who grimaced.

"I can't wait to hear about that," he said.

"Well," Nora said. "I was sitting on a bench in the square reading a book and eating a sandwich from the drugstore and this old lady sat down beside me. She had a sack of groceries, and I asked if I could put them down against the bench for her, and she turned and looked at me and said, 'I know you. I saw you coming in a bowl of tomato soup.'"

"Oh, Lord," Frazier said, closing his eyes. "I'm really going to have to do something about her. I hope she didn't bother you."

"God, no." Nora giggled. Unlike the rich laugh, it was silvery, burbling, flutelike. Peyton felt the corners of her own mouth tug upward.

"I thought she was fabulous. How many of us have been foreseen in a bowl of tomato soup? We talked for as long as she'd let me. We talked about some truly amazing things. Then she raised her fist at a limb full of crows over by the railroad tracks and yelled, 'Go tell the Devil!' and they flew off and so did she. I like her better than anybody else I've met except you all."

"That's a folktale. She's Scottish," Peyton said.

"I know the tale. I loved hearing somebody actually say it. I'll bet the Devil is getting an earful right now."

Peyton looked at her keenly to see if she was making fun of her grandmother, but there was no indication of that. Nora's face was soft with enjoyment.

"She sees things, too. She sees them in fire and water," Peyton said.

"And tomato soup. That's the best of all."

"How did you know she was my grandmother?"

"Oh, she introduced herself," Nora said. "But I'd have known anyway. You look just like her, Frazier, and you're probably going to, Peyton. I thought she was beautiful."

"I'm glad you got along," Frazier said almost primly. "But if she starts to get intrusive, just let me know."

"Not at all. She never could. I'm going down to see her sometime over the weekend. She wants to ride in my car. Peyton, you come, too, if you want to."

"I have a lot of homework," Peyton said. Was this amoebalike cousin going to absorb her grandmother, too?

Presently Nora got up and gathered up a huge straw purse and went out into the twilight, jingling her car keys. Peyton and her father sat in silence while the engine growled into life and then faded away down the street.

"Do you think she ought to do that by herself?" Peyton said finally.

"Why not? She's a grown woman. She's accustomed to taking care of herself. It's not our place to tell her what and what not to do."

"She just wasn't very dressed up. You could see right through that blouse."

"No, you couldn't. Don't be unpleasant. She has a very individual sense of style."

There was no responding to this. The idea of her father's having any opinion at all about style was totally alien to Peyton.

"Are you glad she's going to stay awhile?" her father asked her after a time.

"I don't know. I know Mama didn't like her," Peyton mumbled, feeling her heart pound with her own daring. But this was no ordinary night.

"It was her mother whom your mother didn't get on with. And it was a very long time ago. How did you know about that?"

"Ernie told me. He used to play with her that time she was here. He said she was a sneak."

"Ernie doesn't know what he's talking about."

Her father pushed away his dessert plate and looked at her thoughtfully. In the spill of light from the brass lamp, he looked strange: planes and angles of his face that she did not often notice leapt out at her. She could not see his eyes for the lamp-shadow.

"So you still go to those club meetings of yours," he said. "I'd forgotten about them. Maybe your aunt is right. Maybe you're spending too much time with Ernie and Boot in that shed."

Peyton took her plate into the kitchen and scraped it neatly. She did not look back at her father. Her heart was leaping and battering in the cage of her ribs.

If you make me stop I will run away, she said to him clearly, but she said it far back in her head.

7

*I*n the night the teasing sultriness broke and winter came back. Peyton heard the crash of thunder that broke the spine of the false spring and before she fell asleep rain was coming down in pelting sheets. She wriggled her face deep into her pillow and drew up into a ball. She was not cold, but winter brushed and fingered at her nevertheless. Before she fell back asleep she heard the slam of a car door and the pounding of footsteps on the front porch, then the softer opening and closing of the front door. Nora, coming back from Atlanta. It was, Peyton knew, very late, or maybe even early in the morning. She uncurled a little and relaxed into warmth. Her father wasn't going to like this one bit.

Peyton, lulled by rain and the absence of sunlight filtering through her venetian blinds, slept very late and woke up cross and disoriented. She wrapped herself in her grandmother's afghan and stumbled into the breakfast room, trailing the afghan, blinking into the overhead lamplight.

"Tell Mr. De Mille I'm ready for my close-up now," Nora said from her seat at the table. She was smoking and smiling at Peyton. Her face, too, was crumpled with sleep, and her hair poured into her eyes like a sheepdog's. She wore a black silk kimono, belted tight and crawling with scarlet and gold dragons and tigers. Her clown's smile flashed.

"Who's Mr. De Mille?" Peyton said thickly, slumping down into her seat and looking up at the phony cuckoo clock on the wall. It was hideously ugly and kept abominable time, and its cuckoo had long since flown the coop, but her father kept it in place. Buddy had bought it as a Christmas gift for his parents with the money from his first paper route. Peyton loathed it. The clock said ten-fifteen. Outside, the aqueous light looked like dawn.

"It's from a movie called *Sunset Boulevard*," Nora said, inhaling deeply and letting the smoke drift luxuriously from her nostrils. "It's one of the great movies of all time. Gloria Swanson said that line. Next time it's at an art theater, I'll take you."

"Huh," Peyton said, poking at the curling strips of bacon and the scrambled eggs on her plate.

"These are cold," she said to Chloe in the kitchen.

"They wasn't cold at nine o'clock," Chloe replied, not looking up from the beans she was stringing.

"Well, couldn't you have put them back in the oven?"

"I could have, but I didn't," Clothilde said. "You 'sposed to be up way before now. Your daddy gone out to his office two hours ago."

"So what? Nora was late, too," Peyton said mulishly. "She didn't get home till the middle of the night. I heard her come in."

She looked at Nora, who looked back levelly.

"So I did," she said. "And when you're thirty *you* can come in at dawn if you want to. Besides, I like cold eggs and bacon. I hardly knew there was any other kind."

Defeated, Peyton nibbled at the bacon, making an ostentatious pyramid of the eggs.

"I was going to ride my bike down to Nana's today," she said. "But it looks like it's going to rain for the next hundred years."

"I'll take you later," Nora said. "Right now we are going up to my room and I am going to fix that hair. Don't argue. It looks like a bird's nest caught in a windstorm."

Peyton followed her up the stairs to the big back bedroom without protesting, mainly because her hair did indeed look like a fright wig. She had told herself repeatedly that she did not care how she looked; Ernie had said that true beauty came only from the soul, and that had comforted Peyton for several years. But she did care, and she hated herself for it.

Nora sat her down in front of the mirror at the old walnut dressing table that had been there ever since Peyton could remember. Formerly it had worn only yellowing antimacassars and a vase of dried baby's breath from someone's unremembered nosegay. Now it was littered with bottles and jars and flagons and tubes and brushes, and smelled of spilled powder and some kind of fresh, bitter cologne. Like mock oranges, Peyton thought. Despite herself she studied the array of cosmetics. She had never seen anything like them. There had been none in this house but her father's aftershave since her birth.

"I'll show you what they're for after," Nora said, moving her and the chair beside the window and bringing a towel to drape around her shoulders. "Right now it's show time. Holy shit, Peyton, I can't get a comb through this. It's like a briar patch. Go wet it good and let's go from there."

Peyton did, holding her head under the taps in the old lavatory in this unused, unfamiliar bathroom. It was cavernous, chilling, and filled with a wavery green underwater light, and there was nothing in it but the big clawfoot bathtub and the lavatory and a yellow-stained toilet. But Nora had dragged in a table to stand beside the lavatory, and it held bath powder and deodorant and tubes and bottles, and a wicker basket full of gigantic rollers. There was also a pot of white chrysanthemums sitting on the top of the toilet. Hair sopping and senses open and pulsing, Peyton went back to her chair and sat down.

Nora combed out her tangled hair gently and walked around and around her, studying her head from all angles. Peyton did not speak. She looked fixedly out the window, into the soaked, abandoned rose garden that had been her mother's pride. Now you could tell only that a large square had been dug out of the lawn, its edges now blurred with crabgrass. It made her sad, and she closed her eyes against the garden and the rain.

"Peyton, do you like Audrey Hepburn?" Nora said from behind her.

"Better than anybody," Peyton said. "I sat through *Breakfast at Tiffany's* three times."

"I did twice. You know what I think we'll do? I think we'll cut this hair into a kind of Audrey Hepburn cap. Very short and pixieish, a little curly. It would look wonderful with your features and your long neck. And it would be a snap to take care of. You game?"

"Yes," Peyton whispered, with the sense of leaping blindly into a bottomless abyss.

She kept her eyes closed while Nora snipped and patted and studied and snipped some more. Somehow it was not like the ministrations of Mr. Antoine. As she worked, Nora talked about her night in Atlanta.

"Well, first," she said, as if Peyton had asked, "I went to the movie. It was at the Peachtree Art Theater out in Buckhead. *La Strada*. Have you seen it?"

Peyton shook her head mutely, trying to imagine herself walking alone into an Atlanta movie theater after dark. How did you know whom to sit by? What did a masher look like? It was Aunt Augusta's term, and though Peyton knew it was ridiculous and outdated, she did not know what else to call a man who touched you and unzipped his trousers in a movie theater. According to Aunt Augusta, any man who was not there with his family was suspect.

"No," she said.

"It's another of the truly greats, kiddo. You've got to see it. Maybe I'll take you to a matinee. It's on for a couple more weeks, I think. OK, so then afterward I walked up the street to Buon Giorno's and had my clam linguine and a bottle of awful, wonderful Chianti. That's a red Italian wine, very raw and gusty."

"I know what it is," said Peyton, who didn't. The only wine she knew was the thick, cloying scuppernong wine her grandmother made every autumn. How could anyone in his or her right mind drink a whole bottle of that?

"Did it make you drunk?" she said.

"Nope. Wine doesn't make you drunk if you sip it slowly, and drink it with a meal. Unlike some other things I could name."

"You mean like Tom Collinses?" said Peyton, who had overheard the cheerleaders talking about drinking them at the annual football banquet at the Henry Grady Hotel in Atlanta.

"God, no. That's pure swill. I mean like Scotch. Gin and tonic. And rum. Mostly rum, good old mule-kicking, fire-breathing Cuban or Barbadian rum."

"Does that make you drunk?"

"Like you wouldn't believe. But it's a fine way to go. Well, so then I went down to this little place by the bus station that has the best Dixieland jazz I have *ever* heard outside New Orleans. And I danced and whooped and hollered till about one, and then I came home."

"By *yourself?*" Peyton squawked. "Down by the *bus* station? Aunt Augusta would *die!*"

"Which is why we aren't going to tell her, isn't it?" Peyton could hear the smile in Nora's voice. "Besides, I wasn't by myself. I went with somebody I met at Buon Giorno's. He's the one who knew about the place."

"He!" Peyton's head was literally spinning with the enormity of it.

"A soldier who was eating his dinner alone. So I joined him. It's more fun to eat Italian *with* somebody. He was on his way to Fort Benning and had to catch a two A.M. bus anyway. So we figured we might as well hear some jazz before he left, and dance a little."

"You picked up a soldier and went to the bus station?"

Aside from sitting down on a bare toilet seatin a public restroom, going to the bus station was the number-one taboo in Aunt Augusta's pantheon of crimes and misdemeanors. Prowling soldiers were unthinkable.

"For God's sake, Peyton, he was all of eighteen years old, and home-sick for Tennessee. He was a sweet boy. I wouldn't have gone with just anybody. You get so you can tell who's OK and who isn't very quickly. We had a wonderful time, and he paid for the whole thing, and I kissed him good-bye and put him on a Trailways bus. We both enjoyed it. I really have to do some instructing with you, I think."

"I don't want any instructing in stuff like that," Peyton said. "What if you catch something?"

"You mean like the clap? You don't catch that from kissing, any more than you can from sitting on a toilet seat. I'm not crazy. Wait a minute now. . . ."

She produced a bulbous hand-held hair dryer and aimed it at Peyton's head, fluffing and making finger waves and gently ruffling the hair at the back of her neck. Until the hot air hit her, Peyton did not realize that her neck was completely naked. She looked down. A mat of wiry hair lay inert on the floor under the chair.

"You cut it all off," she wailed.

"Yep. Now look."

Nora stepped back and Peyton looked.

A thin deer of a girl with a short tousle of hair looked back. It was its own color again, with tendrils and points framing her face. Something Nora had done to it made it shine softly, and it was somehow fuller than usual. It did not lie flat on her small head, but had curve and lift and bounce to it. Speechless, Peyton turned her head this way and that. The girl in the mirror was no one she knew, but unlike the succubus produced by Mr. Antoine, she was . . . interesting. Somehow older, yet with a face and neck of tender, unfinished planes and shadows. She lifted her chin and smiled tentatively. The changeling smiled back. Pretty? No, assuredly not. But for the first time in her life Peyton could see what she might look like as a woman. Somehow she had not ever really wondered, had, perhaps, never really thought she would get there.

Nora smiled down at her silently. She lifted one eyebrow: "Well?"

"I . . . gee. I don't know. It isn't me, is it?"

"Yes, it is. It's you like you ought to be. That stuff on your head was like a dead muskrat lying up there. This sort of sets you free. Don't you see? Lord, I can really see your father and your grandmother in you."

Peyton, who had spent her entire life searching for signs of her mother in her undistinguished visage, felt something inside her lighten and lift, as if she had tossed out a heavy burden. At least she looked like *someone* now—if not her mother, then just maybe her mad, beautiful grandmother, her blade-featured father.

Her smile widened in spite of herself.

"Nobody at school has hair like this," she said.

"Precisely," Nora said. "Peyton, take it from one who knows. You aren't ever going to look like Brigitte Bardot or Jackie Kennedy. Not going to happen. Don't waste your time wishing. Go with what you've got. It may not ring many bells at school, but I assure you there *is* a world beyond Lytton Grammar School, and it's a hell of a lot more interesting. You're going to shine in that world like a star. It took me a long time to find that out. See what I'm doing for you, kiddo? I'm letting you in on the tricks of the trade early."

"I feel naked."

"In a way you are naked. You're not hiding behind hair anymore. Hair is a powerful thing, sweetie pie. A headful of it will hide you. Cutting it off means you're offering yourself to the world."

"I don't want to do that!"

"Already done. OK, hold your face up. I just want to see something."

Peyton did. She felt the kiss of a big soft brush on her cheeks and temples and the tip of her nose. She felt a feathering of something along her closed eyelids. She felt a faint slick over her mouth. Feeling the same sick fear that she had felt at the Max Factor counter in Atlanta, she opened her eyes.

It was her, or at least this new her, only more so. There was a wash of color on her cheekbones and across the bridge of her nose, very faint, as if she had been in the sun for an hour or so. Her eyes were . . . real eyes. Deep and alive. You could see the translucent gray of them. Her grandmother's eyes. Her mouth was the pink of the inside of a shell.

"Is it makeup?" she breathed.

"Yep. But it's Peyton's kind of makeup, not *Seventeen*'s or your sainted Aunt Augusta's. Your makeup always ought to look like you're not wearing any, even when you're old. Your bones will carry your face, don't you see? And your eyebrows."

"Nobody will know me."

"They'll be falling all over themselves to get to know you," Nora said. "Come on, let's go try it out on somebody. Is your daddy in his office?"

"No! Not yet," Peyton squeaked.

"Chloe, then."

"She's gone home. She works only half a day on Saturdays," Peyton said gratefully.

"OK, then it's going to be your grandmother. I promised, anyway. Dump that afghan and put on some clothes. Your chariot awaits."

Peyton tiptoed down the stairs, looking sidewise at her reflection in the glass of framed photographs of sundry blank-eyed McKenzies and Peytons. Over their dead faces her own flashed, alive and utterly alien. She went into her room and put on her blue jeans and one of her father's old shirts. Then she took them off and pulled out the slim blue pants her aunt had selected, and the white sweater set she had gotten for Christmas and never worn. The sweaters were too big, but somehow the drooping amplitude of them was all right with the long neck and the small shining head. She pinned up the waistband of the pants and put on her sneakers and went hesitantly out into the kitchen.

"Miss Hepburn, as I live and breathe," Nora said, smiling. She had changed into tight, faded blue jeans like a boy's, and an enormous sweat shirt that said "U. of Miami Crew." Someone had scrawled a gigantic S in front of the "Crew" with what looked to be Magic Marker. It had faded, but you could still read it. Peyton blushed. Nora saw her and grinned evilly.

"There is hardly a soul in all of Lytton over the age of fourteen who hasn't done it at one time or another," she said, and she brushed her heavy hair out of her eyes. They dashed through the rain to the Thunderbird, tethered like a restless roc at the curb. Peyton scrunched herself into the passenger seat, loving the sleek, feral feeling of the car, seeing that its pink fenders and hood shone like the northern lights in the gloom, piercing, almost painful to the eyes, even more so on this gray street of winter-smeared white houses and dripping old oaks.

"What do you call this pink?" she said to Nora as the little car leapt forward away from the curb and skimmed into flight.

"Somebody I used to know calls it vagina pink," Nora said.

Her grandmother was in the kitchen, as usual, stirring something musky and pungent in a pot. There were bunches and skeins of the herbs she grew and dried littering the oilcloth-covered table. Oh God, Peyton thought. It's one of those tea things that she's going to make me drink. One day she's going to kill me.

She dutifully drank the potions her grandmother gave her, mostly because no one else would and she felt sorry for the old woman. Her grandmother would never tell her what they were supposed to facilitate. She would say only, "Well, so far you're healthy and safe, aren't you?"

Healthy, yes, Peyton would think to herself. But safe? Never safe.

Her grandmother heard them come in and turned from the stove. She looked first at Peyton, and a slow smile warmed her wild hawk's face.

"Well, here you are at last," she said. "I've waited a long time for you."

Then she turned to Nora. "It's nice to see you again," she said, almost formally. "Will you stay and have a cup of tea?"

Peyton stared at her. She had never heard her grandmother be polite in her life. Vivacious, maybe; joyful or wrathful or full of a kind of angry glee. But never merely polite. It was as if she had faded like an old photograph. Peyton knew Nora was taken aback, too. This was not the exuberant elemental force she had met in the park the day before. This was an old woman dimly minding her manners.

They sat down before the kitchen fireplace. It was blazing high against the cold rain. Agnes McKenzie brought cups of the steaming brew and slices of seed cake almost shyly, as if offering them to royalty. She sat down then and sipped her own tea, looking down at the oilcloth tabletop.

There was a silence, and then Nora said, "This is good. It's herbal, isn't it? What is it, exactly?"

"Oh, a little of this and a little of that. It's a good end-of-winter tonic, my mother used to say."

"I think I can taste rosemary, and maybe—what? Fennel? But the rest is a mystery." Nora smiled. "So is it going to perk us up?"

Agnes McKenzie looked full at her then. Something flashed out of the gray eyes and then sank back below the surface.

"It's going to give both of you just what you need," she said.

They were silent again, sipping. Finally Peyton could stand it no longer and said, "How do you like my hair, Nana?"

Her grandmother studied her.

"You're not our little girl anymore," she said. "But you're who you're going to be now, and that's a start. I can see the shape of you like a minnow in deep water. Or something in the long grass. Something wild and shy, but the power's there. Oh, yes, it is. I always knew it would be."

"Power?" Peyton said, appalled. She did not want power any more than she wanted wealth or celebrity. She would, she thought, settle gratefully for the old anonymity, so long as no one laughed at her anymore.

"Oh, yes. It'll be a long time until you grow into it, and it won't be any easy journey, but power."

"Is it good power?" Nora said interestedly, looking first at Peyton, then at her grandmother.

"It depends on who guides it," Nana said. "I plan to be on top of it like a duck on a june bug, but I'm not going to be able to go all the way with it."

"Why can't I be in charge of my own power?" Peyton said resentfully. She was accustomed to people's talking about her as if she were not there, but not these two women.

"Because you don't know how," her grandmother said, looking at Nora. "You've never been in charge of your own life. They haven't let you be. It's getting to be time, though."

Abruptly she got up from the table and said, "Peyton, come on in the pantry with me. I need a load of firewood."

Peyton rose to follow her grandmother. Nora half rose, too.

"Won't you let me help?" she said. "I don't want to feel like company."

"But you are," Agnes said, and smiled faintly at her, and went out of the kitchen with Peyton trailing behind her.

In the dim, cold little pantry she fished into the pocket of her apron and pulled something out and dropped it into Peyton's hand. Peyton looked down. It was a strange object, primitive and rather beautiful: an intricately interwoven knot that formed a rough cross on a leather thong. She looked up at her grandmother.

"It's pretty, Nana," she said. "What is it?"

"It's an amulet. It protects you. It's a special one. It's got my hair woven into it, and some herbs that are very old. I want you to put it on now, and I don't want you to take it off again."

"Protects me against what?"

Her grandmother was silent, and then she said, "I saw her again. Your Cousin Nora. I saw her this morning when I built the fire."

"The fire—that's not so good, is it? She wouldn't hurt me, Nana. I know she wouldn't. I don't think I like her very much, but she's always taking my side and doing things for me, and she absolutely hates Aunt Augusta. That can't be all bad, can it?"

Her grandmother shook her head impatiently.

"I can't see bad or good this time," she said. "I just know that I saw her first in the soup, and this time in the fire, and I don't know what that means. I don't see bad; I don't see anything. It's like fog. I don't know what it means."

Suddenly Peyton was tired of all of it—the dark pantry, the visions and the incantations and the mutterings of fire and water and protection. She wanted light, air, normalcy, laughter, the sound of her record player, the smell of supper cooking with nothing in it of bitter herbs.

"I think we need to go, Nana," she said. "Daddy's going to be in before long and Nora's going to make us Cuban black bean soup for supper. We've got to go to the grocery store."

Her grandmother looked at her for a long time and then sighed.

"So it begins," she said. "All right, Peyton. You run on and have your soup. But you put that around your neck right now. I'm not going to let you out of here until you do."

Peyton put the little cross around her neck and let it slide down under her sweater. It felt rough and cool against her collarbone, but not unpleasant.

"Promise you won't take it off?"

"Oh, Nana—"

"*Promise!*" Her grandmother's voice cracked with a kind of urgency Peyton had never heard before.

"I promise," she said. "I really promise."

On the way toward Lytton's small Piggly Wiggly to get black beans and rice, Nora said, "She really does get a little bit peculiar sometimes, doesn't she? Yesterday she was so kind of . . . joyful. I thought—no, I *know* that she liked me then. I wonder what got into her. Did she say?"

"No," Peyton said, the lie coming smoothly and quickly. "I don't know, she just gets funny sometimes. I think maybe she drinks too much of that stuff she makes. She'll be entirely different the next time you see her."

"I hope so," Nora said. "I think she would make a bad enemy."

Peyton looked at Nora under her lashes. It was a strange thing to say, but she knew that her cousin was right. You would not want to get crosswise of Agnes McKenzie.

She wanted to wait in the car while Nora went into the store, feeling suddenly naked with the lightness of her head and the air on her neck, but her cousin jerked open the passenger door and pulled her out.

"Come on. You've got to do it sometime," she said. "You look terrific, and it'll be all over town tomorrow that you do. And besides, you've got your protection hung around your neck, haven't you?"

"How did you know?"

"I can smell it. Rosemary again, and maybe some hyssop. People used herbs for charms and amulets all the time in Cuba. Everybody had something hung around his or her neck. You're lucky it isn't a dead chicken. Is it me your grandmother is afraid of, do you think?"

"No. I don't know. She just gets strange. One winter she made me wear garlic around my neck on a string when I went to bed. She said it was to ward off coughs and colds, but I heard Chloe tell Daddy it was for witches and spirits. It got so bad that I had to take it off. I told her I was still wearing it, but she knew I wasn't. Boy, did I smell."

Nora laughed, her joyous, froggy laugh. "Well, let's go see. If we get through the Piggly Wiggly without being molested by a witch, we'll know she's on to something."

Peyton laughed, too, and the strange dark sense of her grandmother vanished as if it had never been, and together they dashed through the rain into the grocery store.

At supper her father frankly stared at her. He said nothing, only nodded as Nora talked lazily about her trip to Atlanta the night before, and ate the rich, dark soup appreciatively and had another bowl, saying it made him feel as if he were at a real fiesta, and all the while, out of the corner of her eye, Peyton was aware of his eyes on her.

Finally he said, "I really like your hair, Peyton. At first it was a shock to see all that pretty hair gone, but this is . . . right elegant. It suits you. I like the new clothes, too. You remember to thank your aunt, now. She was a little miffed that you never thanked her for the trip to Atlanta."

"She's going to hate the hair," Peyton said.

Her father smiled, a small smile, but a smile nevertheless.

"I expect you're right," he said. "Never mind. This is good. She'll come around. Did you thank Nora for the haircut?"

"She did," Nora said before Peyton could remember that she had not. "We went down to her grandmother's afterward, to show her. I think she liked it, too."

Her father looked at Peyton.

"Oh, she did," Peyton said, bending over her soup bowl. "She really did."

"Well, then, you've got a hard row to hoe ahead of you," Frazier said, but he smiled again. "Nora, tell me where you learned to make this soup. Cuba, you said? Were you there long? I realize Peyton and

I don't have any idea what you were doing so far away from home. I've always wanted to see Cuba."

"It's a wonderful country," Nora said. "I might still be there if the revolution hadn't started to heat things up. I believe in it, but I don't want to live with it. I don't take easily to sacrifice and nobility."

She smiled through smoke, and Peyton thought once again how plain she was, and how utterly arresting. It was hard to look away from her. She had brought out fat wax candles from somewhere, and painted wooden candlesticks, and they ate by the flickering light. In it, Nora looked like some impossible firebird that had alit in a small southern town and decided to stay awhile, unaware that her plumage roiled the air around her. She wore a heavy cabled white turtleneck sweater and the black pants, and her long, thin hands wove in and out of the candlelight as she talked of Cuba.

"I went there in nineteen fifty-two with a friend," she said. "I was just out of school and didn't know what I wanted to do, and I had always wanted to see Cuba. He had a motorcycle. We put it on a ferry and took off, and I was a goner before the first shot was fired. He came back two months later. I stayed five years."

Peyton saw her father remark the "he," though he said nothing. It emboldened her to say, "Why didn't your friend stay, too?"

"He was a priest," Nora said. "He had to get back to his parish."

Peyton thought about it: the hot sunlight pouring down on the fleeing motorcycle, its shadow leaping ahead of it. The huge pile of shining ocean cumulus. Blue seas unrolling beside it like something on a movie projector. Wind in Nora's bronze hair, and the priest's skirts fluttering like black crows. . . .

"Did you ride in one of those little cars beside the motorcycle?" she said. "Did he wear those robes?"

Nora laughed. "I rode behind him sometimes, holding on, and he rode behind me sometimes while I drove. He wore Bermuda shorts and a T-shirt. It was a sabbatical for him. It meant he could wear his Bermudas and drink rum with the cane workers all night if he wanted to. The Catholic Church is kind of vague about that."

"Did he? Drink rum all night, I mean?"

"Once or twice, I think. I don't really know. We didn't keep close tabs on each other. He was a darling and a good friend, but it was really the motorcycle and Cuba itself that got to me. It's funny, he went down there thinking he might stay and find a ministry in one of the really poor little villages west of Havana—God knows there are hundreds of them—and stay. Make it his vocation. In the end the heat and superstition got him, and it was I who stayed on. I liked the heat and I even kind of liked the superstition."

"What superstition?"

"Well, the Catholic Church has had a hard time in Cuba. It's always been the state religion, but there's an older, darker worship, almost pure African, called *santería*, which sort of hovers just under the surface and simply can't be rooted out. It's the worship of saints and spirits, good and evil; everywhere you see the saints' pictures on the walls with the glasses of water under them to trap the spirits. It must have been terribly frustrating for a Catholic priest. In the daylight the old, familiar saints of the church were worshiped, and after dark the Cubans simply named them something else and worshiped them, too. It seemed to me a pretty practical arrangement: nobody had to spend any more money on different saint images, and all the bases were covered. But it drove Tootie wild."

"Tootie?"

"Tootie LeClerc, fresh out of Loyola in New Orleans. I met him on the beach in Miami and we spent the afternoon drinking beer. Once I saw the motorcycle and heard where he was going, I knew what my next move was going to be. I guess I didn't think much further ahead than that."

"So you stayed on," Frazier said. There was nothing of the shock Peyton felt in his voice or face. He looked and sounded merely as if he really wanted to know about this scandalous flight into the sun.

"I did. At first I just wanted to be a tourist—we poked around Havana and did all the touristy things you're supposed to do—but pretty soon we both got restless. There was not enough humble poverty for Tootie and, in the end, too much glitter for me. Living was pretty good then in Cuba. You didn't see the real poor around

Havana. So we got on the motorcycle and headed west, toward
Mariel. It's beautiful country, or it was then—wild and empty, and
the blue, blue water, and those huge tropical skies. And poor enough
for anybody, I guess. That's where we began to see little adobe
shacks with tile roofs and chickens going in and out of the open windows, and rusted old American cars in yards, and the village men
hanging around the lone flyspecked cantina because one or another
of the cement factories had shut down and there was no work. And
the children, some of them naked as jaybirds, some in rags, playing
in the roads and ditches with not a sign of any supervision, or a
school anywhere. Tootie thought he'd found paradise; he went
straight to the Catholic church in the square and asked if he could
sign on sans pay, and the senile old priest almost kissed him. I went
into the cantina and told the barkeep that I would start a little school
for the children, teach them English and some geography and what
all, in exchange for room and board somewhere in the village. I had
a little money. I was going to stay until it ran out. So they found me
a room with a village family and I moved in and fell in love with
them and it and everything else, and when Tootie got a bait of it and
went back to New Orleans, I just stayed."

"For five years," Frazier McKenzie said.

"Yes. Some of the great years of my life. I've never felt so in tune
with a place or a people. It was as if that's what I was meant to be
doing—living there with those people, teaching those children, swimming in that water, eating that food. . . ."

"But you left."

"Things change. One day it was time. I came back to Miami and
got a job with a sort of pre–Head Start program they had for the
Haitian refugees from Papa Doc and his benevolent Tontons
Macoute. They were pouring into Florida by then, dirt-poor and with
no schooling whatsoever. I liked doing that, but it wasn't the same as
Mariel. But you don't want to hear all this. . . ."

"I do," he said. "It's fascinating. Peyton and I both would love to
hear your stories. You've done something really valuable."

"One day I'll tell them all to you." She smiled and got up and said, "Leave the dishes. Peyton, come with me. I have something for you."

The something was a tiny tiger kitten, thin but with a hard little potbelly, slanted green eyes, and a fierce little spike of a tail. Nora brought his box out of the bathroom and set it down, and the kitten scrambled out onto the floor, blinking and mewling furiously. He looked at Peyton and she looked back.

"I found him behind a trash can at the bus station last night," Nora said. "Somebody had obviously dumped him. I bought him a hamburger and brought him home. His name is Trailways, and he needs a friend."

The kitten mewed again. It was not a plaintive sound; it was an imperious demand. Peyton put out a hand and he sniffed her fingers and then climbed into her lap and curled up. Something in her heart softened into a spreading pool.

"Is he for me?" she asked.

"If you want him. He'll need a lot of taking care of. He's eaten now, and has water and a litter box of sorts, but I don't know what else he needs. Shots, surely, and maybe vitamins, and most certainly a flea bath. We need to get a vet to check him."

"We can take him to Dr. Kidd," Peyton said, her voice trembling. "He does mainly horses and cows and mules, but I'm sure he'd know about cats. What does he want? He's yelling so."

"I think he's just saying, 'Here I am. What are you going to do about it?'"

"Can I take him to my room?" Peyton said. Her voice was tight with love for the angry little cat.

"In a little while," Nora said. "You stay with him right now. I want to go down and tell your father about him. I get the idea that there haven't been many pets in this house."

"No. Buddy had a dog, I think, but I don't really remember it. . . ."

"You just sit tight." Nora got up and went down the stairs toward the breakfast room. Peyton wrapped a small towel around the kitten and took it and sat with it on the second step, out of sight but not out of hearing. After wriggling for a while, the kitten curled against her and fell abruptly asleep. She could see his tiny ribs rising and falling and could feel the small thrilling against her chest that meant he was purring. She tightened her arms and closed her eyes.

"... not set up here for a cat," she heard her father say, his voice cool again now, louder. "She's never taken care of an animal before. Chloe isn't going to have time to take care of it when she gets tired of it."

"She's not going to get tired of it, Frazier," Nora said, and her voice was cool, too, and utterly level. "I wish you had seen her face. Do you realize that she literally has nothing of her own? Everybody needs something. Everybody. If it's a problem, I'll find another home for it, but I can promise you it would hurt her badly to take this kitten away from her."

"Did you ever think of asking me first?"

"I did, and vetoed that idea in a second. Would you have permitted it? And besides, it isn't your kitten. It's Peyton's."

There was more talk that Peyton could not hear. The voices dropped and the tight levelness went out of them. Peyton sat on the step and rocked the sleeping kitten against her.

Presently Nora came into the hall and looked up and made a circle with her thumb and forefinger. Peyton felt tears sting her eyes.

She slept that night with the susurration of the wind and rain in the trees outside, and over it, just at her ear, the rusty purr of the kitten.

8

When Peyton woke on Sunday morning the house was still and full of pearly gray light, and the rain was a blanket of sound that muffled wakefulness. She stretched her full length, hearing her joints pop, feeling the new lightness of her neck and head against her pillow, thinking how she would like to simply lie here in this silent, rainy cocoon until she felt like getting up. But Sunday meant church and often Sunday school, though she was sometimes given grudging permission to miss that. Perhaps Nora would be reason enough to miss it this morning. Peyton hated Sunday school. She had once won first prize for being able to faultlessly parrot the books of the Bible, both Old Testament and New, but she was not allowed to receive the prize because it was a Boy Scout flashlight and clearly unsuitable for girls.

"Didn't anybody think a girl might win it?" she had asked her father aggrievedly that afternoon.

He had said little, only smiled absently. But the next afternoon he had brought an authentic Girl Scout flashlight home with him. Peyton could not imagine where he had gotten it. At that time, there was no troop in Lytton, only a straggling band of Brownies.

She was just putting an unwilling foot out from under her covers when she heard Chloe shriek from the kitchen. It was the shriek she used when she was frightened or, more often, driven to extremis by the willfulness and stupidity of children, black and white alike.

"My God and my JEEEZUS!" she squalled. Peyton was halfway into the kitchen before she remembered the kitten and registered that it was not in her bedroom.

"Oh, shit," she said softly.

Chloe was standing flat-footed, arms akimbo, in the middle of the kitchen, glaring down at her skirt. Trailways hung from it, fastened securely by his needlelike little claws, swinging gently and lashing his meager tail.

Peyton ran and unhooked him from Clothilde's skirt and folded him protectively into her arms, where he struggled and yowled. There was blood in Chloe's eye.

"What that sorry thing doing in this house?" she demanded. "I was just standing here fixin' to call y'all to breakfast and he come barreling out of your room and climb right up my leg and grab on my skirt before I even seen him."

"I'm sorry, Chloe," Peyton said miserably. "I thought he was still with me. Nora brought him to me from Atlanta. His name is Trailways."

"Huh. His name mud for all I care. Does your daddy know about him?"

"Yes. It's all right with him."

"Well, I know who ain't gon' feed it and clean up after it. And if it get under my feet one more time I'm gon' stomp it."

"He won't," Peyton said fervently. "I'll keep him in my room. I'll feed him and clean up after him. He won't be a bit of trouble."

Trailways stuck his sharp little head out of Peyton's arm and looked up into Chloe's face. He put out a tiny paw and patted her arm, seven or eight rapid, whisper-soft pats.

"Rowr?" he said.

Chloe's face struggled with implacability but lost. An unwilling grin broke its surface. "Well, he's a feisty little thing, ain't he?"

"He's a good boy. He's going to go everywhere with me. You're going to love him, Chloe."

"I ain't gon' love no flea-bitten stray cat. But maybe I ain't gon' hate him, either," Clothilde said.

When Nora finally straggled down to breakfast it was too late for Sunday school, and Peyton and her father were playing with the kitten, tossing a ball of kitchen twine for him. Trailways leapt high into the air, arching and twisting, batting the twine from one end of the breakfast room to the other. Peyton was laughing aloud, and her father was smiling.

"Isn't he the cutest kitten you ever saw?" she demanded of her father.

"Not by a long shot," Frazier said. "But he's cute enough. He can't be allowed to tear things up, claw the furniture, and things like that, though, Peyton. You're going to have to watch him closely. I'm not going to have him be any more work for Chloe."

"Oh, I will! He won't!"

Peyton looked up as Nora came down the stairs and into the breakfast room. Instead of the dragon robe and the ubiquitous cigarette, Nora was wearing a short black sheath of some stretchy material, and a strand of pearls, and high-heeled black pumps. She had her hair pulled back into a sort of chignon and had tied a red and black paisley silk scarf around it. She looked exotic and absolutely wonderful. She even wore makeup and some sort of coppery lipstick.

Peyton could feel her mouth open and freeze there.

"I thought we'd be going to church," Nora said. "Am I too late? Is this wrong for church?"

"You look just fine," Frazier said. "You just took us by surprise. Here you're all dressed and Peyton's still in her pajamas. I wasn't sure you'd want to go to church, but we're glad to have you."

"I'd really like to. So, I see you've met Trailways. He's a cutie, isn't he?" She picked up the squirming kitten and held him under her chin, crooning to him.

"He's not so bad. Where on earth did you find him?"

"Behind a garbage can at the restaurant," Nora said easily. She

smiled at Peyton, a small smile. We will always have our secrets, you
and I, the smile said. Peyton, who had been about to recount the
story of the bus-station garbage can, did not, and smiled back at her
cousin. Her father, she knew, would have hated the entire idea of the
bus station. Yes, secrets of our own, which nobody else will ever
know, her smile said back to Nora.

She went to dress, and Nora came into her room with her.

"I remember this room," she said. "This is where I slept when I
was a little girl, the time I was here. They offered me one of the big
rooms, but this was the one I wanted. It wraps around you like a
hug, doesn't it? You've fixed it up very nicely. I'll like thinking of you
snuggled in here under the eaves. Now. What are you going to wear
to church?"

Without stopping for Peyton's answer, Nora went to her closet and
opened the door and stood staring in. She shook her head a little and
then reached in and pulled out the dress and jacket that Aunt Augusta
had selected from the Tween Shop. They were just as bad as Peyton
remembered, hanging shapeless and joyless from their padded hanger.

"This," Nora said.

"I hate it. It looks like a maid's dress. It looks like a missionary-
society dress."

"Just you wait. Put it on and I'll be right back."

Peyton slipped on the dark, sleeveless dress. It gaped and billowed
on her, and the skirt flapped like a wet conquered flag at her calves.
She would not look into the mirror on her dressing table. There was
no way anyone was going to get her into the Lytton First Methodist
Church in this.

Nora came back with a shopping bag and began to spread things
out on Peyton's bed, where Trailways dove and scrabbled among
them. First she brought out safety pins and pinned the waist and
armholes of the dress snugly. Then she took a big roll of two-sided
tape and doubled the hem up and secured it with the tape. Peyton
felt it just skimming her knees. She looked down. Her legs were bare
and scabby and covered with downy dark hair. This could not be
happening.

"Dark stockings," Nora said, and brought them out. She turned her back while Peyton grumbled herself into the garter belt, and then Nora showed her how to roll the stockings down and fit them over her feet and pull them taut and fasten them. They felt somehow . . . depraved? No, but something. . . .

Nora clasped a string of irregular freshwater pearls around Peyton's neck. They bumped at her exposed collarbone. Then she produced black suede pumps with low, shaped heels.

"Cuban heels," she said. "Do you think you can squinch your feet into them just for an hour?"

Peyton nodded, wondering how on earth she was going to walk.

"Now the jacket," Nora said, and she slipped it over Peyton's arms and buttoned it neatly at the throat, pulling out the pearls so that they lay just along the neckline. She puffed Peyton's hair and whisked on a bit of the blush and eyeshadow and a slicking of the lip gloss and stepped back and looked.

"Wow," she said. "This is even better than I thought."

Peyton minced in the too-tight heels, her ankles wobbling a little, over to the mirror and looked.

Holly Golightly did indeed look back. At least she did if Peyton used her seeing-not-seeing trick. At the edge of her vision Holly stood poised and straight, her stalk of a neck rising from the collar of her dress, her long legs graceful and coltish. Even the cap of hair, even the dark slant of eyebrows. . . .

Suddenly Peyton did not want to go out of her room.

"I can't," she whispered. "I can't wear this."

"Oh, yes, you can, and you will," Nora said, putting an arm around her shoulder. "You're going to walk into that church with your father and me and you're going to hold your back straight as a stick like Audrey does, and you're going to smile, and I guarantee you're going to hear a great big swoosh of breath from everybody there."

"I'd hate that."

"No, you wouldn't. Once you've heard it, you'll want to hear it everywhere you go. Now let's get at it. Here, carry these white gloves. Oh, yes. Perfect."

Tottering and terrified, Peyton followed Nora out into the break-fast room, where her father sat reading the Sunday *Atlanta Journal-Constitution*. He looked up.

"Why, Peyton," he said, and smiled. "Who is this? You look mighty pretty, baby. You really do. Nobody at church is going to know you. They'll think we've got two cousins visiting us."

"Daddy, I don't think I . . . could I maybe just skip church this once? I need to look after Trailways."

"And waste all this? Certainly not. Trailways can look after him-self. I'm looking forward to showing off both of you. Get your coat; it's turned cold."

The bells of the Methodist church were ringing as they got out of the car and hurried through the cold rain. People stood in a knot on the porch and streamed into the sanctuary. Two appointed stewards stood at the door shaking hands and looking wet and resigned. Tee-tering drunkenly on Nora's heels, Peyton navigated the steps behind her father and her cousin, her head down. There was a faint hum, as from a hive of bees, from the church. Nora turned around and grinned at her.

"The Methodists are swarming," she said, and then she put her hand under Peyton's chin. "Head up. Shoulders back. Let's see that smile."

Blind, erect, and grinning, Peyton walked into the church she had attended all her life. It smelled of wet wool and dusty heat from the ancient furnace, and moldy hymnals. She knew none of it.

There was no whoosh of indrawn breath as Nora had predicted, but there was a small silence from each pew as Peyton passed, and then a little hum of conversation.

"Let me die," Peyton whispered to the God who never seemed to hear her, and she slipped into the McKenzie pew. When she turned to seat herself, she looked back. Everywhere she looked, there were smiles. Her Uncle Charles, seated in the looming shadow of Aunt Augusta, held up his thumb and forefinger in an OK sign. Only Aunt Augusta was not smiling. She looked as if she had swallowed some-thing rancid.

The sermon dealt vaguely with First Corinthians, thirteenth verse, and seemed interminable. When it ended, Peyton stifled an urge to dash out the back entrance and trotted dumbly up the aisle behind her father. Nora walked ahead of them, head high, a small smile on her mouth. Peyton thought that there had been nothing like her in this church in its living memory, though Nora wore plain black, like half the women there, and pearls, and just the silk scarf. Still, eyes tracked her, heads went together, a soft babble rose wherever she passed. When the eyes turned to Peyton the babble swelled, and there were more smiles. Finally, they gained the cold freedom of the porch, where Dr. Moss was greeting his congregation. He had baptized Peyton. He looked at her without recognition for a long moment, and then he hugged her and said, "Well, my dear, you all grow up, don't you? Only you did it overnight. Next thing you know I'll be marrying you and some lucky young fellow."

Peyton smiled sickly and fled.

Her father and Nora were waiting in the car, the heater blasting out warm air and fogging up the windows.

"You ladies surely kicked up a fuss," her father said. "I never saw so much whispering and eye-rolling and what-all. I thought for a minute they were going to clap."

"Well, maybe they just don't have enough to do," Nora said lazily. "Surely girls grow up in Lytton. Surely people come to visit."

"It's a small town, Nora," Frazier McKenzie said. "Not much changes."

Suddenly Peyton was wild to be home, to skin out of the pinned-up clothes and stockings and toss the gloves on her bed and kick the pumps across the room, to curl up with Trailways under her afghan and read away the long afternoon.

"Augusta has asked us to lunch," her father said. "I thought we'd go and get it over with. If we don't, she's going to be at the house every morning at dawn until she finds out all she wants to know about Nora."

"I think she already has," Nora said.

"*Daddy,*" Peyton wailed.

"It's not for long, Peyton. I know she'd like to see you in your new clothes. You need to thank her. And it's been a while since you've seen your Uncle Charlie. I want Nora to meet him."

"I look forward to it," Nora murmured. Peyton glanced at her.

The faint smile was still in place.

Augusta McKenzie met them at the doorway of her home two streets from the church, on the "new" side of town. It was a rambling brick structure with black shutters and a walkway bordered with barren azalea bushes. They were pretty in the spring, Peyton knew, but now they looked like tatty sheep huddled in the rain. The house was fairly new, and looked it. Aunt Augusta had bullied Charles McKenzie out of the big, ramshackle, once-beautiful house at the edge of the downtown area four years earlier, when the town offered them a sizable lump sum to buy it and tear it down and put up a small shopping center. The money had been used to build this house in a "far better part of town." It was the ranch style that was popular in that part of the South, but it was longer and lower and had more lawn and a pocket-sized swimming pool behind it. Peyton had never understood why. Uncle Charles did not spend enough time at home to swim, and Aunt Augusta in a swimming pool was simply unimaginable. She had been invited to swim there whenever she wanted, and her father had brought her over once or twice to do so, but everything was so rectangular and pristine and chlorinated and blue and white that she barely got her feet wet before she was out and wrapped in a towel, shivering. Her father did not make her go back. Peyton did not really know how to swim. He thought she was afraid of the water, but it was the pool. She did not know how to tell him that.

Augusta kissed Frazier lightly on the cheek and nodded to Nora and simply looked at Peyton.

"Your new clothes suit you very well, Peyton," she said. "I'm sorry you didn't think so much of your pretty permanent. Did your Cousin Nora cut it for you?"

The smile she bent on Nora was sharklike and brief. Peyton knew that her father had not seen the teeth in it. She knew that Nora had.

"Yes, I did," Nora said sweetly. "We thought something a little simpler, maybe. Let her pretty natural color and wave show through. I don't think Peyton quite knew how to take care of the permanent. I know she appreciated it, though."

"I'm sure," Augusta McKenzie said. Her eyes took in Nora's trim dress, the pearls, and the scarf. "Quite a change from your last costume," she said.

"I have one for every occasion," Nora said.

Augusta led them into her living room, done in turquoise and rose and beetling with bulbous brocade pieces that she had once told Peyton were Duncan Phyfe. Charles McKenzie was perched uncomfortably on a wing chair, stiff in a blue suit and a red and blue tie. He clashed with the room. Peyton imagined that her aunt would have had him change his clothes if there had been time.

Charles McKenzie was a squashed and spread version of his older brother. You could see the resemblance in the gray eyes and the dark hair and the ruins of cheekbones, but the rest seemed blurred and sagging, like a melting snowman. His nose was traced with red veins and he had two shiny-shaved chins poised over his starched collar. His stomach pushed unhappily over his belt and the soles of his black shoes were still unscratched. Peyton could not remember ever seeing him in anything but hunting boots or desiccated old moccasins, except on Sundays, when he seemed to her like a captive gorilla, miserably dressed up in human clothes and brought to church. She loved him. When she was very small, he used to toss her in the air over his head and catch her, and she remembered her own shrieks of joy.

He got up and hugged her briefly and hard. He smelled as he always did, of whiskey and cigar smoke and his aftershave and, somehow, of the hunting dogs he kept over at Chief Fletcher's house. It was one of the smells of Peyton's childhood, and she breathed it in like oxygen.

"You look might pretty, honey," he said. "All grown up. You're not going to be our little girl much longer."

"This is Peyton's cousin, Nora Findlay," her father said, and Nora put out her hand, smiling. Uncle Charlie took it, reddening. In this waxworks room Nora seemed pulsing, overflowing with life and energy.

"I'm glad to meet you finally," Nora said. "I've met Cousin Augusta, but I was wondering when they were going to let me meet you."

"Pleasedtomeecha," Charles McKenzie mumbled, looking at the rug with interest.

"Please sit down," Aunt Augusta said. "Lunch will be only a minute. I'd offer you a touch of sherry, but it being Sunday I thought we'd do it another time. Now, Nora, tell us all about yourself. I knew your Lytton cousin, Lila Lee, forever, of course, but I don't believe I ever met her Cousin Carolyn. Your mother. She's passed away, I understand?"

"Yes, she has," Nora said. Peyton knew that Aunt Augusta knew that. She knew also that Nora knew she knew. Her stomach knotted, but Nora only said, "As you know, she was sick for a long time before she died. I don't remember much about my father. So the only family I can come close to claiming is here in Lytton. It's nice to check in with them."

"And you'll be moving on to a job in Atlanta, you said?"

"Well, actually . . ."

"I hope Nora will be staying awhile with us, Augusta," Frazier McKenzie said. "There are plans for a new joint English class with Lytton and Carver Highs, and I've suggested Nora for it. She says she'd like it and I can't imagine the board will be anything but delighted. We'll know this week, but I'd say it was a done deal."

"Staying with you, of course," Aunt Augusta said.

"Well, of course," Peyton's father said. "Look what her influence has done for Peyton already. And yours, of course."

"Of course. Well, Nora, you've landed well, haven't you?"

"Better than I could have dreamed," Nora said, wrinkling her freckled nose at Aunt Augusta.

"Oh, I'll bet not," Augusta said. Frazier and Charles McKenzie turned to look at her, and she said hastily, "I think I heard Doreen say lunch was ready. Let's go on in."

Aunt Augusta's table was spread with linen and china and crystal and silver, most of it in turquoise and rose. A prim tower of artificial fruit rose from a silver epergne in the middle of the table. Rose candles burned on either side of it.

"My goodness, it looks like a wedding with the candles and all," Nora said. "Beautiful, Aunt Augusta. Or should I say 'Cousin'?"

"'Augusta' will do," Peyton's aunt said. "You're a bit too old to be my niece, and we're really not cousins. Thank you. I thought the candles because it's so dreary outside. I know it's not strictly proper before dark, but we can surely bend the rules a little with family."

"Certainly," Nora said.

A young black girl came into the dining room carrying a tureen of something smoking hot. She walked as carefully as Peyton had that morning, balancing the heavy dish, and her pink tongue protruded a bit from her lips. She wore a black dress and a starched white apron. Peyton stared. She had never seen such a costume on anyone but the angry woman in Rich's restroom. Then she looked harder.

"Doreen!" she said. "What are you doing in that thing?"

Doreen was the grandniece of Clothilde, and lived in a small house on the other side of hers. She was a quiet girl only a few years older than Peyton. Her mother had died when she was very small, and she did not know who her father was. Chloe looked after her and her younger brother, Tyrone. Peyton had played in the woods with both of them all through her childhood.

Doreen grinned but did not move her eyes from the tureen. She set it down in the middle of the table, where it slopped a bit of soup onto the tablecloth.

"Towel, please, Doreen," Aunt Augusta said evenly, and when the girl had left the room she added, "I'll never get her properly trained to serve. But she's helpful with the cleaning. And she's very young still. Maybe, with time . . ."

"What's she doing in that apron thing?" Peyton asked curiously.

"For heaven's sake, Peyton, it's what people's maids wear," her aunt said. "Just because Chloe comes to work looking like a ragpicker does not mean it's proper. I bought the uniform for Doreen because I want her to learn how to be a good maid. She didn't go to school past the third grade because she had to look after Tyrone, and I can't imagine she would have had much future otherwise. At least she can always find work if she's trained. We need to help our people when we can."

No one spoke. Doreen came back into the room with a towel, looking as though she would burst into tears. Nora leaned toward her and took the towel.

"Let me," she said. "It's easier to reach from here. No, wait a minute, Doreen, don't go yet. I'm Nora Findlay, Peyton's cousin."

Doreen looked at her wildly. Nora smiled and said, "You're a good maid, Doreen, but I wonder if you might not like to go back to school?"

"No'm," the girl said, casting a look at Aunt Augusta. "I've missed too much now. This is fine."

"Well, look. I'm starting a special English class at Carver, and . . . I'd think you might enjoy coming and sitting in sometime, when you're done with your work, of course. And I do tutoring, too. I think we could catch you up pretty quickly."

"That will do, Doreen," Aunt Augusta said, and the girl fled. Augusta turned to Nora.

"It may not be the custom in some of the places you've lived," she said tightly, and Peyton could see that she was furious. "But in Lytton people do not steal one another's maids."

"I wasn't stealing her, I was emancipating her," Nora said, and there were two round spots of color high on her cheekbones. "It was this notion Mr. Lincoln had, a long time ago. I thought perhaps you'd heard of it."

"You may bring in the plates, Doreen," Augusta called. The girl did, and handed them around. The table was silent.

The meal was heavy and not particularly good, and it seemed to go on for years. Aunt Augusta did not speak, and only Nora ate heartily.

"Good old-fashioned southern cooking," she said. "I don't think I've had it since the last time I was here."

"What sort of meals are you used to, then?" Aunt Augusta said sweetly. "Tropical food, I suppose. African, isn't it?"

"Yes. Much like this. Chicken. Yams. Corn. Tomatoes. Okra. Oh, of course there are a few foreign touches. Goat, for instance. And there's a big lizard they serve in Cuba, tastes just like chicken. . . ."

At last the meal was over, and they went back into the living room. Peyton knew that they would sit there for an hour or so before she could go home, chatting and catching up, as Aunt Augusta said. She wondered if she could say she was suddenly ill and leave. But she knew she could not.

There was another, longer silence in the living room, and then Charles McKenzie said, "Got a new shotgun the other day, Frazier. It's out in the garage. Want to go have a look?"

"Charles, you let Frazier sit and digest his lunch," Aunt Augusta snapped. "Good grief. Frazier, don't you pay any attention to him. He's got a bottle out there. He just can't wait to get out there and start tippling."

Charles McKenzie's ears reddened. He studied his shoes intently.

Nora stood up.

"I would love to see it, Charles," she said. "I learned skeet and trap shooting when I was in Cuba. I'm a pretty good shot, if I do say so. Will you show me?"

Uncle Charles had no choice. He mumbled something and got out of his chair and shambled out of the room. Nora followed him, smiling back at them. "You'll forgive me for a while, won't you?" she said. "It's been a long time since I've been around anybody who knew good guns."

After they left, the silence seemed to swell and shimmer. Even Peyton knew that what Nora had done had crossed some sort of boundary, though she did not know what it was. Aunt Augusta's eyes were almost popping out of her rosy face. Peyton knew, too, that whatever it was she was bursting to spill would not come forth while she was in the room.

"Aunt Augusta, may I go in the den and listen to the radio?" she said.

"Of course, Peyton. You might want to close the door so we don't disturb each other."

Peyton got up and wobbled on Nora's heels into the den, where the big Capehart radio had been banished when the new Motorola TV was given pride of place in the living room. The den had started life as a small screened porch and was barely large enough to accommodate the radio and two battered Leatherette recliners. It smelled of cigars and, faintly, of sweet bourbon whiskey. She knew that this must be her uncle's refuge. Peyton liked the little room, too. It had a huge picture window overlooking a rock garden, dun and soggy now, with two narrow bookcases on either side. The bookcases held mainly bits of china and gewgaws—Aunt Augusta's collection of Royal Doulton figurines and one or two cut-crystal candy dishes—but there was also a small collection of tattered Zane Grey paperbacks. She thought that this was the only room in this house where her Uncle Charles had left his spoor.

She turned on the radio and closed the glass French doors that separated the den from the living room. She could not hear so well with them closed, but she could still hear, and she could see. The volume had scarcely swelled before she saw Aunt Augusta's mouth open and begin to work as if she were chewing gum, though Peyton had never known that to happen. She had not really meant to listen, but there was something so disturbing about the sight of her aunt's mouth working furiously and silently that she found herself straining to hear.

". . . see what I mean now, Frazier? How can you possibly think she can stay in your house . . . want Peyton to learn that kind of thing? You're a kind man, I've always said so, but this is simply not . . . out there alone with a man she doesn't even know, when she knows he's got a bottle . . ."

Peyton looked at her father through the glass. He said nothing. She got up and kicked off the pumps and curled up on the floor next to the big radio and laid her cheek against its fretwork as she had when she was a child, feeling the warmth and the living vibration from the station in Atlanta seep into her like sun. She did not think that she slept, but she must have. The next thing she knew someone had opened the glass doors and she could hear her father saying, "Well, it's been a treat as usual, Augusta, but we've got to be on our way. I don't think Peyton has done her homework yet."

"Yes, I have," Peyton protested. Her father gave her a look.

Nora and Uncle Charles stood at the door, laughing. Nora's hair was beaded with rain and Uncle Charles's coat was damp, so she knew they had just dashed in through the rain from the garage.

"Thank you, Charles," Nora said, her rich voice lilting with pleasure. "What a lovely way to spend a rainy afternoon. Maybe you'll let me shoot it one day. I don't hunt, but I'm a terrific shot."

Uncle Charles said heartily, "It would be my pleasure," and then looked at Aunt Augusta's face and dropped his eyes to study his shoes once more.

"Thank you, Augusta," Nora said, leaning over to give Aunt Augusta a kiss on the cheek; Aunt Augusta flinched as if she had been bitten by a blue-tail fly.

"It was a wonderful lunch, and your house is just extraordinary."

Peyton ran with Nora through the diminishing rain to the car. Behind them, they heard Augusta McKenzie saying to Frazier, in a whisper that was more squall than voice, "I smelled whiskey on her breath, Frazier. Surely that should be enough for you."

Nora laughed and shook out her wet copper hair. "A little shot of Uncle Charles's stash wouldn't hurt her any," she said.

Peyton was silent. In her world, no living white woman had ever been known to drink anything but eggnog at Christmas and a glass of champagne at weddings.

Her father was quiet on the drive home, and as they were putting away their wet things, he said, "I've got a good bit of work to do. I'll be out in my office for a while."

Peyton looked after him as he left the kitchen. Sunday afternoon was always their time to drive up to the Howard Johnson's on the interstate and have ice cream, and afterward to watch television until it was time to eat the cold supper Chloe had left them. Peyton had never known her father to work on Sunday afternoons.

Nora looked after him thoughtfully and then said, "Put on something comfortable and get Trailways and I'll show you some of the things I brought with me from Cuba."

"I think I'll read," Peyton said. Tears were smarting in her eyes.

"This is better than any book, even Salinger," Nora said, ruffling her hair. "I'll even show you my voodoo charms. Nobody has ever seen them before."

Peyton brought the angry kitten, struggling wildly in her arms, to

Nora's room and settled down in the middle of her unmade bed. The room was a mess of strewn papers and books and clothes. Clothilde would, Peyton knew, have a fit.

"I'll clean it up before Chloe comes in the morning," Nora said, as if catching her thoughts. "I'm not going to leave it for her. I'm a slob and a packrat, I admit it. Neatness definitely does not count with me."

Trailways ran about the room sniffing, lapped some water from a little Haviland dish that had stood on the dressing table since time out of Peyton's mind, and dove into the soft, tangled mass of covers. He burrowed under the bedclothes and down to the bottom of the bed, scrabbling furiously, and then curled into a ball. Soon he was a still, small lump there, his buzzing purr loud over Nora's little radio.

"Now there's a guy who knows how to make himself at home," Nora said, smiling. "He can curl up in my bed anytime."

She opened a big box that had been tied with twine and pulled out her treasures for Peyton's delectation. There were bolts of vivid printed cloth, as strange and beautiful as a cheetah's hide, that looked unlike anything Peyton had ever seen—batik, Nora said. "The natives in Haiti make it, and sometimes the Cubans, too. It's beautiful, isn't it? Wild as the jungle. I've got a skirt and a sundress made out of it. Maybe we can have something made for you."

Books came out of the trunk, shabby hardcovers, yellowing paper-backs. Peyton recognized some of the titles—*Tropic of Cancer*, *Women in Love*, *Ulysses*—and blushed. Weren't they banned or something? But most had no meaning for her: some were in French, others in Spanish. Big, bursting scrapbooks—"I'll show you some-day"—and an ornate cigar box holding the voodoo charms, which proved to be merely small carved figures and bound clumps of feath-ers, mirrors, and what looked to be bone, and a dead chicken's foot.

"Yuck," Peyton said.

"Yeah, well, it's got power, no matter how it looks," Nora said. "Chickens are powerful carriers in vodun. That's what they call voodoo in Haiti. The Cubans have got a slightly different pantheon, but the charms look almost the same. This chicken foot will absolutely protect you from duppies and were-tigers. That's probably why you never see them in the South, all those chickens."

Peyton grinned unwillingly. The hurt of her father's defection eased slightly. "What's that?" she asked, looking at a beautifully carved ebony box with a lock. It looked very old.

"That's my private stuff," Nora said. "The things that only I see. The things that mean the most to me. Photos, and my journal, and letters . . . do you keep a journal, Peyton?"

"No," Peyton said, suddenly on fire to open the box and let Nora's secrets fly out into the room like Pandora's furies.

"Well, that's one thing you simply have to do, no ifs, ands, or buts," Nora said. "Every writer keeps a journal. Some have done it all their life. How will you know what you think if you don't write it down? How will you remember who you were? I'm going to get you a good leather one the next time I'm in Atlanta."

The green dusk was falling down outside. The rain had stopped, and long, stabbing rays of brilliant red sun were piercing the clouds at the horizon.

"Look at that. Red as sin," Nora said. "Does your father usually come in for dinner? If he doesn't, I'll fix us something."

"He always does," Peyton said, the pain welling back. "Always. I don't know why he's acting like this."

Nora was silent for a moment and then said, "I do. He's mad at me. I think I shouldn't have gone out to the garage with your Uncle Charles, though God knows what your father and your aunt thought we were doing out there. You stay here and look through this stuff, if you want to. I'm going out there and talk to him."

She pulled a sweatshirt over her thin T-shirt and padded out of the room, her panther's gait more apparent in the soft moccasins that she wore. Peyton sat still on the bed for a time after she left, nudging the snoring Trailways with her toe and looking into the middle distance at nothing at all. Then she got up and went down the stairs and out the back door to the foot of the stairs that led up to her father's office over the garage. This time Peyton meant to listen. It crossed her mind that she had eavesdropped on Nora or on people talking about Nora for the past three days. She had no compunction about that. This was about her, too, and it was a safe bet that no one was going to tell her what transpired.

She was motionless, crouching in the fresh, green-smelling cold.

"... if I've broken any of the house rules, I'm sorry, Frazier," Nora was saying. "But you'll have to tell me what they are. I can't read your mind, and I'd hate to have you running out here every time I cross some border I don't know is there."

"I don't want to set rules for you, Nora," her father said evenly. "But I should think it would be apparent that young women don't go off with men and stay an hour and come back smelling like whiskey."

"Maybe not in Lytton," Nora said. "But they do in the places I've lived, Frazier. In those places, it has always been an honor to be shown someone's private treasures. Couldn't you see how proud Charles was of that shotgun? He wanted somebody to see it—you, preferably, but anybody, I guess. I doubt if Augusta has ever set foot in that garage since he's taken to hiding his bourbon out there. And yes, I did have a drink with him. Just one, but a drink. In the Latin countries, it's an insult to refuse someone's hospitality."

"You're in a small southern town now, Nora. There's nothing Latin about it."

"Nothing Latin in Lytton," Nora said, and Peyton could hear laughter in her voice. "No, there certainly isn't. But Frazier, don't you see what she's made of him? He's like a photographic negative, or like a ghost afraid to haunt his own house. How can a woman do that to a man? I wanted to give him back something. . . ."

"Nora, I'm glad you're here. I thought it was a good idea, and I still do. But there are some things that I just can't have Peyton learning."

"What? Like racism? Like the fine art of inflicting humiliation? Like castration?"

"Nora . . ."

"Frazier, your daughter is withering before she even blooms. She knows nothing, she expects nothing, she doesn't even know how to laugh, as far as I can see. It breaks my heart. It may well be that I'm not the right person to teach her, but someone must do it, someone besides Augusta. I've spent a long time finding out the way I want to live, and if I'm not free to live that way, I just can't stay. I can accommodate some of your rules, of course, but if I do, you'll have to accommodate some of my un-Lyttonly notions. But first we have to be able to talk. If you find you just can't do that, then that's all right; I can easily find another job and a place to live. I'm used to that. But I have to know what your . . . rules for living are."

"I guess I just never thought about it," her father said. His voice was low.

"Then how on earth do you know who you are?"

Abruptly the door leading to the landing opened, and Nora stepped out into the dusk. She took a few deep breaths and looked around her as if she had no idea how she had come to this place. Peyton ducked behind the big camellia bush that sheltered the side of the garage. After Nora went into the house, she crept out and tiptoed through the kitchen and into her small room. She curled herself under her afghan. She did not turn on any lights.

Later—much later, it seemed—she heard her father come into the living room and click on the television set.

"Is anybody home?" he called. "Anybody who wants some supper? Chloe left us something, but all of a sudden I feel like Howard Johnson's fried clams. Have I got any takers?"

She heard Nora's step coming down the stairs, and her voice answering. Peyton skinned out of bed and into her jeans and a sweater, light and warmth flooding back as if it had never been dark.

9

T*he next morning Nora said at breakfast that she planned to* spend the day getting to know the inside of Lytton.

"What inside?" Peyton said, feeding the clamoring Trailways bits of her bacon under the table. He promptly launched an effort to scale the table leg and get closer to the source of the bounty. He kept sliding back down, but he did not cease the attempt. Peyton bent to pick him up, but Nora shook her head.

"Don't. He'll get there eventually, and then he'll know how. If you pick him up he'll get old and fat still howling to be picked up. You've got to let people and cats find out how to do things for themselves. . . . You know, the insides of places and the people who run them. The library. The bank. The hair place. The luncheonette. Who knows? Maybe the cemetery and the pool hall and the barbershop."

"People are going to talk about you if you go in the pool hall and the barbershop," Peyton said.

"People already are," Nora said, smiling. "Your aunt undoubtedly had the jungle drums going about my little fling with your uncle before the door was closed behind us."

"Don't you care?"

Nora blew smoke. "No. I don't give a tinker's damn about what most people think about me; I stopped that a long time ago. Now I only care about a very few. You. Your daddy. Chloe. Your grandmother, though that may be a lost cause. And that about does it so far. I've always had a very strict and selective list of people whom I care about at any given time."

Chloe came in with fresh biscuits and squalled, "Peyton, you get that sorry cat off this table right now!" Peyton turned to see Trailways lapping strawberry jam from the jar Chloe had put on the table. There was a delicate tracery of little red paw prints all over the tabletop. Peyton put Trailways back onto the floor and scrubbed at the prints with her napkin.

"Now I'm gon' have to bleach the tablecloth *and* the napkin," Clothilde grumbled.

Then she turned to Nora. "Doreen told me you said you might teach her a little bit. I sho' would appreciate that. She's a real bright girl. She don't need to be a maid the rest of her life. Maybe just enough to read better. She could go to high school classes at night up to College Park if she could read better. They told her when she went to take the test."

"I'd love to," Nora said. "Let me get a week or so of my new job under my belt—if I get it, of course—and then we'll set something up. Maybe a couple of afternoons a week, after school. She doesn't work in the afternoons, does she?"

"No. She don't go back until right before supper."

"Well, you better tell her not to tell Mrs. McKenzie. She's already accused me of maid rustling."

"She ain't gon' tell. Like I say, she's a smart girl."

Peyton slid her grandmother's little amulet into the neck of her blouse before she went to school. The hair was going to be enough for one day. She still turned her head quickly at her reflection in mirrors and windows, trying obliquely to catch this newcomer reverting to the Brillo-haired Peyton of the week before. So far she had not. The deer-girl with the long neck still looked shyly back at her.

That morning Miss Carruthers said, in front of the entire class, "Peyton, you look very nice with your new haircut. Very chic."

After that no one said a word about her hair. She knew they would not. But they stared. She could feel the eyes on the naked back of her neck. This time, though, the eyes were without heat.

She took Trailways with her to the Losers Club that afternoon. She had to carry him in Chloe's lidded sewing basket because he writhed and howled so. When she got to the shed behind the parsonage, Boot and Ernie were waiting.

"What you got in that basket?" Boot said.

"A king cobra, at the very least," Ernie said sourly.

"Never heard of no cobra spit like a cat." Boot grinned. "Come on, Peyton, let's see him. Mamaw told me about him."

Peyton opened the basket and Trailways leapt out. He stood in the middle of the floor glaring at them in turn, his little bowed legs planted apart, the spiky tail quivering. Then he found himself a spot on the frayed rug in front of the space heater, turned around three times, and settled into a boneless ball of sleep.

As happened often in the South after a spell of sullen rain, the weather had turned clear and cold and wild. A green wind came booming in from the west, tossing the trees and hurling lingering pecans down onto the tin roof of the shed. For a minute they simply sat in the warmth, listening to the wind and the wheezing purr of the little cat. Ernie was heating water for instant cocoa. Peyton knew it would be horrible, chalky and cloying, but it was the only kind his mother allowed in the house, and she was chilled through.

Boot reached out with his big leather foot and nudged Trailways gently. "Thought at least you'd got some kind of fancy cat," he said. "That just a mangy little old barn kitten. They a million of 'em around our house."

"They make me sneeze," Ernie said. "He can't stay very long, Peyton."

"He's a special cat," Peyton said. "He came from Atlanta. My Cousin Nora went up there the other night for dinner and met some soldier, and they were at the Trailways bus station and she saw him behind a garbage can. She brought him home to me. Trailways is his name."

"What she doin' hanging around that bus station?" Boot said, scandalized. "They got bad folks in that place. They got bad ladies. Everybody knows that."

"It figures," Ernie said prissily. "Blood will tell."

"She wasn't hanging around it," Peyton retorted. "She was only there to drop off the soldier. He was on his way to Fort Benning, and anyway, he was only about eighteen. Nora met him in the restaurant where she had dinner. An Italian restaurant."

She cut her eyes at Ernie and Boot to see how her cousin's lone dinner in Atlanta, and in an Italian restaurant at that, was being received. They were silent.

"They went to a jazz place and danced after that," she added when she got no response. "She's going to take me with her to Atlanta next time she goes."

"Man, that is *something!*" Boot said admiringly. "I never seen no Italian restaurant. I wish she'd put me in that fancy pink car and take me to an Italian restaurant. When y'all going?"

"Probably next weekend. We're going to spend the day. We're going shopping, and to the museum, and a bunch of other things."

"Well, you and your new haircut have got a full social schedule," Ernie drawled. It was the first time he had mentioned her haircut. Peyton looked at him.

"Nora cut it," she said.

"It's quite pretty, if you like that kind of thing," Ernie said, stirring hot water into three paper cups. "I've personally always thought that kind of cut looked a little butchy, but that's just my opinion."

"What that?" Boot said.

"Extremely mannish, shall we say."

"Everybody thinks it looks like Audrey Hepburn's," Peyton said, color rising in her face.

"More like Aldo Ray's. But never mind me. If your cousin did it, it must be holy."

They were silent again for a while, sipping the clotted cocoa, and then Ernie said, "I'm going to suspend the club for a while. Nobody's heart seems to be in it, and I've got better things to do."

"Naw," Boot cried. "My heart in it good!"

"Peyton's isn't. She's all tied up with her sainted cousin."

Fear flooded Peyton. Not to have the Losers Club, not to come through the virulent garden to this secret, sheltering place, not to have these constant ears into which to spill her secret humiliations . . .

"No, I'm not," she said. "I'm really not. I'm not going to do things with her much. She's dumb. She does crazy things. And she's staying with us at least until school's out, I think. Isn't that just the pits? Everybody's going to be talking about us because of her. She's already made Aunt Augusta mad as a wet hen. She went out to the garage by herself with Uncle Charlie yesterday, and stayed an hour, and came back smelling like whiskey."

"Holy shit," Boot said reverently. "I ain't heard that."

"I did," Ernie said. "Everybody knows it."

"See why I don't like her?" Peyton said, close to tears.

"It doesn't sound to me like you don't like her," Ernie said, elaborately examining his soft pink hands. Peyton always wondered how he kept them so well, doing the sort of work he did. Once or twice she had thought she saw the gleam of clear polish on his nails, but she could not be certain.

"What if I brought her one afternoon, so you could get to know her?" she said desperately. "You'd see for yourself how awful she is."

"You know we said we'd never let outsiders in here," Ernie said.

"Well, she wants to see you, Ernie. She liked you when y'all played together that summer. She wouldn't have to come more than once, just so you could realize why I'm not going to get tied up with her. Besides, she might fit right in. She does the most awful, embarrassing things. . . ."

She felt a stab of guilt deep under the desperation, but it did not surface. Between Nora and the Losers Club, there was no contest.

"I'll have to think about it," Ernie said, and the conversation gradually faded and died. Presently Peyton picked up Trailways and stuffed him back into the basket and went home with him, her heart heavy, his wails cutting the dusk.

Nora came in pink-cheeked and windblown from her day around the town and went upstairs. She did not put her head into Peyton's room, and Peyton did not climb the stairs to hers. From now on, she thought, she was going to exclude her cousin from her life, as best she could. The club; oh, she could not let the club go, not yet. . . .

Nora wore a white sweater and gray flannel slacks to dinner that night. Peyton thought, but was not sure, that the sweater was cashmere. Lytton did not run heavily to cashmere sweaters. The candlelight gave her face a deeper glow over the slight windburn, and lit her chestnut hair to what Peyton fancied, having lately read Tennyson, was titian. Chloe had made her famous vegetable beef soup and fresh hot cornbread before she left, and there was an apple pie warm on the stove.

"Perfect for a cold night," her father said, sliding into his seat. "We're not done with winter yet, I don't think. You girls look mighty pretty, or is it the candlelight?"

They were back at the table in the little breakfast room off the kitchen, but Nora had brought in the wooden candlesticks and lit the candles. The candles smelled faintly of something musky and junglish.

"Vervain," Nora said. "Wards off Baptists. I brought the candles and the sticks from Cuba. An old man in our village made the sticks, and one of the old women made the candles. I have several sets; I thought Peyton's grandmother might like to have one. She's big on herbs, I know."

Frazier McKenzie nodded. Peyton shot him a look but saw nothing on his narrow face other than mild approval of the dinner and the offer.

"I know she'd like that," he said. Peyton thought that her grandmother would rather toss the candles in the railroad ditch than have anything magical in her house that she herself had not made.

"I had a call from the chairman of the Fulton County Board today,

Nora," Frazier said. "Everybody thinks the idea is a good one. We
can't offer you much in the way of a salary, but I think that could be
negotiated if we do the class more than one quarter. I'd be pleased if
you'd accept. I know Peyton would, too."

Peyton dropped her eyes.

"Yes," she mumbled.

"We wouldn't start for a week or so, but as it happens we need a
substitute in sophomore English on Thursday and Friday. Mrs. Camp
is going to see her daughter's new baby."

"And it's a good chance to look over the new schoolmarm,
hmmm?" Nora said, but she was smiling her Halloween smile, her
eyes crinkled.

"I'd love to substitute," she said. "I'll get her lesson plans tomorrow, or if she'd rather, we could do a book-discussion group. I've had
other sophomores who liked that."

"I think at this point she'd be grateful if you'd simply sit there and
keep them quiet," Frazier said. "She's been trying to get away to see
her grandchild for two months now. I think the book discussion
sounds interesting. Why don't you try it? Give you an idea of how
your class will work."

"I will, then. Did I tell you I was going to do an insider's tour of
Lytton today? I met the most amazing people," Nora said. "This little town is absolutely full of characters and stories. What a novel it
would make."

"Novel?" Peyton said. "I think this is the most boring place I've
ever seen. Why would anybody want to write about it?"

"And just how many other places have you seen?" Nora smiled.
"I'd want to write about it. Any writer would. If you'd been keeping
that journal we talked about, you could look back and see plainly
what's here. It's fully as interesting as Grover's Corners in *Our Town*
or even Maycomb, Alabama. You *have* read *To Kill a Mockingbird*,
haven't you?"

Peyton shook her head.

"Well, then, that's our first priority. In fact, I think I'll use *Mockingbird* for my book discussion and first class. It catches the small-

town South better than anything I've ever read, and it says some things about the South that need to be said."

"Like what?"

"You'll see." Nora seemed to tire suddenly of the conversation. She drummed her fingers on the table and looked abstractedly off into the distance. There was a very faint frown between her brows.

"Who did you meet today?" Frazier McKenzie asked. "What stories did you hear?"

"Well, I met a lady in the library whose ancestors were full-blooded Creek Indians, though she didn't look very Indian to me. She predates even the Pilgrims, she says. She's trying to found an organization like the DAR or the UDC for the descendants of Indian chiefs. Now that's something to think about."

"Oh, that's Miss Ronnie Bates," Peyton's father said. "She's no more Creek than I am. Her people came from somewhere in Iowa, I think. Nobody knows why she's got this Indian bee in her bonnet."

"Well, anyway, and then I went into the luncheonette for a sandwich and I heard two men talking about another man who dropped out of the Masons and took to his house and won't come out because his daughter married a Negro. She's thirty-four years old and lives in California, and I don't see why he thinks it shames him, but the men seemed to think it made sense, though it was a loss to the Masons. Imagine the pain he must feel, never to come out of his house."

"Otis Carmichael," Frazier said. "Not many of the Carmichaels come out of the house much, to tell you the truth."

"What's it going to take to impress you? I took the car to the garage and met this old gentleman who drives a goat cart. He seemed to be having a wonderful time. Everybody knew him. His goat is named Mary Margaret, but he wouldn't tell me his name."

"Lord, Nora, did you meet every eccentric in Lytton? That's Sweetie Sayre. None of the Sayres have been right in the head for generations. His sister, Miss Gertie, wears all white and an ivy wreath on her head. She goes to Atlanta on the bus that way once or twice a week. I think she preaches on Rich's street corner."

"And you don't think all that is absolutely magical? You don't think there are marvelous stories in Lytton? I find the whole town irresistible," Nora said. "There's such a kind of wacky sweetness to it. After Miami, you don't know what a relief that is. . . ."

"I trust that concluded your tour," Peyton's father said. He was grinning.

"Yes, except for the pool hall. I went in there to use the phone to call the garage—the car conked out right in front of it—and I had a great game of snooker with a couple of guys. I won, as a matter of fact."

Peyton felt her eyebrows shoot up toward her hairline. She looked at her father. He opened his mouth and took a deep breath and then let it out slowly.

"Good," he said.

After they ate, they went into the living room to watch television. Nora and her father sat quietly, absorbed in *The Hallmark Hall of Fame,* but Peyton curled into the blue chair that had been her mother's and closed her eyes. Behind them, she saw a different town entirely from the one she had grown up in.

Nora met her substitute English class on Thursday morning, and by lunchtime it had passed into legend. Word leapt from Lytton High to Lytton Grammar like wildfire, and Peyton, eating her sandwich and reading *Little Women* alone in the lunchroom, looked up to find herself encircled by other students like a gazelle ringed by jackals.

"Hear your cousin's over at the high school teaching nigger stuff," Wesley Cato said. Wesley was fifteen and had repeated the seventh grade three times. Peyton merely looked at him.

"She's reading some kind of book about a nigger who raped a white girl and got shot by the police," LeeAnne McGahee said. LeeAnne was twelve and looked eighteen, and was much admired for her immobile blond bouffant and her projectile breasts. Peyton had pointed her out to Nora in town the day they went grocery shopping, and Nora had said LeeAnne looked like the front bumper of a 1953 Studebaker. Peyton did not know what one of those looked like, but the tone of Nora's voice had shattered LeeAnne's Circelike aura for

good and all, at least in Peyton's mind. She was able, now, to regard
LeeAnne with something approaching contempt.

"That's *To Kill a Mockingbird*," Peyton said loftily. "It's won all
kinds of prizes. Nora gave it to me to read but I haven't yet."

They stared at her, uncertain after this unexpected reaction.

"Well, it must be a good book if they shot the nigger," Wesley said.

"It's about intolerance and prejudice in a little southern town,"
Peyton said. "You really ought to like it, Wesley."

"I hear there's a retard in it, too," LeeAnne said.

"Yep. So you'd like it, too."

Shorn of their weapons, they smirked at her and sidled away. Peyton's heart was hammering in her chest, but she was also elated. She
had stood down two of Lytton Grammar's most treasured icons and
had actually come out the better for it. A flame of pure power leapt
in her blood.

Maybe that's the power Nana was talking about, she thought.
Maybe I have power in my words.

By the end of the day the rumors were a conflagration. Nora Findlay was reading tenth-graders a story about niggers raping people and
about other people killing them. No, she was reading a story about
two little kids who were afraid of a retard. No, the story was about a
lawyer and his two motherless children who grew up loving nigger.

And it was the gospel truth that three of the boys—football players
all, repeating the tenth grade for the second time—had offered in
graphic terms to service Nora right there on her desk, and she had
looked at them and laughed and said, "Not on your best day, you
horny little bastards," whereupon the rest of the class had broken
into cheers. And it was also gospel that when the class was over she
had walked out lighting a cigarette, and looked back and grinned and
made a circle of her thumb and forefinger at the remaining students
in the classroom. The entire student body of Lytton Grammar School
was humming and buzzing with Nora like yellow jackets in a wind-
fall of rotten persimmons.

"But when the principal stuck his head in to see how she was
doing, she just smiled like a possum in the middle of a cow plop and

said, 'Just fine, sir. You have nice students here,' and he like to busted his face smiling back," a rawboned bus student told Peyton on the school steps. "My brother said that after he'd gone she just looked at the class and winked. He said everybody hoped nobody tells on her. They thought she was great."

Peyton knew that nobody would tell parents or faculty about Nora Findlay. She was life, rebellion, even affirmation to them. No teacher had ever been anything but the oppressor. They would simply say, "Oh, just fine, thanks. She's nice," to their parents, and the faculty would say to each other what a sweet girl she seemed to be, so deferential to the older ones, not at all like the young girls you were beginning to see around Atlanta now.

Peyton did not think it could last, of course; Nora was bound to be found out in this small, airless arena. But for now she was flying high, and Peyton soared with her, riding her updraft. One of the cheerleaders actually asked her to sit with them at lunch the next day.

"I'm going home, thanks," she said. "My cousin and I always have lunch together."

That evening as they sat at dinner Frazier McKenzie said, "Well, how did it go at the high school today?"

"Just fine," Nora said. "Peyton, please pass the butter."

Peyton went back to the Losers Club the next afternoon. She knew Ernie and Boot would have heard about Nora's first day at the high school. It would be a triumph for her, to have a cousin who had embarrassed her and her whole family in front of the entire town.

But Ernie and Boot said nothing about Nora. They were looking at pictures in a book that Ernie had, with photographs and illustrations in dark sepia and pale tints, as if they had been washed with watercolor. Ernie closed the book smartly, but not before Peyton had seen a remarkable image of a mustachioed man on all fours in what looked to be a Turkish harem, naked except for an elaborate harness of leather and metal around his waist. Behind him stood a massive, simpering lady, also naked except for rolled mesh stockings that came up to her thighs, holding a whip.

"It's Victorian pornography," Ernie said smugly, seeing the blank shock on Peyton's face. "Very erotic. Very rare. This is one of only a hundred ever printed. Not for ladies, though, Peyton."

"I don't care," Peyton said, face flaming. "It's stupid, anyway. Who wants to look at a grown man playing horse?"

"Yeah, my uncle got a better harness for his mules than that," Boot said. "In fact, he got two of them. Your mama know you got this book, Ernie?"

"My mother doesn't know everything about me, not by a long shot," Ernie said fiercely. "I have a whole other life she doesn't know about. A life of the mind, if you will."

"That don't look like no life of the mind to me," Boot said.

"Well, it's considered quite highbrow, a kind of literature really. I wouldn't expect either of you to understand."

"I'm reading literature myself," Peyton said, trying to sound offhanded. "My Cousin Nora gave me a copy of *To Kill a Mockingbird*. She's teaching it to her class, too. It's been printed in a bunch of different languages."

"A nice little book," Ernie said. "Not, of course, the great American novel, but nice."

"That idiot," Nora said, grinning, when Peyton told her that night what Ernie had said. "That's just what it is."

On Saturday morning they went to Atlanta. The fresh cold had given way before the green surf of spring rolling north from Florida, and the earth smelled wet and new and rich. The sun was mild, and there were a few daffodils and snowdrops winking from their mulched beds around the town.

"If you'll put on your sweater we'll put the top down," Nora said. "I'll turn the heater on. I used to do that all the time in the winter in Miami, whenever it got a little chilly. It drove everybody who knew me wild. But there's nothing like spring wind in your face and warm air on your feet."

And there wasn't. By the time the little pink arrow of a car rolled into downtown Atlanta, Peyton was drunk on air and light and wind and warm feet.

"We'll park at Rich's because it's a good starting place. But I assume you don't want to go in," Nora said, smiling sideways at Peyton.

"Never again."

"Never say never."

They walked up Peachtree Street from Rich's in the spring sun. The streets were full of people moving languidly, and the sound of car radios spilled out into the sweet air. Many convertibles went by, motors idling, just drifting.

"None of them as sexy as mine," Nora said. "This is nice, though. This reminds me of a Saturday afternoon in Havana, or maybe Miami in the earlier days. Everybody came out into the streets."

"To do what?" Peyton asked. She was still glancing at the deer-girl in the store windows. The deer-girl, dressed in Aunt Augusta's Villager and flat shoes, looked back. When Peyton averted her eyes, so did the girl. Presently Peyton stopped looking.

"Just to be there," Nora said. "You need to learn the fine art of just being, Peyton. I don't think your daddy or your Aunt Augusta is going to teach you that, so I guess the job falls to me. The first thing you do when you're being is to kind of float around seeing what you can see. Listen hard. Smell the smells—like that peanut shop over there. And exhaust fumes. And the narcissus and daffodils from that lady on the corner selling flowers. Want some flowers?"

"What for? They'll just wilt."

"Ah, but how pretty they'll be until they do." She bought a big bunch of ruffled yellow daffodils, still wet from the morning dew, and gave them to Peyton. "Don't pass up feasts for any of your senses, Peyton," she said. "Dorothy Parker—do you know Dorothy Parker? a poet and satirist who wrote in the twenties and thirties, marvelous—once wrote a poem that said, in part, 'passing by a fountain, wringing at a rock.' Don't wring at rocks. Wait for fountains."

"OK," Peyton said, not knowing what Nora was talking about and yet somehow knowing. She slowed down, consciously slackened her muscles, and sniffed the air.

It's Atlanta in the spring, she thought in surprise. I'll never forget it. I'd know it anywhere. It's not like any other smell.

They stopped in a little stationery store that also sold tobacco and cigarettes and cigars and hard candy. It was in the Peachtree Arcade, a wondrous hall between two buildings, two stories high, completely arched over with glass. Many small shops and businesses lined the aisles. The arcade was full of people, milling and chattering and examining wares spread out on tables. They did not look, to Peyton's eyes, very prosperous. This was just the sort of place Aunt Augusta was always warning Peyton about. Not as bad as the bus station, but in the same arena.

"*Exactly* like Havana," Nora said. "Wonderful. Not a Baptist or a lady in here."

At the shop Nora bought a long, fat black cigar from a beautiful box of red and gold. She sniffed it, then asked the clerk to cut it for her, and lit it and put it into her mouth.

"Mmmmm," she said. "Not a Romeo y Julieta, but not bad for an export," she said, blowing a plume of aromatic white smoke from her nostrils. She closed her eyes, savoring the tobacco. Peyton closed hers, too, but in profound embarrassment. The clerk was staring at Nora, as was a group of ladies obviously up from the country, their chapped mouths tight, and a roving band of young men in tight blue jeans, the red, crosshatched backs of their necks proclaiming them to be country boys in the city for a Saturday.

"Got something bigger than that you can suck on," one of them called to Nora. The rest snickered.

"Not as big by a long shot, sonny," Nora called back through smoke. "And for sure not as tasty. Come back when you've grown up."

The young men hooted and pummeled the speaker's biceps. He turned and strutted out, the back of his neck redder than when he had come in.

"If Daddy could see you he'd have a fit," Peyton said. "If Aunt Augusta could, she'd buy a megaphone and start broadcasting it."

"Who's going to tell them?" Nora said. "I can't imagine your aunt has ever set foot in this enchanting place, and I somehow don't think you're going to tell on me, are you?"

"No," Peyton said, grinning suddenly. Her heart took off in crazy flight, fueled by a kind of reckless joy. "Can I have a puff?"

"Not till you're sixteen. I may be definitely suspect, but I'm not a child corrupter. Come on, let's buy you a journal."

In a far corner of the shop there was a dusty pile of books. They seemed to be very old, some with flakes of yellowing paper spilling from them, some thick with dust. All were leather, and some were stamped with faded gold. Nora ruffled through them, smiling appreciatively.

"Lovely," she said. "Just imagine the hands that have touched these, Peyton. Whole lives, right here in these books. What do you think of this one?"

She held up a green, soft-leather book, faded to a pale sage, with the letters "AMS" stamped on the front. Inside, in a faint copperplate hand, was written on the flyleaf, "Anna Marjorie Stephens. Her book." There had been a date, but it was lost now. The thick ivory pages were edged with dull gold.

Some of the first pages had been torn out, but the rest were blank and ruled with sepia ink. There was a long, frayed gold ribbon to mark the reader's place.

"Do you like this? I think it's gorgeous," Nora said. "It was obviously Anna Marjorie's journal. You'd always have her looking over your shoulder, wouldn't you? She'd be the only one you'd have to share your secret thoughts with."

"It's pretty," Peyton said dutifully. She had thought they would go to the Cokesbury Book Shop and select a fat leather book with a lock and key and flowers on the front, and "My Diary" written on it in script. She had seen them there before. A proper diary. A new one.

"I think you should have it," Nora said. "When you're grown and you look back over this, you'll see that there's a resonance to it that a mass-produced teenager's diary could never have. Usually it's a good policy to stick to the old stuff."

She paid for the book and they went out into the warming street. It was past one o'clock and Peyton was growing hungry, but she did not want to break the dreaming spell of this strange day. The crowds had thickened, but they seemed to have slowed down, like people walking under water. Peyton saw forearms bare under rolled-up shirt sleeves, and for the first time, pale, winter-white feet in sandals. The collar of the hated Villager felt hot and constricting. She ran a forefinger under it and bent her neck.

"Just unbutton it," Nora said. "It's gotten hotter than the hinges of hell. I'm going to." She undid the top three buttons of her silk shirt. Under it Peyton could see the freckled slopes of her breasts. She looked away.

"Come on," Nora said. "Unbutton. It's not as if you've got much to shock the populace with yet."

Peyton unbuttoned a top button, and then another. Cool air and warm sun kissed her collarbone. The little talisman her grandmother had made sent up a drift of rosemary. It smelled wonderful.

"I guess it's about lunchtime," Nora said. "What are you in the mood for? French, Mediterranean? Chinese? Indian?"

"I don't think Atlanta has any of those," Peyton said.

"I know. I was kidding. There's a delicatessen over there. How about a kosher pastrami on rye with potato salad and garlic pickles? Have you ever had Jewish deli food?"

"I don't think so," Peyton said faintly. Aunt Augusta had once told her never to eat in a Jewish household: "They cut the throats of the chickens and lambs and use the blood in the cooking," she had said. Peyton's stomach lurched.

"Well, then, come on," Nora said, starting toward the big delicatessen catty-corner across from the arcade. "Best in the world. But I expect they could rustle you up a hamburger if you'd like."

When they approached the deli they saw a crowd on the sidewalk outside. People were milling and buzzing like bees from a dislodged hive, and there were policemen with nightsticks among them. The crowd had the air of a holiday throng at first glance, but as they approached Peyton caught the tenor of the buzz. It was angry.

"They must hate the day's special," Nora said, pushing through the crowd to look in the window of the deli.

Then she said, "Look, Peyton, it's a sit-in. See those black kids at the counter? Nobody's looking at them, and there's no food in front of them. In fact, there's not a living soul at the entire counter. Looks like we'd have our choice of seats."

"Are we going in there?" Peyton squeaked. She had heard, vaguely, of sit-ins, but they had seemed to have as much relevancy to her world as the practice of suttee. She did know, however, that people went to jail for sitting in. Why, she could not quite remember.

"I thought we might. I think it would be good for you to see how the other half of your country lives. Besides, it's the right thing to do."

"Will we get arrested?"

"Oh, no. It's OK for us to eat there. Just not them."

"Is it against the law? Will they be arrested?"

"Probably not, unless they start a fuss. And I doubt they will. Sit-ins are a nonviolent protest. But the restaurant owner gets to decide if he'll serve Negroes or not. Not many do. Obviously this one doesn't."

"I can't go in there, Nora. There's a television camera over there. What if Daddy and Aunt Augusta saw me on TV?"

"I hope they'd be proud of you. Come on, Peyton. Sometimes it's absolutely necessary to do something that scares you. I think this is one of those times."

"Are you scared?"

"No. But then I've been eating my meals with black people for a long time."

They went inside. The deli was dim and arctic with stale air-conditioning. There was a faint garlicky smell that was strange but not unpleasant, and stratas of cigarette smoke still hung in the air. But there seemed to be no customers. Behind the counter, two blond bee-hived waitresses were sitting on stools and staring fixedly out the windows at the crowd. Their faces looked red and ready to burst.

Nora sauntered to the counter and sat down beside one of the young Negroes. He was dressed neatly in a coat and tie and looked to be about eighteen years old. He looked at Nora, who smiled. Tentatively he smiled back. The other three men, similarly dressed, looked over, too. None of them smiled, but they all nodded.

"What's good here?" Nora said.

"I don't think we're likely to find out," said the first young man.

"How long have you been here?" It was a casual, pleasant question, as if Nora were asking about the weather.

"Since eight o'clock this morning," the young man said. "We came in for coffee."

"Must take a long time to brew," Nora said.

"We got time," one of the others said.

Nora nodded thoughtfully. Then she raised her voice slightly and said, "Miss? My cousin and I would like to order some lunch."

"We don't serve niggers," the waitress said tightly.

"Well, we shouldn't have any trouble, then, should we? I think we'd both like a hamburger, and some coleslaw and garlic pickles on the side. And a cup of coffee for me and Coca-Cola for the young lady."

The woman stared. "You may not be niggers, but you're sitting with them," she said. "I'm not going to serve you."

"Oh," Nora said. "Is this a private club?"

The woman merely glared.

"All we want is a simple hamburger," Nora said mildly. "I thought this was a public restaurant and we were allowed to sit where we liked. If that's not the case, I think that guy out there with the television camera would like to know about it. Looks like he's just waiting."

"The owner won't let the newspeople in," the woman said. Desperation was shading her nasal voice.

"Now I *really* don't believe that's legal. There's this little thing called the Thirteenth Amendment. To the Constitution, that is. That guy out there would be real surprised to find that you all hadn't heard of it."

A fat, bald man put his head around a door at the end of the counter.

"She's threatening to bring the TV people in here if we don't serve her," the waitress squealed.

"Then serve the bitch," he shouted, and he shut the door.

"All right. What was it, hamburgers?" the waitress snapped.

"Yes. Two. And one apiece for my friends here."

"I ain't serving no niggers!"

"Well, then, bring me six," Nora said. "With six sides of pickles and coleslaw and five coffees, and a Coca-Cola."

"Mr. Stern!" the waitress shrieked.

"Do it," he snarled from behind the closed door. "Do it and get that trash out of my place."

When the hamburgers came, they all ate silently and neatly. Peyton, at the other end of the counter, beside Nora, kept her head down. Her face was burning. She was close to choking on the dry bun, but she did not.

When they had finished and Nora picked up the check to go to the cash register, the first young man said, "Thank you. We were getting pretty hungry. I hope we didn't scare the young lady."

"You're entirely welcome," Nora said.

"I wasn't scared," Peyton said, surprising herself.

They pushed through the crowd outside in silence. A reporter and a television cameraman came up and thrust themselves into their faces.

"What's going on in there?" the reporter said. The cameraman started filming. Peyton sidled behind Nora, who merely smiled.

"Absolutely nothing," she said. "Just some people eating lunch. Surely you guys have got better things to do." She turned to walk away.

"Wait a minute, ma'am," the reporter called. "I need your name, in case we use this footage."

"Augusta McKenzie," Nora called back.

They walked back to the parking garage in silence. The afternoon was shading toward dusk, and a chill crept into the air. The sounds of the afternoon city seemed to fade a little. Peyton realized that she was shaking all over, a fine trembling.

When the car came, Nora said, "You still up for an early dinner? Can you eat after that hamburger? Or do you just want to go home? You've had a long day. By the way, Peyton, I'm proud of you."

"I'm still a little hungry," Peyton lied. "I'm really in the mood for some Italian food."

"You got it," Nora said, smiling, and she turned the car north up Peachtree Street toward Buckhead.

*   *   *

"Are you going to tell him?" Peyton asked as Nora swung the car to the curb in front of their house.

"Tell him what?"

"Any of it. You know. The sit-in and all that stuff. That I drank wine."

"You didn't drink enough wine to make a chicken blink. It's a sin to eat ravioli without wine. No. I'm not going to tell him anything, unless you do first. I won't lie, but I won't tell him, either. That's for you to decide. This was your day."

"I don't think I will," Peyton said. The day and night hung glittering like a Christmas ornament in her mind. All hers. Just hers and Nora's.

"Good. Everybody ought to have one or two strictly private things."

The house was dark. It was still early, but her father often went to bed early and read. Peyton's muscles relaxed slightly. It would not be required of her, then, to share this day and night. Her own private thing. . . .

"Well, it's a pity, but let's do it. All good things must end," Nora said, and she flipped her cigarette into the street, where it glowed like a small beacon and then winked out. She had smoked steadily coming home in the car, top down, cold wind rushing past them, warm air from the heater flowing up to embrace them. None of the discarded cigarettes had blown back into the car. Peyton could not imagine why.

"Because they're magic cigarettes," Nora said. "They don't burn anything but themselves. Life lesson number one: Don't burn anything but yourself."

They had sung all the way home, loudly, the bawdy songs Nora said she had learned at college: "The Night They Shagged O'Reilly's Daughter," "Roll Your Leg Over," "Dirty Lil." When they veered off the interstate and swept onto the unlighted farm road that led over to Lytton, the moon spilled down on them so close and white that Peyton gasped. They rode the rest of the way singing "Moon River."

When they stopped in front of the house, Peyton felt tears tremble on her lower lids. It had been a perfect thing, this day and night.

They tiptoed inside, and a light went on in the kitchen.

"Oh, shit," Nora said softly.

Her father came into the room. He was still dressed, wearing his tan Perry Como cardigan and tweed pants and house slippers. His face was remote. Peyton knew he was displeased.

He said nothing, merely looked at Nora. She, too, was silent, only smiling a little.

Peyton heard her voice spilling out of her like a broken water main: "Oh, Daddy, it was just wonderful! We had lunch in a Jewish deli and then we rode through Buckhead—you should see the houses there, Daddy, they're mansions—and then we went to this Italian place and I had ravioli, it's like these little pouches with sausage in them and sauce on them, and dessert called cannoli—"

She stopped and looked up at him. His face remained closed and still, and then he smiled.

"You had a big day, didn't you?' he said.

"Oh, yes," Peyton breathed in relief and exultation.

"It *was* a good day," Nora said. "Maybe next time you'll come with us."

"Maybe I will," he said.

10

That night, and for many, many nights afterward, Peyton wrote in her diary. At first she sat cross-legged on her bed, Trailways snugged into the curve of her thigh, and stared at the first blank page.

I have no idea how to write in a diary, she thought. Do you write what you did, or what you thought, or what you think of other people, or what?

"It's just for you," Nora's voice repeated in her head. "Nobody will ever see it unless you show it to them. Write anything in the world you want to. Write *fuck shit piss* over and over, if you like. Talk about what you're reading. Talk about what Trailways looks like when he lies in that patch of sunlight on the dining-room table. Write who you hate and who you love. The whole point is to have a record of how you really were at twelve going on thirteen. I can promise you you're not going to remember yourself that way. It'll be good to be able to look back and check in with the real Peyton McKenzie circa nineteen sixty-one."

Tentatively, Peyton wrote the date and then, *Today I went into Atlanta with my Cousin Nora and had lunch at a Jewish delicatessen*

and dinner at an Italian restaurant. I had ravioli and cannoli and Chi-
anti wine. It was good. We sang Nora's college songs on the way
home. Daddy wasn't as mad as I thought he'd be.

She stopped, and then she wrote, *I was in a sit-in. There wasn't*
much to it, but I think I'm glad I did it. I've never eaten with Negroes
before, not Negroes I don't know. It was just like anybody else. It's
very late and Trailways looks like a pile of feathers from a Domi-
necker rooster. I can feel his purr all the way up my leg and into my
chest. Good-bye. Peyton McKenzie.

She was at the toolshed five minutes early on Monday afternoon.
Ernie was heating water; that meant the dreaded powdered hot
chocolate. He looked up at her sourly. It struck her that she could not
remember the last time he'd laughed. Ernie *did* laugh, infrequently—
a painful, rusty laugh that sounded as disused as it was. Or at least he
used to. Peyton's embellished stories of humiliation at the hands of
the cheerleaders had once brought a cackle of enjoyment, and he
often laughed outright at Boot's cheerful litany of self-abasement.
Peyton wondered if he was tiring of their stories. He had not himself
volunteered any loser's stories in a while. Either his arachnid mother
had lost her venom or Ernie had developed immunity.

It's not fair that it's just us being losers, she thought. It's no good if
he's not a part of it. It isn't the Losers Club anymore.

"I hear Cinderella had a big time at the ball Saturday," he said, not
turning from his fussing with the chocolate. "I hear she came in so
late that her coach almost turned into a pumpkin, and her coachman
into a rat."

"It wasn't late. We were home by nine-thirty. We had dinner earlier
than we liked, but we thought Daddy might worry."

Peyton spoke with the weariness of one who habitually dined at
nine but was accommodating a doting elder. She did not even ask
where Ernie had got his information. He snorted.

"Where did you dine?" he said. "The Varsity? The S and W Cafeteria?"

"At a little Jewish delicatessen for lunch, and at Biuso's for dinner. It
was quite good. I had ravioli—that's a little dumpling stuffed with—"

"I know what ravioli is," Ernie said.

"Well, and then we had cannoli and some wine. Chianti, actually. It's a pretty little restaurant. It's in Buckhead."

"Don't tell me," Ernie said. "Red-checked tablecloths. Candles in Chianti bottles. Artificial grapevines crawling all over the place. Murals of Mount Etna on the walls. 'Santa Lucia' on the Muzak."

"You've been there?"

"To about a million places like it. Atlanta doesn't have any true Italian restaurants. You couldn't get Tuscan cuisine if you lay down and begged for it. Nobody ever heard of a truffle."

"Huh," said Peyton, who had not, either. "How long has it been since you've even left Lytton?"

He flushed, a dull brick-red.

"You know I can't leave Mother anymore," he said.

Boot clumped in then, slamming the door and yelling in his reedy cricket voice, "Hey Peyton, tell us about your ride up to Atlanta in that Thunderbird. I hear you didn't get home till midnight. Boy, I bet your daddy come down on you like a duck on a june bug."

"I got home at nine-thirty exactly," Peyton said. "The rumor machine must be working overtime."

"Yeah, it is. Tell," Boot said, and he plopped himself down on the spavined wicker armchair that was his accustomed place.

"Well," Peyton said, "there isn't much to tell. We shopped a little at the Peachtree Arcade, and then we walked to a Jewish delicatessen and had lunch—"

"What did you have?" Ernie put in. "Chopped liver? Gefilte fish?"

"What that?" Boot said suspiciously.

"I had a hamburger," Peyton mumbled. It was a rule at the Losers Club that they would never lie. They could embellish, but outright untruths were grounds for expulsion.

"Big whoop," Ernie said.

Peyton's face burned.

"I was in a sit-in," she said, spilling it out. She had sworn never to tell anyone about it. The television news had not aired the brief exchange with Nora, and apparently no one in Lytton had even heard about the four young Negroes who had sat for hours in a delicatessen in Atlanta, staring at an empty counter.

"You were not," Ernie spat.

"I was, too! You ask Nora! We saw this big crowd at the deli, so we looked in and there were these Negroes sitting at the counter and nobody would serve them, and we went in and sat down and Nora ordered six hamburgers and gave them four of them. And when we left the television guy asked her what had happened and she said 'Nothing' and when he asked her name she said 'Augusta McKenzie.' "

They were silent for a moment. Sickly, Peyton realized that she had spilled out everything she and Nora had agreed not to speak of in one spasmodic rush. She did not think Ernie would say anything—oddly, he gossiped only with them—but she had little hope that the ebullient Boot would keep quiet.

"Whoo *Jeesus!*" Boot squalled in delight. "Was that on the television?"

"No."

"You better be glad. Yo' aunt skin you alive if she see that, and Nora, too. Does Mamaw know about it?"

"No."

"Well," he said generously, "I ain't gon' tell her, then."

Ernie drained his cup and put it down and leaned back in his leather chair.

"Peyton, it strikes me that you haven't had a real loser's story in quite a while," he drawled. "All we've been hearing about is your riding around in that sports car and going to Atlanta for lunch and dinner. Oh, and getting a new hairdo and new clothes. Tell me, where's the loser in that?"

Peyton stared at him. What he said was true. She had not had a real moment of humiliation to share since . . . since Nora came. A wind from somewhere far off brushed her heart.

"Well, there was the sit-in. You know what Daddy and Aunt Augusta would say if they knew about that. . . ."

"It doesn't matter about your Aunt Augusta," Ernie said. "She's going to think everything you do is awful. I'm not so sure about your

father. There are some people who would say what you did was a
good thing, not something to be ashamed of."

There was another silence.

"Well, I done it yesterday," Boot said. "I dropped a bottle of cran-
berry juice in the middle of the A&P and didn't have no money to
pay for it, so the sto' people made me mop it up."

He grinned broadly. Peyton, who once would have grinned with
him, winced. Soon after that they went home. Ernie in one of his distant moods was impervious to even the most delectable humiliation.

Nora's first experimental English class was held the following
Monday at Carver High, the black school literally across the railroad
tracks from the main body of Lytton. It consisted of honors English
students from both high schools, grades ten through twelve. It was
held at Carver because the school board thought it only courteous for
the white school to make the first visit.

"Like the home team honoring the out-of-towners," Nora said to
Peyton and Frazier at supper the night before, "or more like testing
the waters and seeing who's going to beat the hell out of whom
before it happens on white territory."

Frazier looked at her.

"Does the idea of any of that bother you?" he asked. "Because if it
does, we can assign a male teaching aide for you until things settle
down."

"My God, no," Nora laughed. "This is small potatoes to the lady
who handled a village full of horny teenagers drunk on rum after the
last cane harvest."

"What did you do?" Peyton asked.

"I told them I was going to summon a *nganga* to come and shrivel
up their peckers and then kill a rooster to make sure it stuck. It
worked like a charm. *Santería* and *brujería* are common out in the
provinces in Cuba. And the Cubans are great natural lovers. It would
be a fate worse than death to any teenager."

Peyton felt herself blush and slid a look at her father.

"I guess that would do it, yes," he said mildly. But there was the
slightest tug at the corners of his mouth.

The class was scheduled for ten in the morning. By noon the news of it was scattering through the grammar school like spilled mercury. Two Negro boys had beat up the captain of the white football team, and there was going to be a full-scale reprisal one night soon. In fact, it wasn't two Negro boys at all, it was Jerry Mooney, the massive, truculent captain of the wrestling team, and he had attacked a Negro boy, much smaller, in the bathroom at recess. Miss Findlay threw him out of class with both hands and a foot on his bottom. Miss Findlay made the white students sit by the Negroes and threatened to fail anyone who opened his mouth about it. When two of the white cheerleaders who had somehow managed to stumble into the class made whispered fun of a fat Negro girl, Miss Findlay put her arms around the sobbing girl and rocked her like a child, and told the cheerleaders she was going to do everything she could to get the cheerleading squad suspended for the rest of the year. Then she sent them back to Lytton High. They left smirking and switching their trim behinds, but there was an unease in their blue eyes that had never been there before. Somehow nobody doubted that Miss Findlay could and would do what she said she would.

After the white students left to go back to their own school for lunch, Miss Findlay stayed behind for her lunch and ate it in the company of the enormous, shining black principal. Both, when last seen, were licking their fingers and laughing.

Students swarmed around Peyton when school was out. Was her cousin going to have Negro teachers over for dinner at Peyton's house? Was it true that she had made the white students use the Negro bathrooms? Would the Negroes use the white ones when they came to Lytton High? Was she going to join Saint John's African Methodist Episcopal Church? Was she dating the Negro principal?

Nora laughed so hard when Peyton relayed these concerns that she choked on her cigarette and smoke exploded from her nostrils.

"Well, here's what you tell them," she said. "A: Maybe, if they ask me over to theirs first. B: If anybody wants to pee, they'll do it in the nearest bathroom, wherever that happens to be. C: I'll probably go to some services at Saint John's. I love the singing. D: Certainly not. He's married. But if he weren't, that would be a different story."

"What did you do for your first class?"

"Well, after I got all the sniggering quieted down, I read to them from *To Kill a Mockingbird*. You know I told you I thought I would. Then I picked out passages and asked them to read them aloud."

"What parts?"

"The earliest parts, where Scout tells us about Maycomb and how it was in the summers in that time, and about the people who lived there and what they thought and did. I wanted them to see how closely literature comes to the lives they know themselves, even though it happened in another time and place. And I think they got it, finally. Of course, none of them reads aloud very well, black or white, but toward the end nobody was embarrassed anymore, and everyone was raising their hand to say how they thought Lytton was like Maycomb. They're very quick, if not articulate. Some of the comparisons were really interesting."

"Will you tell me about them?"

"Maybe one day. Right now I'm going to write them all down and see if I can maybe get a little book out of it by the end of the year. The same pieces of literature, seen through black and white eyes. I love the idea."

"A book! Would it get published?"

"I have no idea," Nora said. "I won't be doing it to publish it. I'm doing it just because it interests me and I like to write. But I'll let you read it when I'm far enough along."

"I wish I could take that class," Peyton said. "My English class is stupid. Mrs. Manning just assigned us *Little Women*. I stopped reading that stuff when I was ten and Miss Laura Willingham let me get books out of the adult section of the library. We never told Aunt Augusta. I've almost finished *Mockingbird* already."

"Well, I can't let you come to this one, but maybe we could sort of review what I've been doing in class every afternoon or so. You can read along with us. Or even better, you write down what you think about it and we'll go over it and compare it to what my high-schoolers said. I bet you'll be way ahead of them."

"Well, maybe," Peyton said, thinking she would rather die than let anyone read anything she had written. And yet, to meet these high-schoolers on their own ground and beat them. . . .

"If you're still here next year, maybe I could take one of your classes," she said. "I'll almost be in high school then."

"My Lord, so you will," Nora said, looking at her and smiling. "I should have remembered. And you have a birthday this summer, too, don't you?"

"In June. Right after graduation."

"Ah, graduation. Is there a commencement? When I started high school all you did was just show up."

"Not really a commencement," Peyton mumbled. She had been thinking with dread about it for some time. "Just this thing in the school auditorium where the school choir sings and a preacher says something, and there are some speeches and stuff. It's not a big deal. I don't even think I'm going to go."

Nora shot her a keen look.

"What sort of speeches?" she said. "Who makes them?"

"Oh, you know. The ones who make good grades and stuff. Mostly they're teachers' pets. It's the teachers who pick them."

"You'll be asked to make one."

"No, I'm sure not. I'm not anybody's pet. None of the teachers even know who I am, really. Besides, I'd hate it. I'd never in the world know what to say. I'd make such a fool of myself that I'd be the winner in the Losers Club for the rest of my life."

Nora tapped her unlit cigarette thoughtfully on the table and studied her. "The Losers Club. Is that the club you go to every afternoon? Why is it called that?"

"We tell each other what dumb things we've done that day, and the one who did the dumbest wins. It's usually Boot, because he likes to win and his foot makes him clumsy. He's always falling over things. It's really nothing. Just something we got in the habit of doing a long time ago. And it's not all stupid stuff. Ernie plays music for us and tells us about the theater and literature and all. He's given me some books. And I think Boot has learned a lot from him."

"Hmmm," Nora said. "Sounds like fun. Can I come sometime? I'm not exactly a stranger. I know Ernie and I know you."

"Well, it's in the bylaws that nobody but us can come. I asked Ernie and he got all cranky about it, but I'll ask him again. Boot would love it. He thinks your car is the greatest."

"Never mind. I don't want to make Ernie uncomfortable. I'll meet Boot sometime here. And I'll tell you all the dumb things I do and you can tell him and Ernie, and that'll make me an honorary member."

Peyton shot her a look. Was she being patronized? But Nora simply stretched lazily. Her green eyes looked past Peyton and into space. No. Not patronized. But something was there, something in the eyes. . . .

Nora met Boot the next afternoon, after the Losers Club. He was, Peyton knew, accustomed to going to the house of an old woman in Lightning who looked after many of the children of the women who worked in the big houses. He usually went after the Losers Club and stayed until his grandmother got home, but sometimes the old woman had rheumatism, or went to visit her daughter in Union City, and then he came to the McKenzie house. When she was much younger Peyton had played with him on those occasions, watching him toddling about crowing, bouncing his ball with him. But at some point they had grown apart except for the Losers Club, and on those afternoons when he was visiting, Peyton was usually reading, and he pottered around the kitchen with his grandmother. It bothered neither Boot nor Peyton. At the Losers Club they were fully equal, and that was what counted.

Boot came in shortly after Peyton had gotten home, slamming the back door and shouting for his grandmother. Peyton heard, from the snug harbor of her bed and bookcase, Chloe starting in on him in irritation, and heard his cheerful, "Well, Mamaw, Miz Liz'beth say she got the high blood bad and I needs to come on over here. She say she be better tomorrow."

"Well, you stay in this kitchen and be quiet, then. Peyton studying and Miss Nora coming in from the library any time now."

"She comin' in that car?"

"Of course she is. You think she flying? You don't need to be studying that car, Boot. She ain't gon' want you hanging around it."

"Maybe if I held the door for her she'd take me for a ride," Boot said ingenuously. "I could probably wash and wax it sometime, too."

Peyton heard the front door open and close, and heard Nora's voice: "Is that the incomparable Meatloaf à la Chloe I smell? Could it possibly be? And biscuits, maybe?"

Peyton got up and went into the kitchen. No matter what her intentions about reading or listening to her records, when Nora came into the house she was drawn out of her room like a moth to a leaping flame. Light and air and noise came in with Nora. The old house had not felt their like in Peyton's lifetime.

It must be what it was like when my mother was alive, she thought.

Nora dumped her armful of books onto the breakfast table and plopped down in her seat.

"Coffee before I die?" she said. "And maybe some of that pecan pie from last night? Peyton, are you game for some pie? I swear I . . ." Her voice trailed off. Then she said, "Well, who have we here?" and Boot's face appeared around the door into the kitchen, fat cheeks split with a grin.

"This is my grandbaby Boot," Clothilde said. "He don't usually turn up here. He promised not to bother anybody. Boot, this is Miss Nora. You know, I told you. She's staying with us for a while."

"Hello, Boot," Nora said, looking at him levelly. "I've been hearing about you."

He hung his head and dug at the linoleum with his toe, and then looked up at her and gave her the full wattage of his smile.

"I been hearin' about you, too," he said. "That your car out there?"

"It is," Nora said, sipping her coffee and squinting at him through the steam.

"I heard you drove it all the way up here from Cuba."

"Well, from Key West, Florida. That's about as far as you can go before you come to Cuba."

"With the top down?"

"A lot of the time."

"You get bugs squashed on you?"

Nora smiled then. "Pounds and pounds of them bugs in my hair, in my eyes, in my teeth. . . ."

Boot's joyous, froggy laugh rang out. "Ain't that somethin'? Boy, I'd like to seen all them bugs. . . ."

It was obviously Nora's move, time for her to say, "I'll take you for a ride sometime," but she did not. "A few bugs go a long way," she said.

There was a small silence, and then Boot said, "You could drive that car to our club meeting sometime. It right up the street. It would look fine sittin' out in front of the parsonage. And if it got bugs on it I could wash and wax it for you."

"Well, I'll think about that," Nora said, and she gathered up her books as if to leave. Peyton watched as Boot's heart leapt into his black eyes, and she knew she had just witnessed that most ineffable of phenomena, the thing they called love at first sight. Because she wanted to show Nora off a bit and because Boot was staring at her cousin with such naked adoration, Peyton said, "Nora says she doesn't think she'll come to club meetings, but she'll tell me about the dumb things she does and I'll tell you and Ernie, and that way she can be an honorary member."

"I bet you ain't never done nothin' stupid," Boot said to Nora. He offered it like a cache of jewels to a queen.

"Dumber than you can possibly imagine," Nora said.

"Tell one!" Boot crowed with joy. This was too much for him, a copper-crowned madonna who drove a pink chariot and did dumb things.

"Maybe one day," Nora said, and she went out of the room and up the stairs. Peyton stared after her. So did Boot, and Chloe.

"Can I tell about the stockings?" Peyton called after her.

"If you want to," Nora's voice came back. They heard the sound of her door closing smartly. Peyton leapt into the silence.

"Nora was sixteen, and this boy she'd had a crush on for ages, a college boy, asked her to go swimming with a bunch of his friends. And she bought a new bathing suit and got her nails fixed, but then when she tried on the bathing suit she thought she looked . . . flat-chested. You know. So she took some of her aunt's stockings and balled them up and stuck them in the front of her suit. Well, she was swimming around having a good time, and she saw everybody looking at her chest, and she looked down, and she saw stocking feet floating out of her bathing suit. She said she like to have died. Everybody was laughing."

Boots yelped happily. "That's dumb, all right. That's better than you or Ernie done in a long time. Boy, she sho' know how to do it, don't she? Did that boy keep on being her boyfriend?"

"I don't know. I don't think so. She hasn't said any more about him."

"Then he the stupid one," Boot said.

After he and Chloe had gone home, Nora came down to Peyton's room and settled onto the end of the narrow white bed as she sometimes did.

"What's happening, kiddo?" she said.

Peyton closed her book. "Did Boot make you mad or something?" she said. "He makes a lot of noise, I know, with that boot thing, but he's a nice little boy, and he can be real funny sometimes."

Nora looked at her and then out the single small window into the backyard, where the first forsythia was beginning to spill like a fountain.

"I'm just not wild about children," she said. "There's no use pretending I am. I'll try to be nicer to Boot, though. I just hope he isn't underfoot all the time."

Peyton saw a curtain fall behind Nora's green eyes. Something in her was closing like a door. Peyton did not know how she knew this, but she was sure of it. There were distances and secrets inside Nora, then, places she would allow no one to go. She felt an abrupt and marrow-deep need to go into those places, to know those hidden

things about her cousin. She realized that what she had been given of
Nora was carefully edited and abridged, that an entire continent lay
underneath. She must think I'm a child after all, Peyton thought. But
she's never acted that way. . . .

As if possessed of some perverse incubus, Boot was indeed underfoot after that. His infatuation knew no bounds. Whenever Nora got
out of her car in the afternoon, Boot would rush to hold the door for
her, to carry her books and her parcels. Whenever, on a weekend, she
set out on one of her slow cruises around town, she would see Boot
in the rearview mirror, thumping after her like one of the Seven
Dwarves. She ran into his smitten grin when she went to the grocery
store, and found him waiting on the front steps in the morning in case
she needed the car door opened or something carried. Nora said
nothing, but she began to disappear into her room the minute she
came home from school, and stopped coming down to breakfast,
where, often, Boot would be lurking like a happy frog.

"Doesn't that child have anybody else to look after him?" she said
once to Peyton, after Boot had offered once more to Simonize the
Thunderbird.

"Well, we all sort of look after him," Peyton said. "And he's with
me and Ernie almost every afternoon. He's never any trouble."

"Maybe not to you," Nora said under her breath, taking the stairs
to her room two at a time. Even the gregarious Boot would not climb
the McKenzie stairs to the bedroom floor.

He began to bring her presents: a sack of pecans, a gay double
armful of pink thrift that he cheerfully admitted he had gotten from
Miss Lucy Jernigan's rock garden—"She got plenty more"—a piece
of quartz that he had shined to a diamond polish, a picture of a
Thunderbird like hers, cut out of the Sunday newspaper and glued
onto a piece of shirt cardboard. Nora thanked him after every offering, but she never failed to say, "Boot, you simply mustn't bring me
any more things. It's too much work for you, and I'm running out of
room for them."

"You can throw the old ones away and I'll get you some new
ones," Boot said. And he did.

Clothilde had, Peyton knew, recently forbidden him the house except in a real emergency. She saw Chloe glance often at Nora, her brows furrowed in her yellow forehead. But Nora never mentioned Boot to Chloe, and Chloe did not speak of him, either.

Not until the honey-sweet day in March when Nora came home early from her tutoring session at the black high school and found Boot in her car, top down, engine running, radio booming out country music audible for blocks. Boot's eyes were squeezed shut, and his face was rapt with bliss. "Vrroomm," he was chanting. "Vroom-vroom-*vroom!*" He did not see or hear Nora until she jerked the car door open and clutched him by his collar and dragged him out of the car. Her face was blanched with fury, and her eyes were slitted. Peyton, watching through the screen door, gasped and went as still as a woodland creature seeing a hawk swoop. This was going to be bad.

Nora slammed Boot up against the car and bent and looked directly into his face, only inches from it. Her hands gripped his shoulders, and she shook him slightly. His face was blank with terror.

"Don't you ever, *ever* touch my car again, you hear me?" she screamed into Boot's face. "Don't come near it. Don't come near me. *Nobody* touches that car but me! Where did you get those keys?"

"They was laying on the kitchen table," Boot whispered. He was trying to pull away from Nora's hands. She let him go abruptly, and he staggered a little, then took off around the house.

Nora stood with her head bent, leaning on the car's fender, her eyes closed. Gradually the labored breathing that had made her chest heave slackened. Then she turned toward the house. Peyton moved away from the door and scuttled into her room. She did not want to talk about this. She did not want to see Nora's face like that. She did not want to see Boot's humiliation.

No one mentioned the incident at supper. Nora ate with relish and chatted of insignificant and outrageous things, and Frazier took out the pipe he had resumed smoking and smiled at them both through sweet smoke.

That night Peyton showed herself her movies. She wrote in her diary, *Even the air hurts.*

Nora finally went to Boot's house and apologized to him, largely, Peyton knew, because Chloe's face was so miserable. She didn't know what had come over her, she said, except that she was terribly tired and had not been sleeping well.

"Of course I'll take you for a ride in the car," she said, and Chloe and Boot nodded in unison. But Boot did not come back to the house. Peyton saw him at the Losers Club, where he dutifully recited his litanies of abasement, but she said nothing about Nora and the car because he did not know she knew about the incident. But he was somehow diminished, like a photograph left out in the sun, and though he could still make her and Ernie laugh, he did not often laugh with them. It was as if somebody had pulled a plug and drained the green sap out of him. He was, somehow, a wise and wizened little man, not a child anymore.

It seemed a long time before Chloe began to sing again in the kitchen.

11

O*n Saint Patrick's Day Nora took Peyton and Frazier into* Atlanta for dinner and a movie.

"I think there's some sort of parade down Peachtree Street, too," she said. "We really ought to see it."

"You want to take a Scotsman to a Saint Patrick's Day parade?" Frazier said. He was smiling, though.

"Why not? Loosen you up a little. Get some of that Hebridean starch out of you. We'll have you drinking green beer before you know it."

"Faith and begorra," he said. Peyton laughed happily. She could not remember her father's ever making a real joke before.

It was a sweet, soft day, and they went in the Thunderbird, all three of them squeezed into the front seat. Nora laughed at the sight of Frazier folding his long body into the little pink car, sitting with his knees under his chin. Peyton, crammed between them, felt a lift and swoop of joy that seemed to have its provenance in nothing at all but the smell of new green and the taste of new-cut grass in her mouth, and the rush of clean wind past her face. It was such an intense, flooding feeling that she closed her eyes against it so as not to cry. Nora looked over at her.

"Pretty fabulous, isn't it?" she said softly.

"Yes," Peyton said.

They parked the Thunderbird in Davison's parking lot and walked up to Peachtree Street. Both sides of the street were crowded with people wearing all shades of green, from emerald to hideous pea-soup. There were many leprechauns in the crowd, shambling along in their short pants and peaked hats, carrying plastic shillelaghs. Vendors on corners were selling paper four-leaf clover pennants and decals. Although Peyton could see no bars or taverns on the length of the street, there must have been ready sources for green beer. Half the people around them were carrying paper cups of it; the other half had obviously just discarded theirs. The smell of beer was thick and yeasty everywhere, and Irish songs were bellowed out nearly continuously. Peyton heard "When Irish Eyes Are Smiling" and "Toorah-loora-looral" and others less sentimental and seemly: "Peg in a Lowbacked Car," "The Night They Shagged O'Reilly's Daughter." She cut her eyes at her father and he looked back with a little grimace, but he was smiling, too. It was impossible not to smile on this day of breezy sun and singing ersatz Irishmen.

The parade itself was modest in comparison with the crowd it engendered. The handsome, white-haired mayor came first, in a green Lincoln convertible, followed by sundry other dignitaries in convertibles, all grinning, Nora said, like possums in the middle of cow plops. There was a float bearing a bevy of green-clad young women, all managing somehow to reveal modest cleavage and a flash of leg under their traditional Irish costumes, or whatever passed for them in the Southern Baptist minds of the parade's sponsors. On a throne draped in green sat the queen of the parade, or whatever she was, in a cloud of virulent green tulle, a headdress of woven shamrocks on her Clairol-red hair and another bouquet of them in her arms. The crowd roared at the float, and some of the leprechauns staggered alongside it, trying to climb aboard. Stern-faced marshals on horseback waved them off.

"Going to be a whole lot of Irish horse crap around here after the parade," Nora said, grinning.

Peyton stared at the green queen.

"You'd make a much better queen," she said to Nora. "Wouldn't she, Daddy? Her hair's real, and her eyes are green. That girl looks stupid with red hair and those black eyebrows and dark eyes."

"Well, there are always the black Irish," Nora said. "And the very first Celts were supposed to be little dark people who came out of the caves into the light. But I agree with you about the hair. It's the color of dry red mud."

Behind the queen and her court came a pipe band. The squealing lilt of the bagpipes touched something in Peyton's heart that she had not known was there, something fierce and wild, like a young raptor trapped there.

"Oh," she breathed.

Her father looked down at her and smiled.

"So you've got the pipes in your blood, too," he said. "I thought it was just your grandmother."

Behind the band a surging straggle of green-clad, beer-carrying people lurched along, waving banners and shillelaghs and singing whatever Irish song they happened to know. It was not a big parade, but it was a loud one, and when they got back into the Thunderbird to drive out Peachtree Street to Buckhead, Peyton's ears still rang with it.

They had dinner in the same Italian restaurant where Peyton and Nora had eaten before.

"I promise it's the last time," Nora said. "We should sample a few of the other ethnic restaurants—if there are any. But you wanted clam linguine, Frazier, and Peyton, this time you're going to let me order for you. You can't eat pasta and cheese forever."

In the twilight the dim restaurant had an undersea look, and with its curling vines and impossibly purple grapes and Etna soaring on the walls, it had the aspect of a chamber in Atlantis, a room in Shangri-la. The Muzak was pouring out "Finiculi, Finicula," and Peyton had the sudden flash of elation and comfort that a traveler in a strange land might have, coming upon a familiar landscape.

"I hope it's as good tonight as it was last time," she said languidly. "Restaurants often aren't, you know. They can be inconsistent."

They turned and looked at her. Her father lifted an eyebrow, and her cousin grinned.

"They can indeed. Has that been your experience here?" Nora said.

Peyton blushed, knowing she had sounded ridiculous. The fact was that Ernie had said the same thing a couple of weeks before and had sounded wonderfully worldly and discriminating.

"No," she said sheepishly. "It's just something I heard."

Nora and her father split a bottle of Chianti, and Peyton had a splash of it in a small glass. It was sour and dry, and she really did not like it, but it made a warm track down to her stomach, so she finished it. Her father ordered clam linguine for two, and Nora studied the menu and then said, "Peyton, I think the scungilli for you. It's light and not so highly seasoned, and it has a nice lemony taste to it."

"What is it?" Peyton said doubtfully.

"Fish cooked with some wine. Really special. I think it's southern Italian, but it's not as heavy as most of that."

"OK," Peyton said. "I'll try it."

"Do," Nora said. "If you don't like it you can fill up on popcorn later."

They talked lightly and lazily in the flickering light of the candle set in an empty Chianti bottle, and the white-aproned waiter hovered over Nora and brought another full bottle of Chianti, "on the house," he said. Nora smiled.

"What movie are we seeing?" Frazier said. He was rolling the wine around in his glass and sniffing it appreciatively. Peyton tried the same thing and coughed as the acid fumes curled up her nose.

"*On the Beach*," Nora said. "It's a couple of years old, and certainly not great art, but I've always loved it. It always makes me cry."

"Oh, well, then by all means, let's see it twice," her father said, smiling. "What's it about?"

"The end of the world," Nora said.

"How uplifting."

"As a matter of fact, it is. It's pretty heavy going, but it says everything there is to say about the human spirit. About how to live your
life when it's ending."

He looked at her quizzically. "Do you think Peyton . . . ?"

"Absolutely. Besides having a message she needs to know, it's just a
fine movie, with wonderful acting. I take full responsibility," Nora said.

Their dinner came then. Peyton's plate was steaming, and a wonderful smell curled up from the delicately browned medallions on it.

"Mmmm," she said, taking a bite. It was not like any fish she had
ever tasted, certainly not the ubiquitous fried catfish with hush pup-
pies offered by a half dozen "family-style" restaurants along Highway 29. But there was about it an ineffable taste of sun and sea salt.
The swirls of lemon butter and wine it was bathed in were exotic and
rich. She finished most of the fish and mopped up the sauce with a
piece of bread, as Nora and her father did with their linguine.

"That was good," she said. "What kind of fish did you say it
was?"

Nora leaned back and lit a cigarette and smiled at her.

"Squid," she said. "Some people call it octopus."

The tender white medallions rose in Peyton's throat and sat there
struggling for expulsion. Her stomach muscles contracted. And then
they subsided, and the scungilli slid back down where it belonged.

"Not bad at all," she said boredly, thinking that the squid was
going to earn her a place of honor in the pantheon of awfulness at the
Losers Club. Let's see Ernie top that, she thought.

"Next time we'll go to Emile's and you can try escargot," Nora
said. "Snails."

Peyton looked at her sickly, and her father laughed. "There's a
limit," he said. "Don't push your luck."

From the minute the theater lights lowered, Peyton was trans-
fixed by the movie. The reality of the great cloud drifting slowly
toward the last survivors of an atomic blast, the sweet banality of
the last lives being lived under that reality, the images—paper blow-

ing down an empty street, a Coca-Cola bottle caught in a venetian-blind cord in an empty San Francisco, randomly tapping out a last lost message to Australia—all lodged in her chest and swelled until there was a great ball of darkness there, an abyss of nothingness as real as the nothingness waiting on the celluloid beach. She closed her eyes as the tears began to come: tears of fear and hopelessness and a kind of fierce exultation born of the courage and grace of the doomed people flickering in black and white on the screen. She tried hard to hide them. Mostly she succeeded, but when Gregory Peck kissed Ava Gardner for the last time and took his submarine out to sea to meet death, a strangled sob escaped her. She felt rather than saw Nora's hand come over to touch hers, and her father silently passed her his handkerchief.

Coming out of the theater, they were silent. So were the other moviegoers. Nobody was saying anything at all, and there were empty faces and wide-staring eyes all around. As the crowd moved into the lights of Peachtree Road, and the sounds and smells of the city in early spring eclipsed the great silence they had left behind, they began to talk among themselves in low voices, but there was no laughter.

"Anybody want ice cream?" Nora said, and they walked down the sidewalk to a drugstore that Frazier said must surely have the last old-time soda fountain left in Atlanta. They sat in curly iron chairs at a small marble-topped table. Nora ordered vanilla ice cream, Frazier had coffee, and Peyton, suddenly ravenous for sweetness and substance, ordered a banana split and then could eat only a couple of bites. She put down her spoon and looked guiltily at Nora and her father.

"I guess my eyes were bigger than my stomach," she said.

Nora studied her.

"How you doin', kid?" she said. "I'd forgotten how tough that movie is. Maybe we should have waited a couple of years. . . ."

Her father said nothing but studied her curiously. Peyton felt her face color under his eyes, and dropped her own.

"It was OK," she said. "I liked it."

"What do you think it meant? What was the movie trying to say?" Nora tossed out for whoever might answer.

Presently her father said, "I think it meant that we might be extinguished but we don't die out. That, and that Ava Gardner has a nice shape."

Nora laughed. "Pretty good. *I* think it's a comment on the futility of modern life and our attempts to make sense of it. What do you think, Peyton?"

Peyton did not lift her eyes. She felt tears, thick and briny, gathering behind her eyelids. They stung in her nose.

"I think it meant that everybody always loses everybody they love," she murmured. "But they need to love them anyway because . . ."

"Because?"

"Because there isn't anything else," Peyton said, and she burst into tears.

Her father gave her a brief hug and produced the handkerchief again. When she had mopped the tears, Peyton looked up at them. Both were staring at her.

"But that's probably not right at all," she mumbled.

"It's exactly right. Exactly," Nora said. "Nobody but you really got it."

On the way home Nora put the top up on the Thunderbird and they skimmed through the dark like a small craft planing over the surface of a black river. The inside of the car was small and dark and warm, and the radio played softly. Nora sang along with Dean Martin: "Return to Me." Her voice was soft and gritty, like improperly mixed fudge. Wedged between them, Peyton closed her eyes and let the roaring of the road beneath them swell in her ears until she slipped off on its tide. Once she lifted her head and saw black, star-pricked sky and knew they were sailing through the fields near home, and heard laughter, and put her head back on her father's shoulder and slept again.

When she came in from the Losers Club the next Monday, Chloe was uncovering a great platter of fried chicken. Its warm crustiness wafted up from the waxed paper that covered it. Peyton's mouth watered: it was one of the archetypal smells of her childhood. It meant comfort, safety, love. She knew the instant she smelled it that her grandmother had made it.

"Your grandma was here," Clothilde said. "She say she made too much chicken and thought she'd bring us some. It was real good to see her. She don't come so often anymore. I told her if she'd wait awhile you'd be home, and then your daddy, and he'd drive her home, but she said no, it was a pretty day and she wanted to walk. She right mad at you, Peyton. You ain't been down to see her in a while. You need to call her and thank her, and you really need to go see her."

"I'll go tomorrow afternoon," Peyton said, guilt flooding her. It was true. It had been at least a week since she had visited her grandmother. She couldn't have said why. All of a sudden she felt a fierce longing for the old woman, for her radiant madness and her hawk-like beauty, and for the absolute acceptance and focus that made Peyton feel, for the moment, totally alive.

She called her grandmother after dinner.

"I wish you'd stayed, Nana," she said. "I've missed you. I know, it's my fault. I'm coming tomorrow. And the chicken was just fabulous. Nobody does it like you. There isn't a scrap left. Nora ate three pieces."

There was a long silence in which Peyton could hear her grandmother breathing. It sounded as if she were gasping for breath, a fish drowning in air. Then she said, coldly and as if from a great distance, "Is that red witch still there, then?"

"Well, you know she's teaching at the high school—"

"She's come for your soul," Agnes McKenzie said, and Peyton flinched at the madness. It wasn't fey and flickering now, it was dark, a thick, escalating coil.

"Nana . . ."

"She's come for Frazier, too, but it's mainly you she wants. Listen, Peyton, listen to me. Get the bones. Get the bones! Bring them to me, all of them. Don't leave even one. Did she take them? Ask her. Ask her now!"

Her grandmother's voice slid up into a kind of weak shriek. Peyton dropped the phone and ran to the living room, where Nora was shuffling through the mail on the secretary. She got a lot of mail, most of it from Miami or Key West, but some from Cuba, too.

"Nana says to ask you what you did with the chicken bones from dinner," she said, hearing the absolute idiocy of her own words.

Nora looked at her. "I put them in the kitchen garbage and took it out to the backyard. Tomorrow's pickup day. Why on earth does she want to know?"

"I don't know. She just does," Peyton said, and she ran back to the phone. "They're in the garbage in the backyard, Nana," she said. "Nora took them out after supper. They'll get picked up in the morning."

"Go get them!" her grandmother screamed. It was a thin, high, falcon's sound. "Go get them right now! Get them all! Don't let her bury them! Has she buried any of them?"

"Nana—"

"She'll ill-wish me! She probably already has. . . . If you bury the bones from somebody's meal so they can't find them and get them back, that person will die! I thought she was gone; I couldn't see her anymore. . . . GET THOSE BONES! BRING THEM NOW!"

"I'll get them, Nana," Peyton said, beginning to tremble. "I'll get them first thing in the morning, before the garbagemen come. I don't think I could find them in the dark."

Her grandmother began to scream something Peyton could not make out. The tumble of words was wild and swift, roiling water from an interior river. They sounded almost foreign, not English at all. Then the torrent faded, and Peyton heard the phone drop.

"Nana," she called. "Nana . . ."

But her grandmother did not answer. Peyton ran for her father's study over the garage.

When the car squealed into the farmhouse yard, he was out of it and running before the engine died. Peyton sat still, frozen with terror. There was a great sense of wrongness hovering over the house, beating in the air like enormous wings. Finally she got out and followed her father into the house.

Her grandmother lay on the kitchen floor, the wounded telephone lying beside her, dial tone buzzing. She lay on her back. Her arms were drawn up to her chest, hands balled into fists. Her eyes were closed, and when she breathed a bubble of spittle formed on her drawn-back lips and in her nostrils. Her face was a doll's broken face, twisted, mouth drawn down. She did not move or speak; there was only the terrible, bubbling breathing.

It was not until they heard the sirens of the ambulance wailing into the driveway that she spoke. Frazier knelt beside her, holding her knotted hands, head bent so that Peyton could not see his face. Peyton had been hovering about the kitchen, first at the sink, then at the stove, unable to settle, unable to find any place in the awful, bright-lit kitchen to *be*.

When they heard the sirens, her grandmother opened her eyes. They were dilated to black, and utterly mad. She made a garbled sound in her throat, a spittle-choked grunt that rapidly rose and rose until it became a wordless shout. Her throat knotted with the effort of it; her chest heaved, her twisted face flushed. Her black eyes passed over her son's face and found Peyton's.

The animal scream strengthened. It seemed to Peyton that there were words hidden in it, words for her alone. She leaned forward, forgetting to flinch.

"What is she saying? My God, what is she saying?" her father said. His voice sounded, incredibly, thick with tears.

"'Go tell the Devil,'" Peyton said, knowing it suddenly. "She's saying, 'Go tell the Devil.'"

The stroke was severe. Agnes stayed in the hospital in Atlanta for weeks. She did not speak again, and all efforts to make her accept therapy failed. She simply set her teeth and closed her eyes and went away inside to wherever it was that she spent most of her days. Once in a while she gabbled something at Peyton, but it was not intelligible, and Peyton's efforts to understand seemed only to infuriate her. When she was able to leave the hospital, Frazier told her that she was coming home with him, to live where people she knew and loved could take care of her.

There would be Chloe and Peyton, he said, and Nora would help out. He would be there every evening. It was what everyone wanted. Agnes became so agitated that her doctor was called and he cleared the room, fearing another stroke. The agitation flooded in whenever Frazier mentioned her coming to their house. Finally he gave up and found a nearby nursing home that seemed acceptable. It was clean, cheerful, and well staffed, and it cost the very earth. Agnes seemed if not happy, then at least content there, dreaming and dozing away the days. Peyton visited often at first, but she could not be sure her grandmother even knew her. Sometimes she slept; sometimes she seemed to focus on Peyton for a moment and gargled in frustration and fury when Peyton could not understand what she was saying. Nora visited once, with Frazier, and her grandmother became violent, trying to rip out her tubes—trying, it seemed, to get at Nora. That night she had another small stroke, and after that she was gone from them, only her elegant slight body remaining.

Peyton did not visit anymore after that, nor did Nora. Only Frazier went, night after night, to hold his mother's hands and say words to her that would never be answered, perhaps not even heard. When he came home from these visits he usually spent an hour or so in his office before he came in to watch television with them.

After her last visit to her grandmother, Peyton wrote in her diary, *I hate her and I love her too; I love the way she was. Why does everything have to change? Why do people have to be wrecked like that? Who will there be in my life like her now?*

In her heart she knew the answer to that, but she could not bear the weight of it, and buried it deep.

12

All through the early days of that spring, Nora incised herself deeply and vividly into the small life of Lytton. It was as if, now content that she had safe harbor in the house on Green Street, she felt emboldened to flash out into the town and the school like a comet, trailing delight and outrage in equal parts in her wake. Everyone had an opinion about Nora Findlay. Almost everyone expressed it at the drop of a hat.

Peyton came to think of the two factions as the Aunt Augusta Camp and the School Camp. Aunt Augusta's tongue, and the tongues of her cronies, chronicled Nora's excesses like a Greek chorus. The talk that careened around Lytton Grammar and High Schools was more in the nature of legend: Miss Findlay was teaching from a book where people did it in the farmyard and said "fuck," "shit," and "piss"; Miss Findlay had them writing essays on their own sexual feelings and never once laughed at any of them; Miss Findlay brought in a small set of drums to class and showed them, graphically and energetically, how to honor and invite the pagan saints of *santería* with dance and percussion.

"They're called *bataa*," she said, flushed and perspiring, pointing to the drums. "They're ritual drums. There are thousands of different rituals you can offer, to any number of saints. The one I just danced was to Chango. The *bataa* is central to modern percussion. There's literally no jazz music in the world that doesn't exist in the *bataa*. Now, does anybody want to try it with me?"

At the end of the class every teenager, black and white alike, was whirling and stamping to the *bataa* drums, inviting who knew what pagan entities into their lives. They loved it. In tacit agreement, none told parents or teachers. Even the dimmest among them knew that that would spell the end of their days with Miss Findlay. None wanted that. In that small arena of indolently virulent small talk and languid torpor, Nora was life. Even the cheerleader-goddesses came into her orbit. Nora agreed to be their sponsor and adviser in exchange for what she called minimally decent human behavior, and spelled out her rules in no uncertain terms. The girls rolled their eyes and tossed their lacquered flips, but they agreed. There wasn't anyone in their lives as interesting as Nora Findlay, and besides, she let them smoke behind the gymnasium.

As if by prior agreement, the late afternoons after the Losers Club became Nora and Peyton's special time together. Much of it was spent up in Nora's room, Nora with her long length curled on her bed, smoking, Peyton in the red canvas butterfly chair her cousin had brought with her, a hectic anomaly in that dim room of polished mahogany and white chenille. Trailways would desert Peyton temporarily to curl into the curve of Nora's waist or legs and knead with his sharp claws and purr his rusty, room-shaking purr. He had become a lank, spidery adolescent with the hind legs of a jackrabbit and the long body of a dachshund and an owl-eyed face that looked, Nora said, laughing, like Pete Seeger's.

"Who's that?" said Peyton.

"Find out for yourself," said Nora.

They talked; they talked endlessly, but almost never about themselves. It was too soon for that. They talked about books, they talked about music, they talked about movies, they talked about clothes and food and sometimes sex. Or rather, Nora talked. Peyton had no sense of being instructed, but she knew in some way that Nora was tutoring her. She blushed often, and she fidgeted, but soon she was laughing a little and began, once in a while, to venture an opinion about whatever it was they were talking about.

"Why do you listen to me?" she asked Nora once in a moment of small epiphany. "I don't know anything about anything yet."

"You will." Nora smiled.

Sometimes, in the warming nights, they did things: they went, the three of them, to a movie in Atlanta occasionally, or a symphony at the Municipal Auditorium, and once to a play put on by an Atlanta company at the Women's Club Auditorium. The play was *Our Town;* Nora said it was sentimental claptrap and overdone to death, but she wept along with Peyton when the dead of Grover's Corners reached out, in vain, to the living. They went to a couple of Georgia Tech baseball games, and sometimes to the antiquated movies at the Lytton movie house, and once to a square dance at the Lytton VFW hut. Frazier laughingly refused to dance, and Peyton would not have done so if someone had held a gun to her head, but Nora danced every set and with every man in Lytton who asked her, whirling and stamping and dosi-doing with her head thrown back and her copper hair streaming, her eyes closed in joy. Peyton heard about that first thing the next morning, from Chloe.

"Doreen heard that Miss Augusta say she gon' speak to Mr. Frazier about Nora being a bad influence. I ain't studying that, but maybe you ought to warn your papa. Nora, too, for that matter."

"My God, what would she say if it had been the Panama City Dirty Bop?" Nora said, laughing, when Peyton told her.

"Augusta doesn't have enough to do," her father said when she told him.

Once, on a tender mothy night heavy with the smell of wisteria and an afternoon rain, Nora woke Peyton in the middle of the night and they took the Thunderbird, top down, out into the country to a small lake that fed into the Lytton reservoir. It was still and pure silver in the misty light of a lopsided white moon, so silent that they could hear the plop of frogs entering the water. As if in a dream, Peyton followed Nora as she took off her capri pants and T-shirt and they slipped naked into the blood-warm water and swam under the moon until a little wind came up and the water turned chilly. Neither of them ever mentioned it, not even to each other, but it lay between them like a chalice.

But mostly Nora seemed to want simply to be in the house on Green Street. Sometimes, after dinner, instead of watching television, she would read to them out of whatever esoteric book she was reading, and once in a while she made martinis before dinner and she and Frazier had one. Peyton ate the olives.

Peyton knew via the grammar school jungle drums that almost none of the female teachers at Lytton High liked Nora, and that most of the male ones did, and that almost every unmarried male teacher had asked her out. But she never talked about it, and she never went out on a date.

"You should get out some," Frazier said. "It's just not right for you to sit in this old house all the time when you should be out getting to know people, meeting people your own age."

"Maybe later," Nora said. "Right now I'd rather just be here with you all. You have no idea how tired of flitting around I am."

"Didn't you date in Florida and Cuba?" Peyton asked her in one of their late-night talk sessions on Nora's bed, where Nora sometimes let her have a drag of a Salem. In her head, Peyton had invented a lavish, exotic life for Nora back in those fabled cities she had left. Men were a large part of it—handsome, mysterious men unlike any she knew in Lytton. There must have been men. Nora gave off a musk of unconscious sensuality that even Peyton could smell and feel.

"She's had hundreds of affairs," Peyton told the Losers Club. "She had lovers in every city, but eventually she got bored with them and left. I think she still gets letters from some of them."

"Tell about that," Boot said, enchanted, but Ernie only sniffed.

"If she had all those lovers it seems to me one of them might have finally married her," he said.

"She doesn't want to be tied down," Peyton said. "She told me that."

Nora had done no such thing, but Peyton thought it was entirely true. She did not consider that she had told the Losers Club her first lie.

Nora would not talk about Cuba or Miami or Key West, at least not about the men she had known there, except to say that of course she had had dates, but for right now no one was as interesting or fun as the people in this funny old house. Peyton could not imagine why anyone would think her or her father interesting, but she was warmed as she could not remember being in her life. She mattered, at last, to someone who did not have to love her; her father, at last, was young and funny. She was afraid to look at this happiness full square, but she would glance at it obliquely, from the corner of her eye. She waited for it to vanish, but each time she looked, it was still there, shimmering like a mirage.

"You know, Chloe," Nora said one morning, "I promised you and Doreen that I'd tutor her in the afternoons so she can get her high school equivalency certificate. Would you tell her that now would be a good time for us to start?"

Chloe looked down at the sinkful of tomato peels.

"Doreen ain't around afternoons no more," she said. "She got a job up in Hapeville at the McDonald's. They likes her a lot. Look like she be able to be an assistant manager in a year or two. Might be one day she could manage."

Nora stared at her.

"Chloe, she doesn't need to sling hamburgers all her life!" she said. "No telling where she might go if she gets that certificate. Why on earth did she leave Mrs. McKenzie's? I know she's awful, but at least Doreen had enough free time to study."

Chloe was silent, and then she said, "She ain't leave. Miss Augusta fired her. Didn't even give her no notice."

"Why?" Nora cried. "Who on earth wouldn't want Doreen working for them?"

"She come home from church early and found Doreen sittin' in the bathtub," Chloe said without looking at Peyton or Nora. "She like to

bust a gut. She tell Doreen to put on her clothes and get out and not
come back. She didn't even give her time to dry off. Doreen come
home with her clothes all wet."

"Oh, *Chloe*," Nora said, stricken.

"Thing is, Doreen ain't never had no bathtub," Chloe said. "We
always washed in washtubs. I guess she just wanted to see how it felt
to sit down in that hot water. It ain't like Miss Augusta was going to
catch anything from her. Doreen is a clean girl. You can get mighty
clean in a washtub."

Peyton watched Nora's face in silence. It was blanched white, and
there was a pinched look at the base of her nostrils. She had a hectic
spot of red high on each cheekbone. She went out of the room silently
and did not open her bedroom door that afternoon to Peyton and
Trailways. Peyton, lingering outside the door, could hear music from
Nora's radio, but nothing else. She went back to her own room and
picked up *Women in Love* where she had abandoned it the night
before. She could read only a few pages before the scandalized blood
suffused her face and chest again, and she put the book aside. But she
was making headway.

That evening Peyton heard her father's car door slam out front,
and at almost the same instant heard Nora's bedroom door slam and
her running steps on the stairs. She went to her own bedroom door,
holding the writhing Trailways, and opened it an inch or so, but she
did not go out into the living room. She did not want the volcano
smoldering just under Nora's surface to erupt onto her. Peyton knew
fury when she saw it.

She heard it, though.

"Do you know what that woman has done?" she heard Nora
shouting.

"What woman? What's the matter?" her father said. His voice was
alarmed.

"Your sister-in-law! The famous Augusta McKenzie of Lytton,
Georgia, social and moral arbiter to a generation, great soldier in the
fight for freedom and equality, font of compassion for the frail and
lowly—"

"Sit down," Frazier McKenzie said. "Tell me."

"I hate her, Frazier," Peyton heard her cousin say. Her voice was trembling. "She is the worst, most evil woman I have ever known; she should be stopped from doing the things she does."

"Nora, what has she *done?*"

"She fired Doreen because she found her in her bathtub," Nora said. "She thought Doreen had contaminated it."

And she burst into tears.

There was a brief silence, and then Nora continued, her voice strangled with sobs. "You know, we said I was going to tutor Doreen in the afternoons so she could get her reading up to par and take the high school equivalency test. You were there that day at lunch. So this morning I told Chloe I'd like to start and she told me that Doreen had been fired and was working at the McDonald's up in Hapeville. Frazier, maybe in twenty years she'll get to manage a McDonald's, or maybe they'll fire her, too, for using the white bathroom or something. What future can she possibly have now? Oh, I *hate* Augusta, I hate that horrible woman. . . ."

There was a silence in which only Nora's muffled sobs resounded. Peyton opened her door a few more inches and peered out. Nora sat on the sofa with her face in her hands. Her shoulders were shaking. Her father sat beside her, patting her awkwardly on the back. His face looked as drawn and weary as Peyton had ever seen it.

"Nora," he said presently. "You need to understand about Augusta. I don't mean to excuse her; what she did was a terrible, ugly thing. A lot of what she does and says is . . . not good. It ranges from simply ridiculous to downright unacceptable. But we do accept it, our family, because we know what she came out of, and we know how hard she's worked building a life for herself."

"What life?" Nora cried. "It's certainly no life for Charlie! It's certainly no life for Peyton. What life are you talking about?"

"She was born in a mill-village shack," Peyton's father said slowly. "You must know what that's like if you've seen the factory and cane towns in rural Cuba. It was worse, in a way, than most of our Negro neighborhoods because the folks who live there have strong family

ties and often white families who care for them. But they didn't have
that in Augusta's little settlement. Everybody was too intent on dig-
ging his own way out to put out a hand to a neighbor. A lot of them
just gave up. Augusta's parents were like that. When Charlie met her,
her father was dying of white lung and still smoking like a chimney,
lying on an old sofa they had dragged out on the front porch, watching the cars go by on the way to Atlanta. Her mother was drunk most
of the time; I think she stayed in bed until late afternoon. There was
an older brother who had long since left and gotten into trouble in
the North somewhere and was in jail, I think. And there was a
younger sister, about eleven, who just stayed out of school and did
whatever she pleased all day. I heard somewhere that she was going
with men even then. Augusta was the pretty one, and the smart one,
and she really is both of those things. She worked at the perfume
counter at Rich's in Atlanta, and she did very well because she was so
pretty and so smart; she taught herself how to act like a lady and
dress like one on the measly little salary she made. It can't have been
much, and she had to pay a lot of the family's rent and grocery bills
every month, and keep her little sister in clothes, because both the
parents were on disability.

"So one day Charlie went into Rich's to buy Mother some perfume
for Christmas, and he took one look at her, and that was that. She
sold herself right along with the perfume. They were married not
three months later. They went to Atlanta to a justice of the peace's
office and then left that night on a honeymoon to Miami. She came
back every inch a Lytton lady and hell-bent on staying one. None of
us could blame her. I guess she thought she was marrying way up
with Charlie, but I think if she'd known him a little longer she'd have
realized that what she saw in Charlie was what she was going to get.
He never went any further than that in his life, and he's not going to
now. I love Charlie; he's my brother and he's a sweet man. But I
know, and he knows himself, that he's no Prince Charming, no res-
cuer of maidens. Augusta never got over that. She'd seen herself as
totally safe and secure, the most socially sought-after woman in this
part of the county, the absolute oracle of manners and propriety and

elegance and whatever. But I guess she's known for a long time now that she's only as safe as Charlie's last paycheck, and the only people she can lord it over are her servants and sometimes my daughter. She hardly speaks to Charlie anymore, and I think she's forgotten that he gave her two things she'd never have had without him: a ticket out of the mill village and his love. He really loves her. Always has. Don't think he doesn't know how disappointed in him she is.

"Anyway, it's made her mean. We all know that. Most of us have learned just to overlook the silliest of her pranks and dodge the really hurtful ones. I sometimes think she really does care about Peyton and me, but I can't think why. . . ."

"Oh, God, Frazier!" Nora said. "If you can't think why, then you're more oblivious than I thought. It's just so obvious that she's got an awful crush on you, and she's trying to get at you through Peyton."

"Oh, I don't think so," Frazier said doubtfully. "But you're right about this thing with Doreen. I don't think we can let that go. I'll try to talk to her about it. Maybe she'll take Doreen back. If she won't, maybe I can find her something closer to home that will give her time to study, and maybe we can help her out a little financially. . . ."

"Frazier McKenzie," Nora said, tears in her voice again. "You are maybe the best man I've ever known."

"Then God help you," Frazier said. Peyton could hear the smile in his voice. "Will you at least try to think a little better of Augusta now?"

"No," Nora said. "She's a bitch, and I hate her. But I'll lay off her unless she does something else this bad, which she'll probably manage to do tomorrow."

Peyton went into the bathroom and washed her face for dinner. She felt lighter than air. She knew that whatever bonds kept her tethered to earth, they were never again going to be of Aunt Augusta's making.

As if she felt the house to be a rock-solid island of safety, Nora began to venture out from it into the town in a way that she had not before. Many of her forays were solo, as if she needed to test new-fledged wings, but Peyton went with her on others. She announced, one sweltering late-April day, that there were two things in the South that nobody thought you could do anything about, and they were the heat and segregation, and she intended to do something about both. She borrowed Frazier's big car and drove alone to Atlanta and came back with four window air-conditioning units in the trunk and backseat.

"I will drip sweat at school and I'll drip sweat watching television, but I will *not* drip sweat when I'm trying to sleep," she said. "Chloe's next-door neighbor Carlyle is going to come and put them in. Whoever doesn't like them can just lug them back to Atlanta."

"There's never been an air conditioner in this house," Frazier said. "I remember my father's saying that if you had thick walls and high ceilings and an attic fan and big trees for shade, you'd never need air-conditioning. I never thought the heat was too bad."

"Well, you don't have to turn yours on," Nora said. "But it's going up there. Nobody in this house is going to sleep in a puddle of sweat anymore. And Chloe isn't going to cook in one, either."

Carlyle did come in and lug the bulky units up the stairs and into the kitchen and Peyton's room, and presently he plugged in the last plug and turned them on, one after another, for a trial run. The units roared into rattling life, sending years-old dust flying from heavy curtains and driving Trailways under the bed, tail stiff, ears skinned back like a stoat's. Cool air poured into the rooms almost instantly.

Peyton stood in front of hers when she changed for dinner, letting the cold wind dry the sweat from her body. It smelled dank and stale, but it felt wonderful.

I think I've been hot half my life and never knew it, she thought.

"I ain't gon' use that thing," Clothilde declared. "It sound like a bus coming through the window."

But when Peyton went in for supper, the room was roaring with cool air and Chloe was spreading meringue on a lemon pie.

"First time I been able to make one of these in the heat without the meringue gettin' soggy and sad," she said. "Maybe this thing ain't so bad."

There was no question but that Nora loved hers: whenever she was in her room the roar of the air conditioner poured down the stairs to the first floor. Peyton grew used to the sound; it made their after-noons and evenings together feel like they were being spent in a hidden cave of sound. It was a nice feeling. Trailways came to love it and often lay atop the unit, his purrs drowned out by the bellowing motor. Peyton slept deeply under her old afghan, in a cave of humming cool, and did not dream.

Only her father did not use his. He said nothing, but they knew he did not. They would have heard. And then, on a night of vicious wet heat preceding a thunderstorm, Peyton, lying in her own cocoon, heard the unit in his room go on and felt its vibrations. She smiled as she fell asleep. It was as if he had capitulated in some obscure but important contest.

That Sunday Nora went to services at Saint John's African Methodist Episcopal Church, and took Peyton with her. Peyton had gone once or twice when she was very small, with Chloe, but instead of seeming merely comical and very loud, the service this time was very nearly magical. It was stifling in the old church, and dim, and funeral-home fans waved in unison, and the choir soared from low, primal moaning to exuberant shouting and clapping and rocking, carrying the congregation with it. Soon the entire church, Nora and Peyton included, was rocking in time to the rich, dark music, and clapping, and even shouting out, "Yeah, Lord!" and "Tell me, Jesus!" The sound and motion engulfed Peyton and swept her away to a place inside her that was wild and free and entirely unsuspected, so that coming back from it seemed deflating, banal. No one seemed to mind the two white faces starring their midst; indeed, everyone, including the preacher, smiled and nodded and asked them to come again.

When they finally drifted out into the sun, Peyton felt a small cringe of shame that she had behaved with such abandon, but under it was a kind of fierce joy. For a few minutes she had been a part of something old, earthen, out of time, and it had borne her up like wings.

"We just don't know anything, us whites," Nora said, smiling down at her. "There's more God in one note of one song in that church than you'll find all year in Lytton First Methodist. The only reason I'm not going to join this church is that it would make your Aunt Augusta so happy."

And indeed, Augusta McKenzie went into a vehement and public snit over the visit and vented her indignation upon her brother-in-law the next morning before he had even finished his breakfast.

"The whole town is talking, Frazier," she said. "Is that what you want? Is that what you want for your daughter?"

Frazier did not answer her.

"Have a cheese biscuit, Augusta," he said pleasantly. "Chloe's trying them out on us."

Aunt Augusta left, speechless and biscuitless. The next Sunday Frazier went with them to the Negro church. Peyton was amazed by the number of dark faces that lit up with real pleasure at the sight of him.

"I've done a little work for most of them," he said by way of reply when Peyton remarked on it.

"All of it pro bono," Nora said, smiling at him. "Am I right?"

The talk around the town ceased for the nonce.

It soon swelled again, though, inevitably, and spilled through the town into the house on Green Street. Peyton heard some of it from Chloe, but most she got from Ernie when she went to the Losers Club. She had not been going so often and felt guilty and somehow resentful on the days when she did. She was tired of having to make excuses to Ernie. She was aware, as she knew he was, that in those days she was lying regularly to the club when she said that Nora was tutoring her after school. It seemed that he reported on Nora's public antics with far more venom and less delectation than usual. It occurred to her that he was punishing her with the stories. No one except Boot took any joy of them.

"You know, of course," Ernie said one afternoon to Peyton, finishing his powdery iced tea, "that that Cro-Magnon Freddy Farmer told his fascinated little cronies at lunchtime at the high school that you were getting tits that looked like flea bites, and when everybody laughed, your dear cousin leaned over and blew smoke in his face and said that it was a real pity that his brain was as tiny as his dick. That might have been funny once. But not in front of an entire high school. At least not to me."

Other stories followed. Nora championed the Kennedys in the bastion of conservatism that was the Lytton High School faculty lounge, saying that grace and style and compassion were obviously apparent only to those who possessed some of those traits themselves. When one outraged maiden lady squalled that everybody knew Jackie was nothing more than a whore, Nora smiled ferally at her and said, "We'd all love to know where you got your intimate knowledge of whores, Eula."

Instead of sitting with Peyton and Frazier, Nora sat one morning at the First Methodist Church in the vacant pew beside the pregnant, unmarried teenaged daughter of a local building contractor. No one else, her father and mother included, would sit beside her. Peyton could hear the hushed swell of offense and scandal rising all around her, and she kept her eyes fixed on the back of the two heads, one red, one blond frizz, bent close together over the hymnal.

"They might as well have hung a scarlet *A* around her neck," Nora said grimly at lunch that day. "Or maybe they could stone her. I remember saying that I thought Lytton was a magical little town. Maybe it still is. Maybe it's just the people who are small and squinched-up."

This time it was Augusta McKenzie herself who breasted Nora as she dashed into the library one afternoon. Augusta was there with her reading circle; they all waited with beaks drawn and eyes glittering.

"Nora, dear, this is not a thing we feel we can let pass," Aunt Augusta said sweetly. "You're a newcomer, so perhaps you don't know, but in Lytton we don't publicly endorse young women in the state that Marsha is in. We do not condemn her, of course, but we cannot reward her behavior, either."

The reading club smiled, waiting for blood to flow.

"Why, Augusta," Nora said, widening her eyes. "Don't y'all do that here? I thought you did. There are so many of you."

"My mama used to be a member of that circle," Ernie said when he had done telling Peyton about it. "They may be terribly naive and proper, those ladies, but deliberately trying to shock them just doesn't wash."

"When you get so prissy?" Boot said. He had taken a job bagging groceries at the A&P two days a week and on Saturday mornings, and he was not at the club so often anymore. Peyton felt his loss keenly. The club felt awkward and pathetic without him, like a three-legged dog.

"I'm not prissy," Ernie said. "I just don't like outsiders coming in here and making fun of our town."

"You make fun of it all the time," Boot said.

"It's not the same thing," Ernie said.

The last story about her cousin that Ernie told her was the one that broke the spine of the Losers Club. Boot was not there; there was a chilly wind where he was not. Ernie told the story with loving satisfaction and corrosive venom, laying the details out with relish.

"Have you met Mr. Lloyd Huey, who lives next door to your Aunt Augusta and Uncle Charles?" he asked, and when Peyton said that of course she knew him, Ernie continued.

"Well, then, you know he owns the sawmill and has a bunch of Negroes working for him. He also has an enormous fallout shelter in his backyard. I have to admit, the shelter *is* funny. But somehow Nora got the notion that he was mistreating his help, and she told him in the drugstore that if he didn't shape up she was going to tell everybody in town that he had asked her down to see the famous shelter and then tried to seduce her. It's the kind of talk that could ruin a man in a little town like this."

"How could it ruin Mr. Huey?" Peyton said, honestly curious. "He's got five children and only one leg and he's in a wheelchair all the time."

"Well, I guess Nora thinks that any man with breath in his body would try to seduce her, and she may be right. God knows, enough of them have."

"I'm going home," Peyton said, sudden anger shaking her. "You've turned the club into a witch-hunt against Nora. That's not fair, and it's not fun any longer."

"The truth is often not much fun," Ernie said unctuously, and he picked up his paperback. It was *Absalom, Absalom.*

Peyton slammed out of the shed and stamped home. A feeling of heaviness and loss hung over her that had nothing to do with the story he had told her about Nora. Great change was waiting for her, hovering near. The shadow of its wing had already claimed Boot and fallen over Ernie.

When she got home her father and her Uncle Charlie were coming out of the living room. Peyton gaped. She could count on the fingers of both hands the times Uncle Charlie had ever visited without Aunt Augusta. He saw a good deal of his older brother, but it was usually in Frazier's office or in his own garage lair. Charles McKenzie was dressed in a stiff sports coat and slacks, looking, as Clothilde would put it, like a mule dressed up in a buggy harness, and his face was miserable. Behind him, her father's face was set. Peyton murmured hello to both of them and slid into her room like a salamander going to earth. On this day of strangeness and endings, nothing good was going to come of this visit. She knew it.

She peered through the almost-closed door of her room at her father, thinking that she was getting quite good at spying on people and not caring. He sat down in his accustomed chair and stared straight ahead. He did not open his newspaper or turn on the television set. This was as strange to Peyton as the fact of his being in the living room at all before dinner, when daylight still filtered through the drawn blinds. This room was his nighttime place. It was their nighttime place, the three of them.

She was about to close her door and curl up with Trailways, to try and lose the uneasiness in D. H. Lawrence and warm cat fur, when she heard Nora's light step on the porch, and the screened door creaking open and shut again.

"Well, what on earth are you doing in here in the daylight?" Peyton heard her say. There was a silence, and then Frazier said, "Come in and sit down, Nora. We need to talk a little."

Peyton froze at her spying post. Whatever great trouble this meeting portended, she needed to know about it. She did not feel that she could bear an ambush.

Nora sat with her back to Peyton. Her father faced her. At the last minute Peyton moved back from her door so that she could hear but not see. Somehow she could handle an assault on one sense but not on two.

"Charles was here," her father said. "He was pretty upset. I've never known him to tell tales on anyone, but he felt like he had to tell me about this. And he was right to do it. Nora, Lloyd Huey came over to see him this afternoon and told him what you said to him in the drugstore. Lloyd was mad and he was hurt. He thought Charlie would be the right one to tell me about it, and then he wanted me to speak to you."

There was a silence. Peyton could imagine them sitting there, her father leaning forward with his hands clasped and resting on his knees, Nora slumping in the other chair and lighting a cigarette.

"This is pretty serious, Nora," her father said. "I don't think we can let it lie. I don't think we can let it go as one more of your . . . escapades. The others have been on the side of the angels, even if they stirred up hornets' nests all over town. A certain amount of that is good for Lytton. But this goes way beyond high jinks. This can really hurt Lloyd, and I think it probably already has. The whole drugstore heard it, and you can bet it was all over town by the end of the day."

There was another silence. Then her father went on: "Nora, Lloyd is a silly man sometimes, and a loudmouth, and insensitive, to say the least. And I think he probably is tough on his help over at the mill. But I seriously doubt if he mistreats Negroes. He may yell at them, but he yells at everybody. We all know that; we let it go because it's a tough life he's living and because his mill has provided jobs for a whole lot of people, Negroes mostly, who wouldn't have them otherwise. That kind of talk can hurt him in the town. Whether or not people believe it in the beginning, they'll talk. Lloyd's a proud man. Charlie said he had tears in his eyes when he came over."

"Oh, Frazier," Nora whispered, and Peyton heard the tears in her voice. "I really did hear that he abused his Negro workers physically, and withheld their pay when they displeased him, and other things. You know we can't let that go by—"

"What is this 'we,' Nora?" Frazier McKenzie said, and Peyton heard the ice in his voice. She knew it would be in his eyes, too, opaque gray lake ice. She had not seen it often, but the times when she had, she had felt frozen to her very core.

"I can't imagine you would sanction that sort of thing," Nora said. Her voice seemed to be losing breath and force with every word.

"I wouldn't sanction that sort of thing if it were true, but it can't possibly be," her father said. "I've known Lloyd since we were kids. He's all bluster and no action. If he was seriously abusing his Negro help it would have gotten out way before now. The Negroes have a better grapevine even than Augusta. I'm not going to ask you where you heard it because I don't want to know. But the fact is that you've jumped to a bad conclusion, and you've taken way too much on yourself. You cannot just come into this town and set yourself up as an avenging angel. It hurts people, and it will hurt you."

"So what do you want me to do?" Nora whispered.

"I want you to go over and apologize to Lloyd," her father said, "and I want you just to stop with the . . . eccentricities. Just give it all a rest for a while. Even if I agree with you, and sometimes I do, I just don't have the energy to go on cleaning up after you."

Nora gave a small gasp of hurt and leapt out of her chair and ran up the stairs. Peyton heard the door to her room close and the air conditioner go on. But before that, she heard the ragged catch of a sob. She turned on her own air conditioner and crawled under her afghan with Trailways and lay there until suppertime. Nora did not come down, and her father did not speak. They ate in silence, and he went out to his office over the garage, and Peyton went back to bed and cried. She could not bear the trouble humming in the air.

For a couple of days Nora avoided all of them, eating her meals standing up at the refrigerator at odd times of the day and night, leaving for school early in the morning, and staying away somewhere until very late. The Thunderbird was not often at the curb. Peyton's father ate his meals silently, the newspaper unfolded before him, and went early to and stayed late in his office. Chloe did not sing, or linger to talk, or make special desserts. It was as if a choking black-dust plague had fallen on the house. Peyton went back to showing herself her movies at night.

On the fourth day Peyton heard her cousin's steps clicking rapidly up the walk and into and through the house to the back door. She pulled aside her curtain and looked. Nora, windblown and scarlet-cheeked, ran up the steps to her father's office and rapped smartly on the door. When she saw the door open, Peyton dropped the curtain and burrowed under her afghan again. This was nothing to spy on.

Nora and her father did not come down for a long time. Peyton was foraging hungrily in the kitchen when they did, lifting the lids of the pots Clothilde had left on the stove, rummaging in the pantry for cold biscuits. Nora was red-nosed and pouchy about the eyes, but the vivid life was back. Coming into the kitchen, she crackled with it. Peyton looked sidewise at her father. His face was still grave and level, as it almost always was, but the ice had gone from his eyes, and the crinkles at their corners looked freshly incised, as if he had been smiling. Peyton's heart, for days bound and shut down in her chest, now broke free and soared. All right, it was going to be all right. . . .

"What are you doing in here munching like a goat?" Nora said teasingly. The rich music was back in her voice. "The least you could have done was heat up supper and set the table."

"I don't know where all that stuff is," Peyton said, pretending it was ordinary talk on an ordinary day. "I don't know how to work the stove."

"That's absurd," Nora said. "I could cook when I was ten years old. Knowing how to cook well is a very sexy thing. This coming Saturday you're going to start learning."

She set the green beans and new potatoes to warm and wrapped the chicken in foil and put it in the oven. Then she made martinis. Peyton heard them laughing desultorily at something when she went in to change for dinner. She snatched up Trailways and danced him around her room and squeezed him until he growled. Then she went into the living room to warm herself in deliverance and eat olives. She would never know what had passed between Nora and her father in his office that evening, nor whether Nora finally apologized to Mr. Lloyd Huey. Whatever it was, it sufficed.

Two nights later her father came home early from the courthouse in Atlanta. She heard Nora's steps come down to meet him, and something low being said between them, and her father's laugh, and then Nora called, "Peyton! Get out here! Your days of innocence are over!"

Peyton went cautiously into the living room. Nora had been almost manic since the trouble had passed; a shimmering like heat lightning was on her. It made Peyton want to hug her and pull away from her at the same time. Nora could burn you as easily as she could warm you, she thought.

Nora had brought her portable phonograph downstairs. She stood in the middle of the room, grinning. Her fresh-washed hair almost gave off sparks. Peyton's father sat in his chair, smiling faintly at her.

"We are about to learn the twist," Nora said. "There is no hanging back and no salvation from it. By suppertime I want to see those hips wiggling like there's no tomorrow."

She put a record on the machine and started it.

"Come on, baby," Chubby Checker growled. "Let's do the twist. . . ."

In the middle of the room, Nora planted her feet and threw back her head and held her hands out as if in a gesture of submission or supplication. Her hips began to gyrate in a circle, but her feet remained planted. She seemed to swell with the music, until her whole body was bobbling on the surface of the insistent beat. She wore blue jeans and a T-shirt, but she might have been naked. Peyton felt her face burn, but something in her own hips and pelvis responded to the tug of the music, too. She smiled, hesitantly.

"Come on," Nora said. "Both of you, get out here. No, Frazier, you aren't going to chicken out of this. I've always thought you could dance like a demon if you wanted to. Keep your feet still—that's right—and just move your hips in a kind of circle, in time to the music, and let your legs take you down and up again. Come on, Peyton."

The music and motion took Peyton and flung her far away, and when she came back she was doing the twist as if she had known how all her life. Her hips seemed to move themselves, knowing this old rhythm. She laughed aloud and looked over at her father. He danced easily and fluidly opposite Nora, his slim hips barely moving, like a good, quiet motor. His dark hair hung over his eyes, and he was laughing.

The record ended, and Nora put it on again. By the time it had played itself out two or three times they were flushed and sweating and moving as loosely as if their joints had been oiled. They might have all been the same age, or no age at all. They had just sagged, laughing, into chairs and the sofa when Chloe came into the room. She stood in the doorway, not speaking. They stopped laughing and looked at her. Her face was ashen under its deep ochre. There were tears in her eyes.

"I don't reckon y'all heard the phone," she said. "Miss Agnes done passed."

Late that night Peyton heard her father come into the living room. He had been to the nursing home and then to the funeral home, making the old, immutable arrangements that one made before consigning a life into the earth. His step was slow and heavy. Peyton did not get out of bed. The abrupt draining of the exhilaration of the afternoon and the cold nothingness of her grandmother's death had tired her beyond rising. She turned into her pillow and hugged Trailways close and closed her eyes once more. Even when she heard Nora come rapidly down the steps from her room, she did not get up. Let them deal with it, this heavy blankness that was death.

Then she heard the sound of sobbing, dry and rough, as though the weeper did not know how to do it, and she did get up then and go to her door.

Her father sat slumped on the sofa. Nora knelt beside him, her arms around him, his face pressed into her shoulder. She was rocking him slightly, back and forth, and her face was pressed into his dark hair. Her eyes were closed, and there were tears on her face, but they were silent ones. Peyton knew that it was her father who sobbed.

She averted her eyes as if she had seen something obscene and, trembling all over, got the long-unworn amulet her grandmother had given her from her jewelry box and dropped it over her head. She felt its cool weight and looked down. She could see it on her chest now, and she never had before. I'm getting breasts, she thought, and my grandmother is dead and my father is crying.

She slept heavily and long and got up aching as if she had been beaten. Neither her father nor Nora was about, and Chloe was silent in the kitchen as she put toast and eggs on the table.

"They gone to pick out a casket," she said, in answer to Peyton's unasked question. "You go on to school, now. There ain't nothing you can do till later."

After school Peyton went as straight and swiftly as an arrow to the Losers Club. She longed with every atom of her being to be in a place where no strangeness was. When she got there, the door was padlocked. She went around to the window and stood on a vine-choked cement block that lay under it. The chairs were gone, and the space heater, and the shelf that had held their small refreshments and Ernie's library. Only the potbellied stove remained, black and empty.

Peyton walked home sobbing aloud. She seemed to hang in midair. Nothing was solid under her hands and feet. Around her, empty space whistled and hummed.

Why is it, she wrote in her diary that night, *that if you have one thing you can't have another?*

13

After that, Peyton became obsessed with her Cousin Nora. She dogged her steps in the daytime, leaned close to her when they watched television at night. When they had their sessions in Nora's room, Peyton steered the talk from books and movies and the casual flotsam of their days to Nora and her life. She was insatiable when it came to the particulars of Nora. Nora's past from childhood on was fair game for this hungry new Peyton, and her questions were endless. Nora bore them with good humor. This time, for the most part, she answered them.

"Tell about that time after your senior prom when you rode home on the fire truck," Peyton would say.

"You've heard it a hundred times," Nora would reply, smiling at her from the big bed where she and Trailways were ensconced. It was the end of April now, and the scent of the mimosa tree outside the window poured into the room like a spring creek. You could get drunk on it, Peyton thought. Maybe I am.

"Tell me again about the man in Miami," Peyton would say. "The one you went to the Yucatán with. Tell about the Yucatán."

"I'm tired of him," Nora said. "I was tired of him before we left the Yucatán. What you know of him already is all there is to know."

"Then tell me something new."

And Nora would cast about in her memory and fish out another bit of exotica for Peyton's relish. Her life and affairs were not really exotic; on some level Peyton knew that. On that level she knew that many women had the same sorts of experiences Nora had had, even if they did not have them in Lytton. On that level Peyton knew that her own world had expanded far outside Lytton, even if she had not actually seen that world.

But everything Nora did and said and thought seemed, in these days, to be touched with mystery and glamour, and Peyton could not get enough of them.

She began listening regularly behind the closed living-room door when Nora and her father sat watching television later than she stayed up, or listened to music, or simply talked. The talk was the grail: Peyton waited for some scrap of significance, some portentous word or sentence, something that would illuminate her cousin to her further, or show her her own place in Nora's firmament. It was a small firmament; it seemed that only she and her father and perhaps Clothilde shone in it. But still, Peyton had to know where her piece of sky was.

One night she heard it, or a piece of it, and it left her sweating and cold. Her father and Nora were talking when she got to the door, and it was obvious they were talking about her. Her face burned, but she did not leave her post.

". . . can't let her just monopolize you," her father was saying. "I've said it before. It seems that you're never without her nowadays."

"I don't mind," Nora said, and there was a smile in her voice. "She's good company. She's better company than anybody I know except you."

Peyton's chest swelled.

"I think it started after her grandmother died," Frazier said. "And it seems to me she doesn't go to that club thing of hers anymore. It could be that with both of them gone, you're the only sure thing she has in her life right now. I only hope it doesn't get burdensome. She has to move out into the world sometime."

There was a long silence. Peyton stood as still as death.

Then Nora said, "Frazier, I can't be the only thing in her life. I can't hold her up; I can't. It isn't good for her, and I can't . . . I can't stand the weight of it. I'm the wrong person for that."

"I think it will all change next year or so," her father said. "Meanwhile, if you need for her to back off a little, I'll put a bug in her ear."

"No," Nora said. "Let's see how it goes."

Peyton crept back to bed and curled up under her afghan with Trailways. The night air coming in her window was almost too warm, but she was cold to the bone. "I can't stand the weight of it," Nora said over and over in her ears.

"What does that mean?" Peyton said to herself, almost weeping. "I don't know what that means."

But in the following days nothing changed, and Peyton gradually relaxed into their old routine. But she did not feel quite so safe anymore, so borne up simply by the presence of Nora. It was as if she went through the days with her muscles tensed for flight.

The obsession deepened.

One Saturday on the cusp of May Nora went in the afternoon to tutor a Negro child in English.

"*Huckleberry Finn*," she said, getting into the Thunderbird. "He's having a hard time with Jim. I think it's the first time he's ever really thought about what slavery meant."

"I thought that was a children's book," Peyton said, swinging on the door of the car.

"You thought wrong," Nora said. "It's one of the great pieces of literature America has ever produced. I think adults need to read it more than kids. Most of us have forgotten how clear and simple the biggest issues are."

"What issues?"

"We'll talk about them when I get back," Nora said, ruffling Peyton's hair. "Maybe we'll make some ice cream and have a seminar on *Huckleberry Finn*."

She drove away gunning the Thunderbird, and Peyton went back into the house, scuffling her sandals in the gravel of the driveway. Her father was in his office, and Chloe had gone home. Peyton sought Trailways, but he was not in his morning place on her windowsill. She knew where he would be, though. He would be on Nora's bed, deep in the down pillow that she had brought with her from Key West, lying on his back with his big paws folded on his mottled belly. It was his afternoon place.

Peyton went up the stairs into Nora's room, knowing precisely what she was going to do and on fire with it. She closed the door behind her and opened the door to Nora's closet and looked on the top shelf. The ebony box was there, behind a warped tennis racket. It seemed to shine like a beacon in the camphory gloom of the closet. Peyton could not have said how she knew where the box was, but she had been as sure of it as of her life. She was trembling when she lifted the box from the shelf and carried it over to Nora's bed and set it down. Part of the tremor was the fear of being caught and horror at what she was doing. Part of it was an anticipation so keen that it took her breath. A mystery was in this place, and it was going to open itself to her.

As she had thought, Trailways was on his back, sunk deep into down and percale. When Peyton set the chest down he grumbled in his sleep and flicked the end of his tail but did not wake. Peyton took a deep breath and felt for the latch on the box.

She had been sure that it would be locked, and had brought a roll of thin wire from the kitchen with which to pick it open, but it was unlocked and opened as easily under her cold fingers as if it were responding to them. The smell of old paper and glue and dried flowers rose to meet her nostrils, and something else, something bitter and pungent and somehow terribly evocative, as if Peyton had smelled it often long ago. But she knew she had not.

She closed her eyes and breathed, "I'm sorry for doing this, God," and looked into the box for the core of her Cousin Nora.

Papers. Nothing but papers and envelopes, some yellowed, some newer, but none new. The papers seemed to be the ordinary documents that limn a life: birth certificate, passport, copy of a driver's license, the sale papers and title to the Thunderbird, some assorted receipts and warranties for things that Peyton knew instinctively had nothing to do with the essence of Nora. Some of the envelopes held letters, but they were disappointing: chatty notes from unknown women friends, a couple that might have been from tepid boyfriends, some very old ones that seemed to have been written to her mother. These were tied in faded ribbon. Peyton glanced at the signatures, looking for the presence of her own mother in the letters to Nora's mother, but there were none. Under the last layer of papers, a plastic bag of dried flowers; Peyton recognized roses and a desiccated orchid, and the grayish powder of crumbled herbs that she had smelled and almost recognized. Nothing else. No photographs, no treasured bits of jewelry, no curls of hair bound in ribbon. Peyton leaned back, disappointment flooding her. Where was Nora in all this? Where was the font of the mystery that was so close it was almost palpable?

She started to close the box, and then she saw that the old velvet lining was slit at its top, some of the fabric rotting away. Her fingers felt the bulk of papers. Without hesitating she reached in and pulled out a thick manila envelope.

Photographs. Here she was, then. Here was Nora. Peyton's heart thudded high in her throat. She shuffled them slowly, looking, looking. The first few were landscapes, undistinguished and rather flat, with a low jumble of industrial buildings in the background. A shot of a generic ocean, clouds massing over its horizon, scabby palm trees in the foreground. Then a square in a town, with people in motley clothes milling about a building whose architecture looked to Peyton to be vaguely "tropical." Children darting about in the dirt street, laughing. Chickens scratching in the dust; black dogs collapsed in pools of shade. Flowers hanging low from trees and vines and bursting from pots and window boxes. Even in its obvious poverty and banality, the square had a holiday air. Peyton's mouth curved up into an involuntary half smile. She thought it was a happy place.

The next photograph was the same view, but in its midst, beside a dry fountain in the middle of the square, stood the virulently pink Thunderbird. Peyton's breath caught. Here at last was the spoor of Nora.

She lifted the photograph and took out the others. They were of people, people and Nora. Nora, her red hair molten in the sun, black sunglasses on her nose, laughing with her arms around a man and an old woman. A small group of people stood behind them. Nora wore short shorts and a peasant blouse. The men wore pants and bright flowered shirts hanging out of them, the women cotton skirts and tops like Nora's. The old woman held a small child in her arms, and there were other children at the feet of the adults. All the people except Nora were black. Against them, Nora burned like a pale flame.

Peyton thought that this must be the family Nora had lived with in the small village in Cuba. They were handsome people, but their blackness was so absolute that it was startling. Peyton had always thought Cubans were white with black hair and mustaches, like Desi Arnaz, if she thought of them at all.

She picked up another photograph and saw the Thunderbird again, this time silhouetted against a beach. Here were the white sand and blue skies and turquoise water she had imagined; here was the paradisiacal backdrop she had built in her mind for Nora. There was no one in the Thunderbird. A faded inscription on the back of the photograph read *The famous Thunderbird, 1955.*

Beneath it was another photograph of the Thunderbird, only this time Nora was sitting in it, smiling at the camera, holding the small child in her arms, her cheek pressed into his hair. The child was reaching out to touch the glittering mirror on the driver's side. The sun was high; Nora's hair shone a pure, burnished red.

So did the child's.

Peyton's breath stopped in her throat. Slowly she turned the photo over.

Madonna and child was written in Nora's slashing backhand. *Me and the baby, summer 1957.*

Whose child it was had not been written there. There was no need. Peyton knew. It was so apparent that it left its stigmata in her retinas.

She closed the box and sat down on the edge of Nora's bed, trembling all over. Trailways woke and came over and poked his nose under her arm, as he did when he wanted affection. Absently, Peyton stroked him. Even as she did, her mind worked feverishly to assimilate the photograph.

Nora had a child. He was a midnight-dark Cuban child with impossible red hair. He was perhaps a year old in the photograph. Nora obviously loved him. He was just as obviously gone from her life now.

Peyton sat there for a long time. She looked at the photo, but she heard and saw nothing. Then she did: the door opening, and Nora's footsteps coming into the room and stopping. Peyton did not lift her head. She wished that she could simply die, sitting there.

She felt rather than saw Nora sit down on the edge of the bed beside her. Nora did not speak, but she reached out and took the photograph from Peyton's fingers.

"I'm sorry," Peyton whispered. Her voice was strangled. She knew she was going to cry.

Nora did not reply, and then she said, "Don't be. I would have told you sometime. I wasn't quite ready to do it now, but now's as good a time as any. The baby is my son. His name is Roberto. He adored that car. I could always stop him from crying just by putting him in it."

"Is that why it made you so mad when Boot got in your car?" Peyton said, knowing suddenly that it was.

"I wasn't mad. But yes, that's what . . . got to me. For a minute it was like seeing Roberto when he would be eight or nine."

"Like Boot?"

"Yes. Roberto is very black, as I'm sure you've noticed."

"Where is he?" Peyton said, and then wished she had bitten out her tongue before speaking. It was obvious that something had happened to the baby, or else he would be with Nora.

But no: "He's in Cuba, with his grandmother," Nora said. "If you've seen the other photographs, she's the old woman. She loves him very much. When I was about to bring him back to Miami with me, she hid him away somewhere, and she's never told me where. I get letters from her sometimes, telling me about him. I know that he's safe and happy. I probably never will know where he is, unless he finds me when he's older."

Peyton struggled to get her mind around it.

"Weren't you scared for him?" she said. "Couldn't you have called the police or something?"

Nora laughed. There was little of amusement in it. "The police probably helped hide him. The law in Cuba is very flexible. It expands to fit whatever it needs to. No, I wasn't scared for him, and I'm still not. Cubans adore children; they're little royalty. They're all that most of them have. The whole village will be Roberto's family. They'd never have let me take him away. Oh, they wouldn't have harmed me; they liked me, as far as it went. The family I lived with loved me. But I was essentially an outsider, and Roberto wasn't. He's the jewel of the family. He's set into their crown with cement. He'll have a better life in Cuba, even in that poor little village, than I could have given him here in the South. His color, you know. His color would have made him a pariah, no matter how hard I tried to protect him. I couldn't have borne that."

"Don't you miss him?"

"Like my arms and legs," Nora said. "Like my heart."

Peyton felt a pang that was different from the shock of surprise and the surge of pity for Nora. It was jealousy. She knew it absolutely, just as she knew it was unworthy of her. But it did not go away.

"Will you go back there?" she said finally.

"No," Nora said.

The silence spun out.

Hesitantly, Peyton said, "Does your husband help take care of him?"

Nora turned her head and smiled down at her.

"He's not my husband," she said. "He's the son of the family I lived with. He is a beautiful man, a sweet man. He adored me, and the baby is simply his heart. The Cuban men and their sons! But when I . . . knew I had to come back, he wouldn't come with me. He was very angry. He had assumed I would stay in Cuba with them always, and . . . I guess I just never told him that couldn't happen. He helped his mother hide Roberto, and then he went into the mountains with Castro. He doesn't write, and his mother doesn't tell me about him. I presume he comes down to see Roberto occasionally, but I don't know where he is."

"Maybe he'll come here one day," Peyton said. "Maybe he'll bring Roberto, and when he sees what a good country it is he'll want to stay."

"He'll never leave Cuba," Nora said.

They were quiet again. Peyton could smell mimosa and new-cut grass, and she could hear songbirds and Trailways's raucous purr. But over them were the hot, sweet smells and sounds of Cuba.

"It's awful," she said at last.

"Yes, it is," Nora said. "It wasn't smart of me. But I don't regret it. Raoul was the lover of a lifetime, and Roberto is in the world now. I'll always have those two things."

Another silence, and then Nora said, "You mustn't tell anyone, Peyton. Not anyone, not even your father. I'll have to decide when I'll do that, or even *if* I will. If anyone else knew I'd have to leave."

"Daddy wouldn't care!"

"Maybe not, but there's no way it wouldn't get out eventually. Augusta would ruin both of you in a minute, just to get at me. You may not think so, but I couldn't stay. The rural South simply will not have it. I could never stay and let that kind of thing happen to you and him."

Peyton's heart hurt.

"I promise," she said. "I'll never, ever tell anybody. It'll always be just our secret."

After a time Nora stretched out on the bed and gathered Trailways to her and smiled up at Peyton. Her eyes were wet. Peyton was so giddy with shock and deliverance and pity for Nora and pride that Nora had confided in her that she could not speak. She knew that if she did she would cry. She smiled back, tremulously.

"It seems to me that it's mainly your secret," Nora said. "You know mine now, but I don't know any of yours."

"I don't have any secrets. I've never done anything," Peyton said, feeling inadequacy crest over her like a tsunami. Never, not even at the Losers Club, had she felt so utterly bereft of anything to offer.

"The best secrets can be the ones that you make with your mind," Nora said, reaching across the coverlet for her cigarettes. "Didn't you ever have a secret dream? Didn't you want to be a ballet dancer or a spy or something when you got older? Didn't you ever have a great love affair in your mind?"

"No," Peyton said, wincing.

"Oh, Peyton," Nora said, blowing smoke. "The day that you will isn't far away at all. Don't be afraid of it. It won't happen until you're ready. And it's just the greatest thing, to be crazy in love with somebody. You wouldn't want to miss that."

"I'll never get married," Peyton said.

"I'm not talking about marriage," Nora said, smiling through the smoke. Peyton blushed.

"I do have a secret," she said suddenly. "I have a huge one. I don't know how I could have forgotten."

"And it is?" Nora said.

"I killed my mother," Peyton said, and this time, unlike the time at the Losers Club, she did not feel dizzy with the enormity of it, only as if she had handed off something heavy to Nora, and Nora had taken it.

Nora stared at her.

"What are you talking about?" she asked.

"Well . . . she bled to death after she had me. Didn't you know that?" Peyton said.

"Who told you that?" Nora's face was whitening as she spoke. Her cheekbones were reddening.

"Aunt Augusta, I guess. Or maybe Chloe. But I think it was Aunt Augusta. It was a long time after Mother died. I must have been seven or eight."

"And she told you you killed your mother?"

"Oh, no. Nobody had to tell me that. I mean, if I came and then she bled to death, what else could it be?"

"Peyton, did you ever talk to your father about this?"

Peyton looked down. "No. We never talked about her. Not much, anyway. Every now and then I'd ask Chloe about her, and I have some old home movies with her in them, but I never asked Daddy about her."

"Why in the hell not?" Nora cried. Peyton flinched. There was hot anger in Nora's voice.

"I thought he was grieving for her too much. And then Buddy . . . I thought it would be just too awful to remind him. I guess I thought it was enough that he thought about it every time he looked at me."

She felt the old salt in her throat.

Nora sat up and reached over and took Peyton's face in her hands. Peyton tried to twist her head away, but Nora held firm.

"No, now listen," she said. "I have something to tell you, and I want you to be looking at me when I do. It's about your mother, and you have to know it now. It's way past time."

Peyton looked steadily at her cousin, unable to move her head, unable to close her eyes. It was here now, this great change that had cast its shadow before it. She had never wanted to hear anything less in her life. Please, she said in her mind, please just let's go back to the way things were this morning. Please don't let this be my punishment for snooping in your things. She said nothing aloud.

Still holding her face in cupped hands, Nora looked away, and pursed her lips and blew air through them. Then she said, "Peyton, you did not kill your mother. Your mother was just fine when you were born. She was bleeding a little, but a lot of women do that. I did. The doctor propped her legs up on a pillow and told her not to get up until the next morning, and he gave her a shot of something. She was asleep when he left. Your father and your aunt were taking care of you. Your father was ecstatic."

Peyton's heart filled. He had held her, then, had looked down at her, had rejoiced that she was in the world.

"What happened, then, if she was all right?" she said in a low, fearful voice.

"What happened was that she got out of bed that afternoon and slipped out and drove to the country club and shacked up with the tennis pro," Nora said calmly. "She'd been doing it for months. She must have been out of her mind. It knocked something loose and she came home and bled to death in the bathroom. The professional asshole was gone the next morning."

A great whispering whiteness, like snow, filled Peyton's heart and mind. She looked into it as if she were looking at a blizzard through a windowpane.

"How do you know?" she said, thinking with incredulity that she sounded as if she were asking Nora about her morning.

"My mother told me. She told me not long before she died. I don't know how she knew, but someone in the family obviously got wind of it, and told her. She said she didn't want me to go worshiping Cousin Lila Lee like an idol, when she was just as human as the rest of us. But I think now she just told me out of spite. They were always enemies."

"Did . . . does my father know?" Peyton whispered. Her voice was dying.

"Yes," Nora said.

"But he couldn't have told me," Peyton said, as if arguing with Nora. "He loved her so much. Everybody knows how crazy he was about her. And he must have thought it would have hurt me awfully if he told me. . . . It was a kind thing, really."

"I don't happen to think it's too terribly kind to let your child think all of her life that she killed her mother," Nora said in a constricted voice.

"He didn't know I thought that. I've never told anybody that, except the Losers Club and now you."

"Well, anybody with eyes in their head could have seen that something's been bothering you for all these years. He damned well should have found out what it was, and the hell with his tender sensibilities."

"Please don't be mad at him," Peyton said, beginning to cry. She felt nothing about her mother, only the terrible possibility of the loss of Nora.

Nora shook her head swiftly and then got up.

"I'm going out and have a talk with your father," she said, cheeks flaming. "I want you to stay here until I come back and call you. I do not want you listening at the door this time. Oh, yeah, I know you do. I don't usually care, but I care about this. Hear what I'm saying, Peyton: if you eavesdrop on us I will know it and I will leave here this afternoon. Do you understand me?"

"Yes," Peyton said through thick, stinging tears.

Nora had reached the door when Peyton cried, "Wait! Could he be my . . . could I be . . . ?"

"God, no," Nora said. "You're every inch a McKenzie. He was a Neanderthal. His eyebrows met over his nose."

She flung herself out of the room and slammed the door. Peyton pulled the muttering Trailways to her and curled into a ball around him and turned on the air conditioner. Its whumping roar drowned out all sound, even the cat's affronted growl. Even the slam of her father's office door. She stayed there until the cat fell asleep and the light outside the window went from yellow to blue, until she finally dozed.

She did not wake until Nora opened the door and put her head into the room.

"Your father and I are going to get a hamburger," she said. Her voice was level, even light. There were silver snail tracks on her cheeks, though. She had been crying.

"There's cold roast beef in the fridge, and some potato salad," her cousin said. "Or we'll bring you a hamburger. But this time you can't come with us."

Peyton could think of little on earth she wanted to do less.

"A hamburger would be nice," she said meekly.

But she had fallen asleep again on her narrow bed long before they returned. She slept until morning, and she did not dream, and when she woke she felt so much lighter that she thought she might float. Whatever else she had been—and Peyton knew that she might never catch the sense of it—her mother was not, after all, a saint, and she herself was not a killer.

14

*S*he did not float, though. When she got up that Sunday morning and put her foot on the rag rug by her bed, it felt as if she had stepped onto a suspension bridge high over cold space. She stood holding on to her bedpost for a moment, rocking with the frail bridge and trying to get her bearings. Everything around her—the little room, her clothes strewn about, the window and the slice of backyard beyond it, the door into her tiny bathroom—seemed too bright by far, flaring in her eyes and making her blink, disorienting her as if she stood in a world made of glass. Strangeness hummed in the air like a hive. She put a tentative foot forward, almost convinced that she would crash through this brittle, transparent floor into whistling nothingness.

She crept into the bathroom and washed her face and then crawled back into her bed. The lightness continued; she drew up the covers so that she would not simply waft away like milkweed silk. Trailways jumped up on her stomach, purring in her face and kneading his big paws on her chest. She buried her face in his spiky ruff and closed her eyes.

"I don't know what's the matter with me," she whispered to him. "I feel so funny. Everything feels funny."

He backed out of her grip, tail lashing angrily. Then he made a circle of himself and found his place in the hollow of her bent knees and settled down. This was right, this was so familiar that Peyton was afraid to move lest she lose this tenuous anchor to the known world.

Presently Nora tapped on her door and then came in before Peyton could call out. She was dressed in her church "lady" outfit, a soft yellow linen suit with a short buttoned jacket. She had bought it at Rich's after, as she said, it became obvious that it made Aunt Augusta far angrier to see her properly and demurely clad than decked out in tongue-clucking exotica. She even carried short white gloves, and her fiery hair was pulled into a shining bundle on the back of her head. The yellow linen cast a glow upon her neck and washed her tawny face faintly, as if she had held a bouquet of buttercups under her chin. Peyton thought she looked wonderful. Somehow she was free to think so now. Another strangeness on this strangest of days.

"You OK, kiddo?" Nora said, sitting down on the edge of Peyton's bed. "You had a big day yesterday. I was thinking last night that maybe I should have saved the stuff about your mother. Roberto was probably enough for one day."

"I feel funny," Peyton said dreamily. Her head felt disconnected from her neck. It felt as if it were floating above her shoulders like a balloon on a string.

"Funny how?"

"I don't know . . . kind of floaty. Nothing seems very real. Everything looks all bright and lit up. It almost feels like I'm in a place I don't know."

"Well, in a way you are," Nora said. "Everything that shaped the world for you all your life changed yesterday. Of course things seem strange. But I think that when you get used to them you may feel better than you have in a long time. That was a hell of a load you were carrying on your shoulders. You want to talk about any of it?"

Peyton considered. If she could not think about her mother in the same way that she had all her life, how then must she think of her? It did not seem very important or very real. What seemed real was Nora, right now, sitting on her bed in yellow linen.

"I guess there's a lot I want to know, but I can't quite think what it is," she said. "She just seems like somebody I only heard about, and what I heard was wrong."

"Well, that's what she was. That's how it was. Don't push it. You'll find just the right place for her in your mind. Then you can love her for what she really was."

"Will I ever know what she really was?"

"If you want to—as much as anyone knows anyone else. I'll tell you everything I know whenever you ask. Your father will talk to you about her, too. He hasn't before now because he thought it would be too hard for you. But he's promised that he will, when you want him to."

"Did you all have a fight about this?"

"Mmmm-hmmm. A monstrous one. We were furious with each other. We yelled and screamed. Finally it occurred to both of us that this was not about us, it was about you, and then everything seemed just to fall into place. He knows he should have been closer to you all these years; he knows now what he's let you carry on your shoulders. It hurt him terribly when he realized. He wanted most to spare you any pain, and so he just didn't talk to you about anything. He thought it would upset you. In the long run he didn't talk to you about anything much at all. That's going to change, though."

Peyton felt uneasy. Did she really want a volatile new father who bared his soul to her and invited her own this late in the game? She rather thought not. It was enough to know that it was not, after all, she who had struck him to chilly silence all those years. She would have to live her way into that.

"Maybe Daddy and I can talk later," she said. "I just don't feel like I know what to say yet. I was that other way for so long that I don't know what way I need to be now."

Nora laughed and hugged her.

"Point taken," she said. "I'll relay the message. Do you want to come to church with us, or would you rather just piddle around here and collect yourself?"

"Piddle," Peyton said gratefully. The thought of Aunt Augusta's drilling blue eyes trained on her made her faintly sick. Her aunt would smell the profound change, she knew, even if she could not see it. She would be relentless in her pursuit of it.

Nora went to the door and looked back.

"She did love you, you know," she said. "And she loved your father a great deal. What she did had nothing to do with that."

"How could it not? How can you leave people you love and go off and . . . do that?" Peyton's voice shook.

"They're not at all the same thing," Nora said. "Not at all. One is like scratching an itch. When the itch stops, the scratching ends. But the other is better in every way. It lasts. And the other is what she felt for you and your brother and your father. Your father knows that. You will, too, when you're older."

Peyton heard her father's voice then, calling from the living room. "You gals ready to go?"

"Let's let this gal sleep in," Nora called back. "She had a big day yesterday. She'll have lunch with us. Maybe Howard Johnson's fried clams again. Are you buying?"

"I'll flip you," he said, and he came into the room.

He moved to the bed and stood looking down at Peyton. She could not look back. She felt stricken to stone, her tongue cleaved to the roof of her mouth. Her heart hammered. What if Nora had been wrong? What if the faint, cool distaste she had been sure he felt for so long was still there, and he now felt that he had to disguise it with little pats and hugs and chats about her mother? Not talking about anything of import had served them well for a very long time. Suddenly Peyton wanted desperately to keep it that way.

Frazier sat down on the edge of her bed as Nora had done, and looked at her. He lifted her chin with his hand so she would have to look at him. He was smiling faintly; his gray eyes were crinkled with it.

"I let you think a terrible thing, and I didn't even know it," he said. "We'll have to talk about that. But right now I just want you to know that you are my dearly loved daughter, and my best thing, and that I am very, very proud of you, and that I promise not to put my hands over my eyes again if you promise not to put yours over your mouth. OK?"

Peyton nodded. She thought hopelessly that if she cried again her throat and nose would finally burst with it.

He leaned forward and hugged her hard and then got up and stood beside Nora. The scent of his pipe and shaving soap lingered.

"Your mother would have loved you totally," he said. "It would have been impossible for her not to. I'm telling you the truth about that. Can you be dressed and ready for clams in an hour or so?"

"Yes," Peyton whispered. "I can."

The crystal shell burst, and the world came flooding back in, rude and loud and charged with joy.

Peyton went through the next week with the careful deliberation of the newly sighted, carefully placing one foot after another on the earth, not quite trusting it to bear her up, not quite believing that the old blindness would not strike her again. It was not the profound dissociation of the past Sunday, but it was strange enough to keep her preternaturally aware of everything around her, of her own body. When did the cheerleaders stop looking celestial and start looking as though they needed to wash their faces? When did the bank of wild honeysuckle drowning the fence by the schoolyard begin to smell like the breath of heaven? Why had she never noticed how the golden dust motes danced in the slanting afternoon light in her last class? Why had she not noticed that people nodded to her, and many spoke, and some even smiled when they passed her in the hallways?

Why did the very weight of her body feel different, as if its center had shifted to her hips? At Nora's suggestion she had reluctantly pulled out the loathsome training bras, which she had hidden in a shoebox in the top of her closet. When she looked down she could see her chest, like a shelf. When had that happened? Jeremy Tucker from the tenth grade had run up and kissed her on the cheek at recess, obviously on a dare from the other applauding sophomores. What was she supposed to do about that? Her cheek burned all afternoon.

But it was not a particularly fearful, threatening time, only a confusing one. If Peyton did not know what to do about herself and this new world, she had a dim but certain sense that she would soon. For the moment that was enough.

When Nora came in from her last tutorial that Friday afternoon she found Peyton and Trailways curled up on her bed, air conditioner thundering, record player braying out Brahms. Peyton was in a tight ball with her eyes closed.

Nora sighed.

"Who stole your bubble gum, toots?" she said, coming across the room to sit beside Peyton. The smoke from her Salem curled around Peyton's head like incense. Peyton opened her eyes.

"I have to make a speech," she said through stiff lips. "I have to write it. I have to get up onstage and say it at graduation. It's supposed to be some kind of honor, but I told Mrs. Manning I couldn't do it. So she made it an assignment. I'll get a 'barely passing' in English if I don't. But I'm not doing it. I don't care about the grade."

"You could do it wonderfully," Nora said. "You'd be better than anybody I can think of. We could practice it until you weren't frightened anymore. It would be a really grown-up thing to do."

"I'd die. I'd forget what I was supposed to say. I'd throw up onstage. Everybody would laugh at me. They already think I'm drippy. You know I look like a stork."

Nora leaned back and blew smoke and studied her.

"No," she said finally. "I don't know you look like a stork. Haven't you looked at yourself lately? Really looked? You have a waist and hips and breasts. They may be small, but they're there. Your legs are starting to fit the rest of you. Your hair is great. You're a pretty girl; you have your grandmother's cheekbones. You have your father's wonderful profile, and his eyes. Lord, Peyton. Lots of girls would kill to look like you."

"Can you see me leading cheers?" Peyton said bitterly. She

looked down at her bare legs, though. They were faintly tanned from the late-spring sun, and there did not seem to be quite so many knobs on them. The old scar on her knee from a long-ago bicycle collision was gone.

"No, and you should be glad. Is that really what you want to look like? Is that really what you want to do? Come on, Peyton. Let's do this thing. We can work on your speech together. We can practice it. I'll stand in the wings grinning and juggling plates on speech night. We'll get you a knockout new dress. Something you and I pick out this time."

"Oh, God," Peyton whispered, and she turned and buried her face in the pillow. Trailways swatted her desultorily and curled back into sleep.

Nora waited, silent.

Peyton turned back over and looked at her.

"I can't write," she said. "What would I write about?"

"You've *been* writing," Nora said. "You've written every night in your diary. If that's not writing, I don't know what it is."

"I can't get up there and read my diary!"

"I'll bet you could, come to that. But I wouldn't ask that of you. Look, I have an idea. You know how much you liked *Our Town*. What if you did an *Our Town* about Lytton? You could be the Stage Manager and read all the other parts. It could be short, and it would be about things you know in your own mind and heart. That's what a writer works with."

"You mean write about dead people? I don't know any except my mother and Nana. Nobody wants to hear about dead people at a graduation. They want to hear all that stuff about the future and going forth from Lytton Grammar ready to lick your weight in wildcats."

"Wildcat shit is more like it." Nora grinned. "So why not give them something different from anything they've ever heard? Dead people don't have to be tragic. You'd make them up to fit what you wanted to say. A young girl like you talking about how sweet it was to be young in Lytton, Georgia, and about making the most of your precious time. An honored old man telling about the past here, and all the things he witnessed while he was alive, and what he learned over a long lifetime. A person who thought Lytton was small potatoes and left, and wandered the wide world over, and then came home at the end because there was no place better. A mother who grew up here and is overjoyed because she watches her children grow up as happy as she was. You'd talk about the things they remembered—that *you* remember: the long summer twilights, rollerskating in the fall, the town Christmas decorations, old people rocking on white porches in green chairs, teenagers on their way to dances at the teen center, dogs trotting home to supper. You know; all that. . . ."

"Oh, Nora."

"Your father would simply burst with pride," Nora said.

After a long silence, Peyton said, "Would you absolutely and positively be there in the wings? Would you help me all the way, and tell me when it gets silly, and fix the things that are wrong with it?"

"I'll most certainly be there," Nora said. "But I'm not going to tell you it's silly unless it begins to sound like the Marx Brothers. And you're going to have to fix the wrong things yourself. I'm not writing it for you. But I'll read it all along the way, and I'll rehearse you. You might just surprise yourself by having a good time."

The next morning Peyton went to the library and checked out *Our Town*. She had known when Nora mentioned her father that she was going to do it. She was trembling, though, when she brought the book home, and it took her days to work up enough courage to open it.

Finally she did, and she had not read more than two pages before she picked up her pencil and school notebook and began to write. She wrote so fast that the pencil slashed through the flimsy paper in some spots, and the words tumbled over themselves and piled up on the page. She wrote for a long time, and when she looked up it had grown dark and she could hear the voices of Nora and her father out on the front porch, where they sometimes sat after dinner in the soft, fragrant night. She shook her head as if she were coming up from the ocean's floor. She could smell the cool bite of Nora's cigarette, and a sweeter, thicker scent that meant her father was smoking his pipe.

The old porch glider creaked. All at once Peyton was powerfully, giddily happy, and very hungry.

She went out onto the porch. She could not stop smiling.

"Hey," she said to them.

"Hey, yourself," her father said. "Did you just wake up? We saved you some supper."

"I wasn't asleep," Peyton said.

Nora looked at her keenly and then reached over and picked up her hand and squeezed it. "We're off," she said, grinning.

"Off where?" Frazier said.

"Off to see the Wizard," Nora said, and she laughed joyously. "Off our rockers. Off down Moon River. You just wait and see where we land."

"I gather I'm not supposed to ask."

"No. But you'll hear about it soon. Literally. Chicken salad in there, Peyton."

And Peyton went off to eat her late supper and find a way to think about herself that was not, perhaps, so drippy after all.

It was as if she had two sets of eyes in those first days of working on the speech. The first set was the one she had had since birth—more educated now, perhaps, more focused on the rapidly expanding world. But still her own vision.

The other set was somewhere inside her, and it filtered everything through the scrim of her writing. She was usually unaware of this second set, but occasionally it would surface and blast her awake with the urgency of its vision. She would see a canopy of old roses on a crumbling well-house, so vivid in the sun that they seemed to burn there, and she would think, That has to be in the speech. It could be where the young girl is talking. Or no, I think it would be more what an old man would remember. The farm, and the well-house, and the roses.

She would hear the two teenaged Crowell sisters from three houses down walking in the spring dark toward town, and their laughter would sound like running water. Something would tug at her heart, and she would think, This is what the young girl would remember.

Coming back from Atlanta in the Thunderbird in the late afternoon she would see the Lytton water tank before she saw anything
else of the town, and the setting sun would strike the metal into a million facets of glittering color, and she would think, This is what the
person who went away and came back would see first.

She spoke of it to Nora, shyly.

"It's like everything I hear and see and do wants to go into the
speech," she said. "I saw two horses in Mr. Milam's field the other
day and I actually thought I might write about what the dead horses
would remember. What they saw in their lifetimes. What they
thought about the people in the town."

"That's what makes a writer," Nora said. "That you see the story
in everything. That you go through your life with all your senses
open, that you think 'what if' a thousand times a day. I knew you'd
be good with words, but I didn't know about the seeing. It's not given
to many people."

"What does it mean?"

"It means you could be a real writer if you wanted it badly enough.
Not many people who have just the words can. You can learn the
craft, but the vision is a gift. Either you have it or you don't. It's your
choice what you do with it, Peyton, but you can't ever again think of
yourself as a loser, as you say. Or even ordinary."

Peyton's head swam. Pride and fear in equal measure flooded her.
To be a real writer . . . but then you'd stand naked before all the eyes
that read you.

"Do you have it?"

"Not really. If I did I wouldn't be teaching other people about it. I
envy you, I really do. To know this early what it is you're meant for—"

"But maybe I'm not! I don't have to be! There's nothing that says I
have to be just because I've got this thing you're talking about. I can
be just . . . a person if I want to."

"Absolutely. But I can tell you that if you don't use those other
eyes they'll pull at you all your life. They won't give you a minute's
peace. Have you read Frost yet? If you haven't, we'll read 'The Road

Not Taken.' Frost knew. By the way, the thing about the horses is wonderful."

And so Peyton went back to her notebook and wrote furiously through the warming afternoons of May. Five weeks. She had only five weeks before graduation.

It was as if Nora's words had opened the second pair of eyes, and everything Peyton saw flamed with life and import. There had never been a more beautiful spring, she thought. The mimosas and early roses almost burned her eyes and took her breath. It was as if she saw for the first time the fountains of white spirea in Mrs. Cuddy's yard next door, or tasted for the first time the nectar in the honeysuckle that grew wild in a vacant lot on the way to school. The sound of the tiny frogs in the lily pond at night, and the thwacking of tennis balls on the old dirt courts at the recreation center, almost made her weep. The last of Trailways's baby fur, on his speckled belly, did.

"Where did you go, you silly kitten?" she sobbed into his stomach. "I wasn't ready for you to grow up yet."

She might have been speaking of herself. Everything that spring was underlaid with the poignancy of impermanence. For the first time she felt keenly the passage of time. For the first time she thought, many times a day, The last time. This could be the last time I see this as I am now. This could be the last time the Peyton I know hears this. The next time maybe I won't be the same person.

She drank in the days like a person dying of thirst. It all went into the notebook, which by now bulged with scribbled pages.

"When are you going to show some of that to me?" Nora would say.

"Soon. Real soon."

"Well, don't wait too long. I know you've got a book's worth in that notebook, and we've got to pull a ten-minute speech out of it, and then you've got to practice it."

On a warm, cloudy Saturday they went with Frazier down to the farm where her grandmother had lived all the days that Peyton knew her. She had not been back since Agnes McKenzie died. She had hardly thought of the house, or even of her grandmother. It was simply too painful to remember the mute, clawing, furious thing she had become at the end.

The house put its arms around her and drew her in. She followed as her father walked Nora through the dim, musty rooms, and in each one she felt, so vividly that she almost saw it, the presence of her grandmother. She and Agnes McKenzie had sat in this parlor on winter Sundays after lunch, Agnes talking of the old days in Scotland and the more recent past, when her father and uncle were children, warming themselves before this fireplace. She wondered if they had seen the firelight making of her grandmother's face something mythic, archaic, like the face of a goddess in the days before there were words to write about such things. She had watched her grandmother shelling peas and stringing beans on this screened porch in the cool of late-summer afternoons, the tink of the vegetables in the old tin bucket providing the only sound for long, companionable minutes. And the kitchen . . . how many times had she sat in this kitchen while her grandmother measured and stirred and listened to her with her whole being and smiled at her, and told her more stories? She realized now that her grandmother had been a storyteller in an old and tribal way. The old person in her speech had to be Agnes McKenzie, Peyton realized, picking up one of her grandmother's aprons and holding it to her face, smelling vanilla and the wild, musky scent of the herbs she grew. It was here that she told me I would have power, she thought. The day I showed her my haircut. I wonder if she could have meant the writing? How could she know about that? But she knew about almost everything. Peyton felt a great salt lump in her throat.

"I feel like she's here," she said, and her father smiled.

"Me, too. Like she was before the stroke. We're lucky we have this house. We'll have her as long as we have it."

"Would you ever sell it?" Nora said, fingering the old spice rack that hung on the wall. In it, among the basil and thyme and block-hard oregano, were unlabeled glass pickle jars full of powders and liquids: her grandmother's tools.

"I don't think so," Frazier said. "We might rent, I suppose.

Although the day may come when we have to sell. Charlie says he doesn't want to, but I expect the land is worth a good bit of money now. His half could keep them for a long time."

"Augusta will be all over him to do it," Nora said. "Maybe they could come and live here. Sell that overblown monstrosity. Of course, the only way you could get Augusta onto a farm would be to bridle her and tie her to a stake in the yard. Not a bad idea. Well, then, maybe Peyton will want it one day. Or her children. It's a wonderful house. I'd love to live here myself."

"Would you?" Frazier said, smiling down at her. "You and your pink Thunderbird all alone down on the farm. What on earth would you do in this isolated old place by yourself?"

"I didn't say I would be by myself," Nora said, and she looked up at him obliquely.

"I'll never have children," Peyton said. "I'm never going to get married. I've never met anybody I would want to marry. And who would want to marry me?"

"Well, I heard via the grammar school grapevine that Jeremy Tucker kissed you the other day." Nora grinned. "That's a start."

"I'd as soon kiss a pig," Peyton said sullenly.

"What's all this?" her father said, smiling at her with one dark eyebrow raised. "Anything I should know about?"

"Not for several years yet," Nora said. "And not Jeremy Tucker, I don't think. It is widely accepted that he is what is commonly known as a creep. Or maybe a jerk. I forget which is worse."

On their way home Peyton was silent in the backseat. When they got out, Nora looked at her questioningly but said nothing.

"The old person will be like my grandmother," Peyton said that afternoon. "The things she would love and remember wouldn't be like anybody else's."

"Rule two of writing: The art is in the particulars. There never was a good generic character in all of literature."

Peyton worked in her notebook every afternoon and did not once think about the Losers Club. At night, when she came out for supper, she felt as if she were breathing air and seeing lights for the first time in a long while. Suppers now were near-magical times. Chloe laughed and sang in the kitchen and made enough pies and cakes and cookies to stock a bakery. They sat long at the table, talking about their days, or rather Frazier and Nora talked and Peyton listened, and when they finally got up it was to move onto the screened porch and sit in the mothy dark, hearing the ghostly nighttime dissonance of the katydids, breathing the fragrance of the hardy early roses that grew wild in the bed that Peyton's mother had tended. Nora and her father almost always lingered when Peyton got up to go to bed. Where once she would have spied on them, now Peyton wrote more in her notebook, or read over what she had written earlier. But once she went to the window that gave onto the porch and saw her father putting out his hand to Nora to pull her up out of the glider, and saw Nora hold his hand longer than necessary, and saw him reach out and touch her cheek. Peyton scrambled into bed with her heart beating hard, but there was a small smile on her mouth, too. Another time she went into the living room to ask Nora how to spell something and saw her sitting on the couch watching the soundless television. Her father was stretched out on the sofa with his head in Nora's lap, fast asleep. Nora heard Peyton and looked up and put a finger to her lips.

"Don't wake him. He's had an awful day," she whispered.

Peyton felt as though she were walking on tiptoe in those days, afraid she might crush something fragile. It felt like waiting for Christmas when you were a small child, she thought. You knew in your mind that it would come, but you were afraid in your heart that you would do something so clumsy and awful that there would be no Christmas at all that year.

"Please," she would whisper over and over to herself, without having the slightest idea what she pled for. "Oh, please."

Nora and Chloe undertook to teach her to cook, and were successful enough that she produced, amid choking laughter from all three of them, a glutinous pot of macaroni and cheese and a pear salad with mayonnaise on it. She put a maraschino cherry on top of the mayonnaise and laid the whole thing on a leaf of iceberg lettuce.

"Ah, the dreaded iceberg," Nora said, licking mayonnaise off her fingers. "Next we're going to learn about really good lettuce. Boston and romaine and red leaf. Iceberg is for the Rotary Club."

"Where would you get those in Lytton?"

"Where, indeed? It'll be worth a trip to Atlanta to get them. Once you taste them you'll never go back to iceberg."

Her father gamely had two helpings of the macaroni that night and pronounced it as good as her grandmother's. Peyton knew he was lying, but she basked in the praise anyway. It made her feel strangely nurturing and wise, a woman capable of sustaining multitudes.

"You can take over some of the cooking now," her father said. "Give Nora a break when Chloe has the night off."

In her mind's eye Peyton could see it unrolling like a movie: night after night of suppers at this table, salted with laughter, warmed with wonderful smells. Her father praising her chicken and her rolls and her pecan pie, Nora smiling at his appetite.

Peyton did not try to see the end of the film. She was content just to let it roll down through months and years of suppers.

She saw Boot one afternoon in the parking lot of the A&P. He was pushing a cart teetering full of groceries, gimping along behind a large woman headed purposefully for a dirty Pontiac. When Peyton came out of the store with the eggs she had been sent for, he was waiting for her at the curb.

"Hey, Peyton," he said cheerfully.

"Hey, Boot," she said, sweetness and familiarity flooding over her. She had, she realized, missed Boot enormously.

"Mamaw says you learnin' to cook." He grinned. "Whooee. I'd like to see that. I ain't sure I'd like to taste it, though."

"I'm doing better," Peyton said. "I'll send you some of my biscuits next time I make 'em, if I don't ruin them. The last ones were like rocks."

He laughed delightedly, and Peyton realized she had fallen unconsciously into the mode of the Losers Club. The thought made her uneasy.

"Have you seen Ernie?" she asked.

"Don't you know nothin'?" Boot said, swollen with the impor-

tance of real news to impart. "Ernie gone. His mean ol' mama broke
her hip and he had to put her in a home up to Hapeville. He sold that
little old house and moved in a 'partment to be near her. I think he
workin' at McDonald's, like Doreen, only not the same one. He a
manager; you know he real smart."

Ernie in a little paper cap, taking orders from empty-headed teens
and fat, blue-rinsed old women who would never in their lifetime
know as much as one hundredth of what Ernie's brain held. Ernie in
a costume. Peyton felt tears start.

"Oh, Boot, when?"

"Week and a half ago. It was real sudden. He came by to see me
before they left. I asked him if he couldn't find him a graveyard up in
Hapeville to take care of, and he say it don't bring in enough money.
That home cost an arm an' a leg, he say. He working double shifts."

Peyton would not look at him. She did not want him to see the
tears pooling on her lower lashes.

"Did he say anything about me?" she whispered. Guilt choked her
voice.

"Naw. He ain't said nothin' about you since the last time you was
at the Losers Club. We shut it down right after that. I miss it, though.
It was a lot of fun."

"I miss it, too," Peyton said, and she turned away. The tears were
streaking down her cheeks now. If Boot saw them he would broadcast
it that Peyton McKenzie was crying in the parking lot of the A&P.

"I'll see you soon, Boot," she called over her shoulder.

"Yeah," he called back. "Tell Mamaw I say hey."

Peyton did not write in her notebook that afternoon. She lay on her
bed and cried and cried, and when the tears finally stopped and she
washed her swollen face, she saw for a moment the watery reflection
of the pale, pigtailed girl in the too-large blue jeans who used to cut
through the undergrowth every afternoon to reach the sanctuary of
the Losers Club, and she began to cry again.

"Wow," Nora said, shuffling pages. "I don't know whether we need
an editor or a surgeon."

They were sitting cross-legged on Nora's bed on a Sunday after-noon, surrounded by drifts of tablet paper. It was thickly hot, and air-less with a coming storm, but they could not turn on the air conditioner because the pages would scatter like leaves in a tornado. Trailways had been banned because he insisted on rolling joyfully on the piles of paper, and he now howled dismally from the other side of the closed door. Peyton was dripping sweat in one of her old sleeve-less blouses—too tight across the chest now—and a pair of the cut-offs Nora had showed her how to make. Nora wore underpants and an enormous, frayed blue oxford-cloth shirt. She was smoking and turning pages intently.

"Is that Daddy's shirt?" Peyton asked, more to forestall the announcement that the pages were no good than to solicit information.

"God, no," Nora said, not looking up. "This shirt belonged to the priest . . . you know, the one I told you about, whom I went to Cuba with."

"A priest's shirt," Peyton said. "Maybe it will make you saintly."

"Not likely. Not this priest, though he did give me the shirt off his back," Nora said, and she finished stacking paper into piles and thumped the last one smartly.

"Now," she said. "We're going to have to cut so much that it will make you weep, but you can save the rest for a book of essays. The thing to do first is decide what you want this speech to say."

"Say?"

"What do you want people to remember about it?"

"Well . . . I guess just . . . how good it was to live in Lytton years ago, and how everybody sees it differently, but it's still Lytton."

"Good. You have your theme. Everything has to have a theme, a central spine. Now how would you go about telling that?"

"Through the people who are talking from the cemetery," Peyton said.

"Yeah, but which ones? And what's most important about what they remember? You've got ten minutes, you know."

"I can't choose," Peyton said. "I like all of it. How do I know which ones are best?"

"There's no best. There's just what works best to accomplish your intention, to show people about that early Lytton. It's all good, Peyton. I'm not kidding you."

"You choose," Peyton said, wanting to cry. No one had ever said that writing meant amputating your work.

"I'll help," Nora said. "I've been an editor, and I'm good at it. A lot of times an outside person can see things better than the one who wrote it. But you're going to have to help me. Let's start with the beginning. Since you're the Stage Manager, what do you want to say?"

"I want to say what the Stage Manager in *Our Town* says."

"Well, you can't use his exact words, or you'd get sued, but you could say that the play inspired you to think about Lytton and how it must have been long ago, and that you wanted to show people that, because that Lytton won't come again. And you might tell them a little about the form of the play, and that the people who'll be speaking are in the cemetery, but in one way are as alive and present as they ever were."

"I want to say exactly that," Peyton said.

"OK. But it's the only part of it I'm going to write for you. Now let's get into the body of it. I think you could handle maybe three soliloquies. The old woman and the girl are perfect. Whom do you want for your third? The young mother?"

"No," Peyton said, knowing suddenly how it should be, seeing the shape of it. "The horses. Their field is on the edge of town, and it would be a way to show Lytton as you came into it back then, and to talk about how it was when people were mainly farmers. And then the young girl, who lived in the middle of town. And then the old woman, because she lived on the other edge of it. It sort of takes you through the town, see?"

"I do indeed." Nora smiled. "You ready to start pruning?"

They worked all that afternoon and into the night. Frazier was at a board of stewards' meeting at the church, and Chloe had left cold chicken. They ate it on the bed, licking greasy fingers, tossing shreds to the liberated Trailways. His howls had finally worn them down.

When at last they stopped, Peyton was amazed to see that it was nearly midnight, and her head was pounding. They had culled out the three segments, though. It remained only to put them together.

The next afternoon Nora wrote out the brief introduction, and Peyton read it aloud for the first time:

"More than twenty years ago Thornton Wilder wrote a play called *Our Town*. I went to see it this year in Atlanta, and it made me cry and laugh and wonder. It takes place mainly in the cemetery of the little town, where the dead talk to the Stage Manager, but to me they are as vivid and real as if they were alive. In a sense, they are, through their memories, and I'd like to show you what I think Lytton might have been like through the eyes of some of us who aren't here anymore, and yet are totally here."

Peyton looked up at Nora, her eyes brimming.

"It's just right," she said. "I could never have thought of it. I sound stupid, don't I? My voice is just . . . silly. And the stuff I wrote just sounds so young."

"I'm a good voice coach," Nora said. "And you *are* young. You should always sound like who you are."

She was a good coach. Before long Peyton was not mumbling anymore, and she was beginning to find the cadence and the sense in the words. In the beginning sequence, when the good, big horses were speaking of their masters and their work, her voice broke, and she had to stop. In the young girl's segment she found the essential, lovely foolishness of the young and laughed aloud with it.

"'Scuse me," she said to Nora. "I won't do that when I'm onstage."

"I wish you would," Nora said. "It's charming. You'll have people crying and laughing with you."

"Oh, Nora, what if I mess it up? What if I stammer or mispronounce something? It's just so different from anything I've ever heard of at graduation."

"Precisely. If you screw up, grin and go on. But you won't. I'll be right there in the wings. All you have to do is look at me. I'll be your lucky charm."

Over the next few days the speech took shape and Peyton grew if not easy, then at least familiar with it. She stopped dropping her eyes and looked out as if at an audience. She paused to allow phrases to have their effect. She let her voice swell when the prose did, and fade when it faded. Nora listened and smoked and applauded.

"Fabulous," she said. "Just right. Nobody I know could do it better. You'll be a sensation."

And Peyton, flushed with success, began, hesitantly, to believe her.

Two weeks into their practice sessions, Nora came home and dumped her books loudly on the secretary and stood rubbing her forehead as if it ached.

"What's the matter?" Peyton said in alarm, coming in from the kitchen. What if Nora was getting ill, and could not be with her onstage?

"Oh, nothing. Just a fuck-up at school. I threw a kid out of class and I didn't want to do it, but I didn't have any choice."

"Was it one of the Negro kids?" Peyton said.

"No. It was one of the cheerleaders," Nora said, and she began to laugh.

"You didn't! How wonderful!" Peyton said. "Which one? What did she do?"

"Mary Jim Turnipseed. She's been asking for it for weeks. This time she called one of the black kids a dimwit, and the child cried in front of the whole class and ran out. Mary Jim started to laugh. I'm afraid I yelled at her."

"Mary Jim! Lord, Nora, she's the cheerleader captain, and homecoming queen, and editor of the paper. Her father's a judge."

"And she's a spoiled brat," Nora said. "I don't care if her father is the lord high executioner. I will not have that kind of thing in my classroom."

"She'll tell her father."

"No doubt."

"Are you scared?"

"No."

Mary Jim not only told her father about the incident, but also

informed her parents that Nora had been teaching them pornography
for the last few months, and took home her heavily underlined copy
of *The Tropic of Cancer* by way of proof. When her outraged parents
asked why she hadn't told them earlier, she said that Miss Findlay
had said she'd flunk anybody who told his or her folks. Margaret
Turnipseed was on the phone before the words died on Mary Jim's
trembling little lips.

They had finished supper and were sitting on the porch talking of
the coming summer when the people came. Later, Peyton thought
they must have walked; she had heard no cars. Frazier heard them
first, and looked up. They stopped at the bottom of the porch steps.
There must have been ten or twelve of them, people he had known all
his life, neighbors, clients. He did not speak. It was easy to see that
they had not come in friendship.

"All that's missing is the lighted torches," Nora muttered, standing
and moving up beside Frazier. Peyton instinctively stayed where she
was, sitting still and silent.

Horace Turnipseed stepped out of the small knot of people and
said, "Frazier, we don't like doing this, but we can't let it go on. Your
. . . cousin, or whatever she is, expelled my daughter from her class
today and said some pretty hard things to her. That might not be such
a bad thing if Mary Jim deserved it, but she's always been a good girl,
a quiet girl. I can't imagine what she could have done to warrant that
kind of behavior. But the main thing we can't let pass is what Miss
Findlay is teaching our children. It's pornography pure and simple. I
never read anything so dirty. The idea that my child—anybody's
child—is reading this stuff is absolutely unacceptable. I'm afraid that
we're going to have to ask that you see that Miss Findlay is relieved
of her position immediately."

Frazier was silent, looking at them.

"What book are you referring to, Horace?" he asked. His voice
was even and mild.

"This." Horace Turnipseed held up the book. "This *Tropic of
Cancer* thing. It wasn't even allowed into this country until a year or
two ago. There's filth on every page. Every single one."

"It must have been a real trial for you to have to finish it, Horace," her father said. "Every page, think of it. And it's a pretty big book, too."

Horace Turnipseed's face reddened. You could see it darken even in the urine-pale light from the street lamp.

"Have you ever heard of this book, Frazier?" he said.

"I've read that book," her father answered. "I didn't find it in the least offensive. Pretty basic and earthy, but not offensive."

Peyton goggled. She knew her father had not read the book. She doubted he had even heard of it. Moreover, she had never known him to lie. Beside her father, Nora stirred and opened her mouth to speak. He put his hand lightly on her arm, silencing her.

"I will not ask her to resign, Horace," he said.

There was a shuffling, murmuring silence, and then Aunt Augusta stepped forward into the lamplight.

"Why am I not surprised?" Nora muttered.

"Frazier, you are a good man and my brother-in-law," Augusta McKenzie said. Her voice was burdened with lugubrious sadness. "But we believe you are not seeing this situation clearly. We think perhaps you're . . . too close to it. This young woman is a troublemaker. I've said so from the beginning. She is a terrible influence on our young people. How can you subject Peyton to all that? It makes us all wonder just exactly in what capacity you keep Miss Findlay in your house."

Peyton saw her father stiffen. She heard Nora gasp. He took a deep breath to answer, and this time it was Nora who tugged at his arm. But he stepped forward and crossed his arms over his chest and looked at his sister-in-law, and then he let his gaze slide over all their faces. Many looked away.

"Miss Findlay is in my house in any capacity she wishes to be," he said. "And it is my fondest hope that she will remain so—in any capacity she chooses. It is you who are the troublemaker, Augusta."

Augusta McKenzie gasped and turned on her heel and clicked rapidly down the walk. Horace Turnipseed cleared his throat.

"Then we have no choice but to go to the whole school board, Frazier," he said.

"Go," her father said. Peyton could see that he was trembling all over, a fine shivering. Nora backed away from him and stood as still as a wild creature caught in headlights. The small crowd sensed that there was nothing more to say and melted away as silently as it had come. In a moment there was only lamplight and the smell of grass and the sound of crickets.

Her father turned to Nora and took her by the shoulders.

"I meant what I said," he said. "I want you to stay. I want you with us. We need you. Don't let these idiots run you away. Any capacity, Nora. Any at all."

Nora's face was as white as a lily in the dimness. Her eyes were wide and white-ringed, and then she shut them.

"Don't do this to me, Frazier," she whispered. "Don't need me. Don't. I can't carry the weight of it. I can't stay."

And she wheeled and ran up the stairs to her room. They heard the door shut behind her, and the air conditioner go on.

"Daddy . . . ," Peyton said, near tears. "Daddy, go get her. Don't let her go."

"I don't think she'll go," her father said. His voice was flat. "All this business upset her. I don't blame her. She's like a bird. You have to hold her in your open hand. I landed on her too hard tonight."

"Did you want her to stay . . . you know, like my mother or something?" Peyton could not say, "Like your wife."

"Go to bed, Peyton," he said wearily. "We'll straighten it out in the morning."

But they did not. Nora eluded them like a wild thing. She got up early and stayed late at school. When she was not there she was in the library. She went often to Atlanta alone and did not ask Peyton and Frazier to go with her. When they did see her, she was noncommittal and pleasant. Her face was pinched and the fire seemed to have gone out of her hair. She still rehearsed Peyton in her speech, but she did it with the mechanical capability of a paid coach.

Peyton couldn't speak to her of the night on the porch, mostly for fear of what she might hear. But she fretted about her speech, over and over.

"But you'll be there, won't you? Nora, you *will* be there?"

"Peyton, you've gotten so good at it that you could do it by your-self in a New York minute," Nora said. "But yes, I'll be there. I promised, didn't I?"

The silence in the house spun out. Frazier was once more in his office until all hours. Clothilde trudged heavily about the kitchen and shooed Peyton out whenever she came dawdling unhappily in. Even Trailways felt the emptiness: he stayed on Nora's bed until far into the night, curled up, as if his leaving would mean that she would leave, too. Peyton did not show herself her movies; there was no com-fort for her there anymore. But she ached for the Losers Club, at the same time knowing that even if it were still meeting, she had some-how traveled beyond it and could not go back. It was a cold, dull time. Peyton remembered the days of joy only distantly, as she might a sunny, idyllic slice of her childhood. Whenever she closed her eyes, nothingness roared under her.

We're all back to where we were before, she thought bleakly. Only then we didn't know that there was any other way. Now we do, and it's gone, and that's a million times worse than the other way. I don't know how I'm going to stand this.

And then Sonny Burkholter came home, and everything changed.

15

Sonny Burkholter was Lytton's claim to fame, its shining star. He had been born to the town's seamstress, a nervous little woman known in Lytton simply as Miss Carrie. They lived for many years in a tiny, neat cottage beside the railroad tracks on the south side of Lytton, on old Highway 29. There had been a Mr. Burkholter, but he had apparently tired of nerves and neatness and trains early on and had disappeared, leaving Miss Carrie to bring up Sonny. She idolized him. He had the mark of greatness on him from the moment of his birth, she said repeatedly, to whoever would listen. There was no doubt in her mind that this golden changeling of hers would touch the world in a very special way.

And he did. After an undistinguished academic career at Lytton High, during which he played so-so football and made marginal grades and went through the female population of the town like a dose of salts, Sonny cut and ran. For months his frantic mother did not know where he was. After she collapsed at the A&P, the First Methodist Church had a Krispy Kreme doughnut sale and made enough money to send Miss Carrie to a rest home for a few days. She emerged, sedated and gentle and somehow broken, about the same time Sonny surfaced. In a letter to his mother, in which he did not mention his absence or inquire after her well-being, he told her that he was in Los Angeles and had just been cast in a new Western drama as the second lead.

I'll see you soon, he wrote. *I'm going to come back and build you the biggest house Lytton has ever seen. Watch for me Tuesday night. It's called* Pecos.

Miss Carrie and the whole town watched, and there was no doubt in the collective consciousness that Sonny was going to be a very big television star. Besides his rather ordinary good looks—sharp, diamond-blue eyes, shock of yellow hair, square jaw, chiseled nose—Sonny had something ineffable and immediate on the little screen. As his mother said proudly afterward, "The camera loves him." Sonny had only to grin and the set lighted up along with the hearts of half of America; when he spoke in his slow drawl sighs were heard from L.A. to Bangor, Maine. He was nineteen years old at the time. Sonny didn't have the sense God gave a billy goat, but he didn't need it. The role in the Western was small, and the character simple to the point of near idiocy. But it propelled Sonny into the small-screen stratosphere, and there he had stayed for all the years since, ending up the season before in a turgid drama called *The Southerners,* in which he played a "modern Rhett Butler born to raise hell and break hearts." From the first episode the ratings were off the charts. Raising hell and breaking hearts became, to his adoring public, the very quintessence of southernness. Sonny played it so well that he came to believe totally the silly script, and became a southerner the likes of whom had never trod the red earth of the South. There were talks of movies, of a remake of *Gone With the Wind.*

His name and photograph appeared in every tabloid and even some reputable magazines and newspapers several times a week. He was seen with more starlets than there had been on the old MGM back lot. Speculation about his love affairs was rife and lurid. But Sonny did not settle down. When he came back to Lytton for the first time since he'd left, to install his mother in the mammoth new house

he had had built on an artificial lake just outside Lytton and to speak
at the high school career-day program, he was unmarried, thirty years
old, and richer than Croesus.

Lytton went berserk with pride and joy. There had long been a sign
at the city limits that said, "Home of Sonny Burkholter." Now signs
sprouted all over town. *Welcome home, Sonny,* the neon marquee at
the Howard Johnson's up on the freeway read. "Sonny, come have a
cup of the world's best coffee," a cardboard sign in the window of the
café said. The Locksmith beauty shop put up a banner saying, "Girls!
Come get ready for Sonny!" More banners and bunting went up on
Main Street, and there were plans under way for a parade and a
Sonny Burkholter Day, during which the mayor would present him
with a key to the city. Every motel within a forty-mile radius was
booked solid with media.

But Sonny's publicist sent word that he wanted no special treat-
ment, no parades, no keys to the city, no marching bands and
majorettes. He was, she said, coming back to find his roots and see
his mother into the home they had dreamed about during the years in
the cramped little railroad cottage. He would appreciate it if the town
would treat him just like anybody else.

It was an inspired public-relations ploy. It let the town worship him
for his down-to-earth humility and his devotion to his old mother—
"That sweet boy hasn't changed a bit"—and laid the groundwork for
Sonny to get out of town afterward as fast as his limousine would
take him.

He and Nora collided like meteors. After they met, in the high
school cafeteria on Career Day, Sonny decided to stay awhile.

Peyton heard about it from Chloe. Chloe had heard it from her
cousin's daughter, who worked in the school cafeteria and witnessed
the whole thing. Peyton thought bitterly that by the time she heard it,
half the town knew. She burned with resentment. Nora should have
told her herself.

As local legend had it, Sonny was escorted to the cafeteria where he
had once eaten hot dogs and baked beans by the tongue-tied presi-
dent of the student body and the grinning principal. He went through

the line "just like anybody else," spoke to all the servers, ate his meal seemingly unaware of the breathless giggles chiming around him, and pronounced the lunch the best thing he had had since he left home.

"There's nothing in the world beats good old-fashioned southern cooking," he said, crinkling his blue eyes and smiling his white smile. This was perhaps a stretch, since the school had sprung for flaccid gray steaks and uniformly yellow frozen French fries in his honor, but it was appreciated and widely quoted all the same. He was just getting an Eskimo pie—"We used to call 'em hunkies"—out of the freezer when Nora came into the room.

"She had on that yellow thing that makes her look like a birthday candle," Chloe reported, "and somebody had brought her a yellow daylily, and she'd stuck it in her hair. That boy put down that hunky and got up and walked straight over to her and said, 'Will you have lunch with me?' And she said, 'Sure,' just like he was one of the teachers or something. And they sat down together and he ate lunch all over again. They left together, too. Maureen says somebody saw 'em going off in that little pink car. Maureen say it just like something in the movies."

Before the day was out, Nora was back with them. Not the coltish Nora who had climbed Peyton's tree in the beginning, not the gleeful Nora who had outraged and overjoyed Lytton in equal parts. And not the languid Nora who had coiled herself bonelessly on the porch glider with them in the spring nights, listening to and telling stories, smoking. But nevertheless, Nora. The dulled, dimmed stranger of the past few days was gone.

This Nora was not often in the Green Street house, nor at home for meals, and spent virtually no evenings with Peyton and Frazier. She dashed in and out, hair a brazen banner behind her, green eyes sparkling, face flushed underneath the russet freckles. She sang in the bathroom and gave Peyton whirlwind hugs on her way out to meet Sonny and paused to kiss Frazier on the cheek and straighten his tie, and rubbed Trailways's stomach until he bit her in an excess of bliss. There was about her an electricity that was unlike her usual cheeky vibrance. She seemed to give off sparks. Looking at her, Peyton had the notion that if Nora stuck her finger into a light socket, all the fuses in the house would blow. Despite the hugs and kisses and laughter, there was something about her that was out of control, almost dangerous.

"Fly too high toward the sun and you gets your wings burned off," Chloe muttered, watching as Nora whirled through, grabbed a biscuit, and ran out into the fresh morning.

"That's Icarus," Peyton said. "We studied him. He was this Greek who had wings made of wax, and he flew too high near the sun and they melted."

"I ain't studyin' no Icarus, and there ain't no Greek gods around here. That's for sure," Clothilde said.

Chloe disliked Sonny Burkholter and was not polite about it.

"He look like an ol' yellow pug dog, with that squished-up nose," she said after Nora made her watch Sonny's TV program. "And he don't act like no southerner I ever seen. Who you seen lately kissin' hands all over the place, or tippin' that hat what looks like a lady's?"

"That's a plantation hat." Nora smiled, refusing to be baited. "People used to wear them on the big plantations."

"Ain't no plantation around here I ever seen."

"Well, you just wait till you see the house Sonny built his mother. It's got everything: columns, oak alleys, white fences, horses, everything."

"She gon' keep slaves?"

"Don't be a butt," Nora said, and hugged her, and dashed out in a flurry of skirts and petticoats.

The skirts were new. They were not the blazing tropical prints that most of Nora's others were, nor were they willowy and snug, like the rest. They were wide and sprigged with small flowers, or made of candy-striped seersucker. Nora had abandoned her T-shirts and peasant blouses for neat white sleeveless blouses or oxford-cloth shirts. She had not worn her shorts or her Jesus Is Coming T-shirt in a week, and she no longer slouched about barefoot. Most amazing and troubling of all, she had stopped smoking, except in her room late at night. It made Peyton crawlingly uneasy. She could never have imagined that Nora would alter her own essential Noraness for Sonny Burkholter or anyone else, but it seemed that she had.

Peyton knew about the smoking only because she smelled the cool, sweet smoke—forever Nora's smell—drifting down the stairs and into her room. They had not spent an afternoon or evening together in Nora's room since Sonny came home. Pride and pique kept her from begging Nora to rehearse her on the speech, but anxiety about it mounted daily.

Finally she said, "Could you possibly listen to my speech tonight? It sounds funny to me and it's only a week away."

"I can't tonight, kiddo," Nora said, shinnying into a new white dress that drifted around her like a snowbank. "We're taking Sonny's mother into Atlanta to Emile's. She's never had dinner in Atlanta, much less at a French restaurant. Besides, it's time for you to rehearse alone now. You'll be alone when you give it, and you really need to get used to it."

"But you'll be there. . . ."

"Sure, but I can't give the speech for you. Now's as good a time as any to start standing alone. You can do it."

No, I can't, Peyton said inside her head. She was suddenly very angry at her cousin. This was to have been her special time with Nora, but Nora had given it all to Sonny without a backward glance.

"You're going to look pretty silly, all of you jammed into that little car," she said.

"We're taking Sonny's limo. He hates to use it, but with his mother and all he has to, and besides, his driver is dying of boredom."

"He could always watch TV."

Nora shot her a look.

Peyton could not leave it alone.

"I'd have thought a big TV star could drive his own car," she said. "Can't he drive?"

"Of course he can, but he doesn't like to drive the limo around here. He thinks it looks ostentatious. Knock it off about Sonny, Peyton. He's a nice guy. You'll see when you meet him."

"I don't want to meet him."

"Well, then, you can sit in your room all night, because I've invited him to dinner."

"Daddy's just going to love that. Did you ask him? What did he say?"

"He said he'd be honored to meet any of my friends, and by all means to ask him."

Peyton thought of the night on the porch when her father had taken hold of Nora's shoulders and said, "I meant what I said. I want you to stay. I want you with us. We need you. . . . Any capacity, Nora. Any at all." She remembered his face as he said it. He had looked younger by far than she had ever seen him. He had looked happy. He did not look young now, or happy. He looked like an actor playing a part.

"I bet he didn't mean it," she said to Nora.

"Well, if he didn't he'll never let me know about it, because he's a gentleman, and the kindest man I've ever met."

Then why isn't that enough? Peyton said in her head. Her heart hurt as if someone had hit her in the chest.

Still, Nora's sheer vivacity animated them. She swept them all up with her energy. Once again they flew high with it. Only now, Peyton felt the breath of the abyss beneath her. If she misstepped, she would fall forever.

She plowed stolidly on with her rehearsing. At first the space where Nora was not swallowed her voice and her will, but after a few days she saw that given no mishaps, she could probably read the speech competently. The magic and music had gone from it, though. But Nora would be there in the wings, and perhaps the magic would come back.

The judge and his coterie were as good as their word. Nora was dismissed only days after the confrontation on the front steps. She never spoke of it, did not seem to remember that she had had a job. She lived entirely in the wake of Sonny Burkholter. A day came when Peyton could not really remember a time when she had not.

Her father did not, this time, shut Peyton out or pull away from her. He spent his nights with her on the porch or in front of the TV, and he never missed breakfast or dinner with her, and sometimes he teased her gravely. She could tell he was trying manfully to enter her world, to make himself one with it. He asked about her days and she answered, trying desperately to inject some particularity, some glamour, into them. But it was Nora who had done that. Peyton imagined that it must be a great struggle for her father to maintain his concentration on her affairs, and she felt guilty about it. Why should he try so hard? There was nothing of interest there.

But he hugged her frequently, and sometimes held her hand as they walked together, and made a small game of her graduation speech.

"Still not going to tell me?"

"No."

"I know. You're giving it in Japanese."

"You're silly."

"Then it's going to be in blank verse."

"No."

"Well, then, you're going to tap-dance and twirl batons while you're speaking."

"*Daddy . . .*"

But she laughed. They both laughed. They laughed much louder and longer than the badinage warranted. If they laughed enough, Peyton could not hear the emptiness where Nora's rich laugh should be. Once it would have been enough just to be this close to Daddy, she thought bleakly. Almost, it was.

She was still angry with Nora in those days, and not the least of her anger was for her father.

She had to know that he wanted her to stay, she thought. If she wasn't going to be with us like she'd always been, she should have moved out so we wouldn't have to watch her carry on with that jerk. Let him support her; Daddy shouldn't have to do it if she's not going to stay with us.

But then Nora would fly through again, and the house would ring with laughter and shimmer with life, and Peyton would toss away the anger swiftly and gratefully. It did not take much. She ached to rid herself of it.

Sonny came to dinner the week of graduation. Chloe had been in the kitchen all day, muttering and slamming pots and pans. Nora had asked for a completely southern meal and had presented Chloe with the menu: fried chicken, turnip greens with cornmeal dumplings, fresh corn, sliced tomatoes, biscuits, and chicken gravy. And there had to be peach cobbler for dessert. These were all the things Sonny pined for out in California, she said. He'd missed them terribly.

"They ain't got chicken in California?" Clothilde grumped.

"Nobody in California fries anything, and they've never heard of turnip greens. Please, Chloe. He's really just a southern boy at heart. I'll clean it all up."

Chloe relented. "Just don't go asking for none of them bean sprouts," she said. "I ain't cooking no sprouts."

"You don't cook them; you eat them raw. And Sonny hates them. Thank you, Chloe. You're a darling." And Nora was off up the stairs to dress.

Promptly at six o'clock the long black limousine slid up the curb in front of the house and Sonny got out of the backseat—or one of the backseats, Peyton thought. She was watching from the screened porch, behind a big fern. There was something about him that drew the eye like fire, or a wild animal. He looked gilded, or sculpted from golden marble. He looked enormous, though he really wasn't. He was actually rather short. Peyton did not know if he seemed bigger to her because she had seen him on television. But the sight of him was intimidating. Could Nora really laugh with and tease and sing with this colossus? Could anybody?

Sonny came up the steps and Nora stood in the doorway to greet him. She wore yellow pique and he wore a bursting blue T-shirt, white pants, and black sunglasses.

Maybe it's so his reflection in mirrors won't put his eyes out, Peyton thought.

Sonny nodded toward the limousine, and the unseen driver eased it soundlessly away. Peyton knew that their neighbors would be talking about it for months—but not to them.

Nora took him by the hand and led him onto the porch.

"Frazier, this is Sonny," she announced. "He's heard all about you. He said he was almost afraid to meet you. Sonny, this is my Cousin Frazier McKenzie."

"We're pleased to have you," Frazier said, standing up and putting out his hand to Sonny. "We've seen a lot of you on TV."

"The pleasure is mine, sir," Sonny said. He took Frazier's hand in both his own and pressed it, and looked into his eyes.

"Needless to say, you're all Nora talks about," he told Frazier. "You and Miss Peyton here." He smiled over at Peyton behind her fern. His teeth were blinding white and his voice was small and high, as if he had a bee trapped in his jaws. They must do something on TV to make it sound lower, Peyton thought. She was so delighted with his voice that she came out from behind the fern and let him take her hand and bow over it and kiss it. She looked up at Nora to see if she was successfully concealing her laughter, but Nora was not laughing. She was smiling tenderly upon Sonny.

"Didn't I tell you they were special?" she said.

"Better than the Cleavers, even," Sonny said, and he laughed at his little joke. His laughter was not much lower than his voice.

It was an awful dinner. Peyton felt as if it went on for eons; she felt that she had been listening to the bee buzzing in her ears for ages. Perhaps she had. Sonny did most of the talking. He began the moment they sat down.

The table was set with pink linen and flowers, and her mother's silver candlesticks held pale-pink candles, and Sonny had brought some white wine that he said was the hottest thing in Hollywood: he had brought a bottle with him in his suitcase because you never knew when you'd need a really good bottle of wine. To Peyton it tasted like sour grape juice, but she finished a glass of it. Nora and her father had several. Sonny himself drank only Chloe's iced tea with fresh mint.

He drained his first glass and smiled broadly at Clothilde when she brought in the pitcher. And when she came in with their plates, he rolled his blue eyes and mimicked a swoon. When Chloe had left again, he turned to Frazier and said, "It's what I've missed most, this good old-fashioned southern cooking. And nobody does it like these good old Negro mammies, do they? You be good to her; she's worth her weight in gold."

At first Peyton thought she had not heard correctly. Then she looked at her father. He was looking down at his plate with interest. She looked at Nora. Surely she would demolish him with the cold knife of her tongue. "Mammies" indeed!

But Nora merely smiled and said, "She's the best cook I've ever known. She's teaching me and Peyton, isn't she, Peyton?"

"I guess," Peyton said. She could not look at anybody.

From then on the talk was a monologue. Sonny talked of Hollywood and the show; he talked casually and knowingly of people whose names they had only heard and read; he talked of the artificiality of Los Angeles and his need to get back home to his roots. He tossed out words and phrases like *production schedule* and *hiatus* and *ratings* and *syndication*. It was a foreign language to Peyton. Sonny spoke it fluently and lovingly. Her father looked gravely interested. Nora looked as if she were hearing an Ave Maria.

What is *wrong* with her? Peyton thought incredulously. He's a jerk.

When Chloe came to clear away the dishes and bring the cobbler he said, "I wish I could steal you away to Hollywood, Chloe. I wonder, do you know anybody who can cook like this who could take care of my mother? I've been looking around, but nobody has quite suited yet. It's a big house, but Mother has a housecleaner, so whoever it was would only be doing the cooking. It would be nice if she could live in, though. Mother needs somebody with her, and the housecleaner won't even consider it. I thought maybe an unmarried girl. . . ."

"I don't believe I know anybody," Chloe said, and she turned to go.

"Chloe, what about Doreen?" Nora called after her. "She's not married, and I know she can cook like an angel. You told me that yourself."

"Doreen working at McDonald's," Chloe said, not looking back.

"I'd pay her enough so she wouldn't miss McDonald's," Sonny said. "I think it's safe to say that I could offer her more than any of the"—he did not say "Negroes," but it hung in the air—"domestics around here could ever hope to make. And she'd have a beautiful room and bath to herself. It looks over the pool."

Will you let her use the pool? Peyton thought. I bet you will, just like Aunt Augusta let her use the bathtub.

"She night supervisor now," Chloe said to Sonny. "She thinks she can be a manager in a year or two. She wants to save enough to go on to school."

"Well, providing she's clean and honest—and of course she is, if she's your niece—she's as good as hired, and I can tell you she'll never once look back at McDonald's or school, either."

"I don't think she gon' want to live in," Chloe said.

"Oh, Chloe, I bet she would," Nora said. "In that beautiful house? Anybody would. And she wouldn't have that awful commute, and she could save up for a little car. . . ."

"Mother has two cars," Sonny said. "I just bought her a new one. She's never going to use the old Fairlane again. I think I could promise your niece the use of that."

"I tell her," Chloe said, and she went out.

That night before she fell asleep, Peyton prayed. She had not done so in a long time. But now she begged, "Please, God, don't let her go off with him. Please don't let her leave." She fell asleep still mumbling the words over and over.

The day after the dinner Sonny flew to New York for a few days and Nora was back in spirit as well as in flesh. It was as if she had never been away. No one remarked about it; they simply slid into their old life as if they were sliding into warm water. It felt like that, too.

On one of the days they went into Atlanta, and Frazier did some business at the courthouse while Nora and Peyton shopped. Nora had trimmed Peyton's hair and it was back in its lustrous tousle, and they found, at Rich's, an ivory polished-cotton sheath with a standaway collar that made Peyton look, as Nora said, like a lit candle. Even Peyton could see that it was an extraordinary dress. The girl in the mirror was no one she knew. In this dress a person could do anything, even make a speech on the stage of Lytton Grammar School. Nora bought it for her.

"My treat," she said. "And it didn't come from the Tween Shop, either."

They drove home in the late afternoon, singing at the top of their lungs. Oh, yes, Nora was back.

"Do you think she's trying to say she's sorry about taking up with that jerk?" Peyton asked her father that night when he came in to tuck her in. He'd been doing that every night, and after the first embarrassed stiffness, both of them had enjoyed the ritual.

He was silent for a moment, and then he sat down on the edge of her bed.

"No, I don't," he said, looking at her. "I think she's saying good-bye."

"No," Peyton cried. It came out as involuntarily as breath.

"You know she never said she'd stay," he said, smoothing the hair off her face.

"But she wanted to, I know she did . . . she always talked about how safe she felt here, and how she just wanted to be with us."

"She needs to be able to do what's right for her," Frazier said. "We can't hold her if she wants to go. She might try to stay, but she'd end up resenting us, and that would be bad for everybody."

"Do . . . you want her to stay?"

"I want her to do what she needs to do."

"But do you wish she'd want to?"

He smiled. "How many angels can dance on the head of a pin? Let it be, Peyton. Try to be happy that she's happy."

"I bet she's not. I bet it's just his stupid money. She'd hate living in Hollywood. Can you see her out there?"

"Yes," he said. "I can."

On Thursday of that week Nora listened to a last run-through of the speech Peyton would give the next night. Peyton dressed for it in the ivory dress and the Cuban-heeled shoes Nora had bought her, and her mother's pearls. The run-through was faultless.

"That was perfect," Nora said. She was back in her old priest's shirt, smoking, with Trailways buzzing ecstatically in the curve of her hip. "And look at you. That girl's got the world on a string. I'm going to have to hogtie Sonny; he'll try to make a play for you for sure."

"Is he coming?"

"Yes. He wouldn't miss it for the world. He's coming back tomorrow afternoon. I'm going to meet him at the airport and we're coming straight to the auditorium. It's practically his last night before he has to go back to California, so you should be honored."

"Are you going with him?" Peyton said, elaborately examining her hemline in the mirror.

"He hasn't asked me," Nora said.

"He will. You've already made yourself a real southern lady for him. He eats that stuff up. He'll ask you."

"Well, if he does, you'll be the first to know. But it certainly wouldn't mean I'd go. . . ."

"He's awfully rich. You'd never have to worry about money again."

"I don't worry about it now. That's not worthy of you, Peyton. Let's drop this right now." Her tone was chilly. As she left the room, Peyton took a last look at her reflection in the mirror. The candle's flame had gone out.

Nora was not there the next morning.

"She gone to Atlanta to do a little shopping," Chloe said. "She say she don't have no decent underwear."

"I didn't think she wore any," Peyton said sullenly. "What does she need new underwear for?"

"It don't do to think about it," Chloe said, slamming plates.

But Peyton did think about it. It was a part of the southern girl child's catechism: Always have nice underwear. You never know when you'll be in a wreck. "Or when somebody eligible might see you in it" was implicit.

I bet he already has, she thought, and she pushed away her plate. The looming speech had sickened her before she even got out of bed. Her stomach felt as though she would throw up, but that relief did not present itself. Her head felt light and her ears buzzed. Why had

Nora left her on this morning? She didn't have to leave for the airport until late afternoon.

The day at school was agonizing. They were dismissed at lunchtime to prepare for the night's festivities, and a raucous celebratory atmosphere held the entire building fast. It was salted with the sense of endings, of leavings. Girls hugged each other and cried. Boys pounded each other on their biceps and smoked cigarettes in the restroom. Peyton put her head down and plowed through it as if through a quagmire. Over, just let this day be over. Let this night be over. The fragile beginnings of confidence, even anticipation, that she had felt the night before dissipated like fog.

Nora was not back in the afternoon, either. Peyton stayed in her room, with Trailways fretting at the closed door. He wanted Nora's big bed, she knew. But she hugged him close. She looked at her watch a hundred times. Finally she saw that Nora would be on her way to the airport to retrieve Sonny now, and knew that she would not see her until that night in the wings. When she had dressed and sat down to put on her makeup the way Nora had taught her, her hands shook so that she could manage only clownish red spots on her cheeks and a crazy slash of lipstick, so she washed it all off.

"You look beautiful," her father said as they got into the car to go to the school. "I can see you when you're grown up. It makes me a little sad."

Me, too, Peyton thought desperately.

The honorees sat in tiered rows on the stage, on bleachers borrowed from the gymnasium. There were potted ferns at the end of each row, and swags of cheesecloth draped around the curve of the stage. The school choir sat in chairs just below them. The graduates fidgeted in high heels and stockings and dark suits. It was very hot; the auditorium had never been air-conditioned. Sweat rolled down smooth cheeks and budding Adam's apples. Peyton could feel it dampening her hairline and her bra. She felt lightheaded and removed, stricken with terror.

The choir got up and mooed "You'll Never Walk Alone." That's a lie, Peyton thought. She remembered Nora's saying she had no idea why people thought the song was appropriate for school graduations. It sounded, she said, more like a dirge for middle age.

Nora. . . . Peyton slid a look under her lashes at the wings. There were the principal and the drama coach, but Nora was not there. But she had thirty minutes yet. . . .

They had the prayer. The principal stood up and welcomed everyone. The salutatorian, a gangly boy with the appearance of a spectacled weed and the mind of a Fermi, got up and bade everyone think about the solemnity and portent of the occasion. The audience rustled and fanned; the smell of chalk and the oil that periodically darkened the wood floors rose cobralike in the thick air.

Nora did not come.

Peyton heard the principal telling the audience that the valedictory address would be given by Miss Peyton McKenzie, well known to them all since babyhood, and that he was sure they were all eager to hear what she had to say.

Nora did not come.

Peyton stood up and walked to the lectern. She could not feel her feet and she could not get her breath. Her hands were so wet that they left prints on the pages of her speech. She looked out into the audience and could see nothing but the dusty haze of lights. Then she made out a white blur that resolved itself into her Aunt Augusta's face. Beside it, her father smiled. He winked and made a little victory gesture with his clasped hands. Peyton felt the floor swing and dip, and closed her eyes, and opened them again.

Nora did not come.

"More than twenty years ago Thornton Wilder wrote a play called *Our Town*," she whispered. Her voice shook. In the wings the drama coach cupped her hands to her ears and smiled.

"Louder," she hissed in a thunderous whisper.

Peyton plowed ahead. There was no sound from the audience. All she could hear was her own voice in her ears, and it was the voice of a sick child, silly and fretful and high. Bile rose in her throat.

She finished the introduction and started into the segment about the horses.

"We are horses," she faltered. "We died fifty years ago. Our names are Samson and Delilah, and we lie now under the green fields where we worked in the summer sun and the autumn rain. Let us tell you how it was then, on the farms of Lytton, Georgia. . . ."

From the audience there was a muffled whinny, and a patter of smothered laughter. Peyton's hands and lips numbed. She did not look up. She read on. Nora was not there. Peyton would have felt her if she had been.

"We were happy here," she finished up. "Our farmer was kind to us. We were fed and groomed with love, and nobody ever beat us in our lives."

"You can't beat a dead horse," a voice in the audience said. This time the laughter was not muffled.

Sickened and dizzy, Peyton started into the segment about the young girl. She knew she was whispering. She did not care. Just get through it. . . .

Nora did not come.

"My name is Elizabeth," Peyton quavered. "I was sixteen years old when I died, and I loved my life. I think of it often now, up on my hill. I look down at Lytton and I see not Lytton today, but the town that was my town all those years ago. There were no streetlights then, but there were gas lamps, and I used to walk in their soft light in the spring nights, smelling the honeysuckle and mimosa, laughing with my friend, all dressed up. We did not always know where we were going, but it did not matter. Sometimes we just went to the little meadow behind the bandstand and lay in the cool grass. . . ."

"Must have been a real good friend," someone called.

"Yeah," another voice, a boy's, yelled. Peyton could tell by its roughness that it belonged to one of the bus kids, a farm boy. "I've had a lay behind that bandstand, too. I never knew you could die of it, though."

There was an airless hush, as of the held breath of a crowd, and then the auditorium exploded into laughter. Peyton saw her father stand up and turn and glare at the audience, saw him hold up his hands for quiet, heard the principal sternly exhorting silence. The laughter spiraled up.

Peyton turned and walked off the stage. She left the pages of her speech behind. She did not turn her head right or left as she went through the wings. The handful of people there stared. The drama coach put out her hand.

"Peyton, honey," she said. "It wasn't you. It was those idiot boys."

In the schoolyard Peyton broke into a trot. By the time she was a block from home she had taken off her new pumps and tossed them into the grass beside the sidewalk and was running flat out. Her stockings were shredded, and the cement of the sidewalk abraded her feet. She did not feel it. The wet band of her new brassiere bit into her chest. She did not feel it. She felt nothing but a simple, one-celled need to be in the tree house. In the dark.

Where Nora was not.

Without hesitation she went up her tree and huddled on the floor of the tree house. She felt the slimy mold of a recent rain under her cheek and knew it was staining the candlelight dress beyond repair. The tree house felt cramped, too small, a toy. She knew she would not come to it again.

She laid her head on her crossed arms and sank down into the leafy darkness of the tree branches. She waited. She knew that they would come soon.

In what seemed like an eyeblink she heard her father's voice under her tree.

"Come on down, honey," he said, and his voice was thick with what sounded like sorrow. "Come on down and let's go in and have some hot chocolate. It's not the end of the world, and it's not your fault. Those boys will be punished. The principal promised me. It was a kind of nervous laughing. It wasn't your speech. Your speech was just beautiful. . . ."

Peyton burrowed her head deeper into her arms.

"Peyton, come down from there," Aunt Augusta's voice shrilled. "You're way too old to be up that tree now, and in that pretty dress, too . . . come on down and just hold your head high and smile and everybody will have forgotten about it before you know it."

She did not reply. I wish I could be dead, too, she thought. In a quiet cemetery somewhere, looking down on a little town. But not Lytton.

"Peyton, I can't just leave you up there," her father said pleadingly. "Please don't make me come up and get you."

She did not reply. She had waited him out before, until the morning. She could do it again. It was the morning when Nora first came, she remembered. Something that was not tears nor anger, exactly, formed in her chest and pushed at her eyes. She kept them closed.

"Let me get her," Nora's voice said. "I did it once before. She'll come down for me, and we can talk this business out."

Peyton lifted her head and looked down. Nora stood at the foot of the tree, hands on hips, looking up. She had on the yellow dress, and she shone in the darkness like foxfire. The lights from the house touched the clownish planes of her face. She was smiling. Beyond her, at the curb, stood the little pink car; she and Sonny must have come home and Peyton had not heard. Sonny stood beside Nora, looking serious and concerned.

"I apologize, kiddo," Nora said. "We just got hung up and couldn't get back. Listen, you don't care about those goddamned cretins. They think the backs of cigarette packs are literature. I'm just going to come up now. That's how we met, remember?"

She put her hands on the lower limbs of the tree to swing herself up. The yellow skirt belled out around her. The other faces stared up like water things in an aquarium.

Peyton was on her feet before she even knew she was rising. She leaned far out over the railing of the tree house.

"Don't you come up here!" she screamed. The force of it scalded her throat. "Don't you dare come up here! What makes you think you can just come up here and take care of me like a baby, like nothing even happened? YOU TOLD ME YOU'D BE THERE AND YOU WEREN'T! You can't take care of anybody! You can't even take care of your own baby!"

The silence was absolute. In it Peyton could hear the katydids start up, and her own blood thundering in her ears.

"Did you all know that Nora has a little boy?" she called down, in a voice of such ugly gaiety that it hurt even her ears. "He's five years old and his name is Roberto and he lives in Cuba with his grand-mother because Nora went off and left him. He's black, and his father is black, and he was never Nora's husband. . . ."

A blindness was roaring down on her, but through it she thought she saw her father's face go still and blank, and saw Sonny Burk-holter's slight recoiling, and heard Aunt Augusta's gasp. Nora said nothing; her face did not change. Then she turned and walked away toward the house. She did not look back. The others did not move.

"Go tell the Devil!" Peyton screamed after her, leaning further out still. "Go tell the Devil!"

The sodden railing gave, and Peyton followed her rage and anguish down into darkness.

16

There was a song they used to sing in the car, Peyton and her father and Buddy. "There's a hole in the bottom of the sea," it started. Peyton knew now that it was true. There was a hole in the bottom of the sea, and that was where she was.

It was as if she lived and moved and slept in deep green water. There was sunlight dappling the surface of it, far above her, and just under the surface people and things swam in and out of the sunlight, sometimes reaching down to her, sometimes simply looking. She did not reach up to them. She was happy to be where she was.

There was a time when she was in real darkness. It seemed like an eternity after she broke free of it, but her father said that it had been only three days.

"You have a doozy of a thing called a cranial hematoma," he said. "It knocked you out for three days. But you're fine now, and there won't be any aftereffects as long as you behave and stay quiet. You've got a broken collarbone, too. And a couple of cracked ribs. Boy, when you take a dive you really take a dive."

His voice was light and warm, but Peyton could see, through her clear water, that his face was slack and his gray eyes were ringed with deep circles. She remembered thinking that he must have been worried about her, and was sorry for that, but it did not seem to touch her. She remembered, too, dimly, about the night of the graduation and the tree, but she did not let her memory take her any further.

The fat, perennially unshaven young doctor who attended her told her and her father that there might be lapses in her memory for some time.

"That was quite a thump," he said. "You're a lucky girl."

"Yes," Peyton said tranquilly, and she went to sleep again.

When she came home from the hospital she asked to be in the upstairs bedroom. Nora's room.

"You sure?" her father said.

"Yes. The other one's too small. And Trailways won't stay in any room but this one."

So Chloe aired the room and turned it out, and it became Peyton's room, with nothing left in it of her Cousin Nora Findlay. Peyton lay in it, floating on pain medication, and slept and waked and watched the little television her father had brought her, and ate the tray meals Chloe brought, and stroked Trailways, and never thought of the room's last occupant except once or twice, on close, still nights when she had not turned the air conditioner on. Then she thought, in that place between sleep and waking, that she smelled the bitter green smell of Nora's perfume.

It did not bother her, either.

Later she dressed and tottered about the house and yard, feeling too tall and not quite connected to the earth, blinking in the light. Her collarbone no longer hurt, but her ribs still did when she took a deep breath, and sometimes her head throbbed under the bandage. It had been a large bandage, covering her head turbanlike, when she first awoke, but now it was only a small patch in the stubbly field of her scalp where they had shaved her head. She thought once or twice that she must look pretty awful with one side of her head shaved and her hair an untended tangle. And her clothes were too tight across her chest now, and her old shorts too short. She did not care. She had not

looked into a mirror since she came home. She brushed her teeth and
washed her face and combed her hair without raising her head from
the washbasin. She saw in her father's eyes, and in Chloe's, that she
looked beautiful to them, and that was enough.

June seeped away, and July came, hot and stopped and still, as
underwater as the hole in the ocean she lived in. Peyton felt as peaceful as a fish hanging still in sunlit water. She did not ask about Nora.
She did not ask about Sonny. She did not ask about graduation. She
did not care. She read and slept and watched TV and slept again.

"There's nothing organically wrong with her," she heard Dr. Sams
say to her father one evening, after he had brought his bag to the
house and checked her over. He had been her physician since birth.
"It's not unusual after a severe head injury. She seems comfortable,
and she smiles and talks, and isn't confused or irrational. I'd say she's
just resting. Let her do it, as long as she doesn't complain of
headaches, or start sleeping all the time."

"Good," her father said. "I've been awfully worried. She hasn't
seemed like herself."

I'm not, Peyton thought. Why did you think I would be?

The succoring sea held her almost until the end of July. On a still,
hot day in the third week of that month Peyton raised her head from
her toothbrushing and looked into the mirror. A bleached, yellowed
stoat's skull looked back, with shapeless, lank hair on one side of its
head and stubble like a wheat field over white scalp on the other.
There was a long, welted red scar in the stubble. Peyton put her hand
up and touched the scar.

"I need a haircut," she said, and then she realized that there would
be no haircut because Nora was gone.

She began to cry, and she cried, on and off, through the afternoon
and most of the night. Her father lay on her bed beside her, holding
her face to his shoulder. Gray light was just showing under her
venetian blinds when she stopped.

"You better now?" her father said.

"I don't know," she said. "Daddy, do you pray?"

"Yes, I do."

"Does it always feel to you like God is listening?"

"I don't always feel Him, but I think He does listen. Most of the time, anyway."

"What good does it do if He's not listening all the time?"

"I think He wants us to handle what we can on our own. Why do you want to know?"

"Because I prayed for Nora to stay, and she might have, but then I ran her away myself. I thought maybe I'd done it wrong."

And she began to cry again.

"Once I told Nora that sometimes when I prayed it felt like I was praying to God, but sometimes it felt like I was praying to my own need. And she said as far as she could see it was the same thing," her father said. His voice was peaceful.

The pain lanced at her again. She longed desperately for the green sea, but she knew that she would not be allowed to go back there.

"I hate her," she sobbed. "She ruined my life!"

"Well, you didn't do such a bad job of ruining hers," he said.

"What do you mean?"

"I mean old Sonny was out of there and gone before you hit the ground. And Augusta was on the phone before then, too."

"When did Nora go?"

"I'm not sure. She was gone when I came home from the hospital the next morning."

"She didn't even care whether I was badly hurt or not."

"She did. She called from Alabama late that day to see about you. We knew then that you'd be all right. Chloe told her."

"Have you talked to her?"

"No."

"When you said . . . that Sonny was gone, you mean gone back to Hollywood, without her?"

"Precisely. I think he hit the road before daylight."

"I don't understand."

"How would it look if the new Rhett Butler was keeping company with a lady who had a black baby out of wedlock?" her father said. Incredibly, there was laughter in his voice. Peyton smiled tentatively, and then she began to laugh, too. Her mouth was stiff, as if she had forgotten how.

"Rat Butler," she said, and collapsed against him in weak laughter. Presently she stopped.

"So you know where she is?" she asked.

"Texas," he said. "I had a letter the day before yesterday. She's working in a library there. She says it's a funny little town but it doesn't hold a candle to Lytton."

Peyton felt fresh pain flooding her. She closed her eyes against it. Nora, in a dusty little town in Texas, working in a library. . . .

"What about the car?"

"She sold the car. She said she didn't like it anymore. She has a Plymouth now."

Peyton shook her head back and forth, grinding her face into her father's shoulder.

"I loved that car," she said.

"There was a message for you in the letter," he said. "I've been carrying it around for days, waiting for you to want to hear it. I think now's the time."

He pulled a much-folded sheet of stationery from his shirt pocket. Peyton closed her eyes and waited.

"Here's your part," her father said. "'Tell Peyton it wasn't her fault. If I know her, she'll carry around a wagonload of guilt for the rest of her life if somebody doesn't take it away from her. But it was all me. Tell her it's what I do best, run. I've been doing it all my life. I preach freedom and spontaneity; I know better than anybody in the world how to draw people out and get them to trust me. It's one of the only talents that were given to me. And when I have them hanging on to me, naked as jaybirds, I run. I leave them twisting in the wind. The truth is that I'm dying for safety, and a place to be, but I can't stand it when somebody offers it to me. I can't handle the responsibility of that. I punish the people who open themselves to me. Tell her that she was born with the gift of a constant heart, and that's worth a hundred of me. Tell her to stop feeling guilty and start writing, and that she did me a favor. Ol' Sonny is nothing but a redneck with money, and he'll be a real hog when he's forty. I knew that even when I was following him around like a puppy dog. He was my ticket away from the love and trust you both offered me. I deserved him, but I'm mighty glad to be rid of him.

"'Tell Peyton I love her, just as I do you.'"

It was signed, simply, "Nora."

"What does that mean?" Peyton said.

"I think it means that you grew up and Nora didn't."

Peyton's heart cracked. Nora stood before her whole and living and vivid, laughing. Peyton could count every copper freckle. Loss drowned her.

"I hate her," she said, weeping, but she said it doubtfully. Surely hate did not hurt like this.

"Well," her father said, "you'd just as soon hate a butterfly. We didn't give one single thought to what *she* might need. We just climbed up on her wings. We loved it there; it was a wonderful ride. And she tried to hold us up, but we were too heavy. Finally she had to drop us and go. All the time she wanted an anchor, a place to light, and we were too busy riding her wings to see that."

"She said I'd always be safe with her. She *said* that!"

Her father put his chin down on her head and began to rock her like a child.

"Nobody's safe, Peyton, and nobody's free," he said. "There's only somewhere between safe and free, and what people are. The only thing we can ever be is just human, and that ends up breaking our hearts. We all try so hard to be strong, or free, or safe, or whatever it is we think we need most . . . and in the end all we can ever be is just us. And it's enough because it has to be. There's not anything else."

"I don't think I know how to do that. I'm not even sure who me is."

"Well, this is what we do," he said. "We try to give what little we have to somebody who hasn't got it, and maybe they try to give us back some of what they have that we haven't got. That's what love is. That's all it is. You can do that. You already do it."

Between the slats of the blinds the sun burned rose red. "Look," he said. "It's one of Nora's suns. Remember? 'Red as sin over that green roof. I think the sun comes up redder there than anywhere else on earth.' "

"I remember," she said.

They were silent awhile longer.

Then he said, "We both still need her, I guess."

"No. We don't."

"Yes. For one thing, you need a haircut." He smoothed her hair back from her forehead.

"Let's go get her," he said.

"Are you *crazy?* After what she did to you? After the speech?"

He rocked her silently. Whatever was thickening in her chest began to prickle and fizzle like a great bubble of ginger ale.

"Go get her?" she said. "You mean to Texas—go to Texas?"

"Yep. You and me and even Trailways if he'll behave himself. Drive to Birmingham and then New Orleans and then on over to Texas."

Peyton saw it in her mind, the empty, heat-shimmering roads, the drone of the engine, the murmur of the radio as stations faded in and out. Small diners and gas stations and neon cactuses and Burma Shave signs. Hamburgers and milkshakes in the car at McDonald's and Burger King.

"When would we go?"

"Now. This afternoon."

"She wouldn't come," Peyton whispered, the bubble stretching and shining, filling her chest. "Not after what I did. . . ."

"Bet she would. She needs us, too. She really does. I should have seen that sooner."

"What if she doesn't think so?"

He grinned suddenly.

"Then we'll pester her until she changes her mind," he said. "We'll plonk our guitars under her window and yowl like a couple of tom-cats until she gives up. She'll come."

Peyton hiccuped and began to laugh. The ginger-ale bubble exploded. She ran to the window and jerked the clattering blinds up. Red-gold light smote her. Joy took her then, and hurled her, still laughing, out into the brightening day.